The Doll from Dunedin

A Genealogy Mystery

ML Condike

keys arts

FLORIDA KEYS
COUNCIL OF THE

Research for this novel was funded in part by a grant from the Florida Keys Council of the Arts.

Chapter One

Our Keurig had just finished spitting out my second cup of coffee when my phone vibrated on the counter next to me. The display showed a New York area code in an exchange matching those at Murbeck, a huge law firm that handled New York's elite clients. I recognized the last four digits as Austin Bradley's extension. A law partner there, he often hired me to help with his difficult inheritance cases.

"Hey, Austin. What would have you calling me this early on a Friday morning?" We'd become good friends as well as business associates.

"A problem, as always. We have a case where we could use your help." I heard voices in the background, and, unusual for Austin, he sounded anxious.

"What's the problem?" I hoped he didn't have another project involving the dead. I preferred to search for the living.

1

"Hang on, RaeJean. I'm in a meeting with my partners. Coffee and doughnuts just arrived." I heard a door open and close. "I have a great opportunity for you. You may have seen the story in *The Times*."

"Opportunity?" I frowned. I hated when lawyers used that word. It usually meant they had a bird's nest on their hands and needed someone to sort out the snarls. Or, worst case scenario, take the fall as a scapegoat.

Austin moaned. "It's a mess. A jogger found a dead woman in Central Park with a dog lying next to the body."

"I know the story. Sam and I adopted the dog." I glanced out the back door at two corgis barking as they circled our pool. Sam had just scrambled out of the water.

"You have the dog? How'd that happen?"

"While collecting data for your Rogers case, I met the woman in Central Park. She approached me with her corgi in tow and stopped to rest on the same bench. During our chat, she asked me if I worked. I explained my job as a genealogist. She confessed she'd reached an impasse with her family research, so I gave her my Bloodline Forensics business card. The police found it in her purse and called to see if I knew her name. I—"

Austin cut me off. "The police identified her as Jill Harriet Hamilton, one of our oldest clients. This new project's an inheritance issue. We need to track down the primary beneficiary of Ms. Hamilton's estate. He's named in the will, but we can't find him. Should be straightforward, not like the last case. I'll email you the specifics and you can let me know what you think."

"That will work."

Austin cleared his throat. "There's a stipulation in her will. If the beneficiary isn't found in a year, the entire estate goes to the Columbia University Scholarship Fund. The bad news is that six months have already elapsed. We tried using other resources."

"That sounds ominous." I didn't like having deadlines on these types of cases. Sometimes it took years with a lot of waiting in between leads.

Austin laughed. "It isn't meant to be. I'll wait to hear from you. You're the best genealogist I know. It shouldn't take you long to discover the whereabouts of the missing heir."

"Thanks for the confidence, but I won't commit until I review what you send."

Although I had worked with Austin on his inheritance cases before, I'd never had a tight deadline, or the stress associated with one. Sam and I had reached our mid-thirties, our planned time to start a family. I didn't need unnecessary pressures right now if I hoped to get pregnant.

To ease back to work after my six-month hiatus, I'd refused the tough stuff and accepted a few simple projects, family trees or inheritances. Rejoining the workforce on my terms. However, the first case I undertook nearly killed me, literally and figuratively. Unless this case looked routine, I'd refuse it. I'd learned the hard way that people didn't always appreciate me snooping around in their family business. Sometimes, it became downright dangerous.

Plus, today, Sam and I had an important doctor's visit that could impact my decision to accept Austin's offer.

Chapter Two

The kitchen door swung open, and the familiar trio of Sam and our two corgis crowded through the opening after his polar dip in our pool. A towel covered the bottom half of Sam's firm body. My heart rate elevated at the sight. I resisted the temptation to give his coverup a tug. Instead, I let the dogs lap water droplets from his legs while he used another towel to dry his hair.

Our first priority after we purchased our historic home had been to install a pool. For the five springs we'd owned the house, one of us would sneak outside and jump into the frigid water once the ice melted. A shiver ran through me recalling the last year I'd made the plunge. I'd awakened that March morning feeling alive again, ending my malaise and my six-month hiatus from work. This year, Sam leaped first.

Sam slipped into his terry robe, tossed his wet towels into the laundry room, kissed my cheek, and pulled up a chair at our kitchen table. "Thanks for making breakfast. Polar dipping makes me hungry."

Fortunately, Sam would eat anything. I'd thawed several ready-made frozen pancakes. I'd never learned to cook from scratch. My mom, being a single mother, had stocked up on microwavable pre-cooked foods.

Sam never complained. He couldn't. His dinner prep involved ordering pizza.

My stomach turned as I watched Sam smother his stack in butter, then drown it with maple syrup before digging in. After poking mine a few times, I stared out the window.

"You're quiet this morning. I expected to find you in the pool," Sam mumbled through a mouthful of pancakes.

I shrugged. "The nursery door was open."

He stopped eating and looked at me. "Thinking about what the doctor might say?"

"I'm scared. Excited, but scared." I'd fallen apart after we lost our first baby at the fifth month of its development a year and a half ago. In clinical terms, I had an early stillbirth, since the baby had moved. During my downtime, I had learned to cope, but the hole in my heart hadn't healed—if it ever would.

"The doctor said it wasn't you. Don't blame yourself." Sam brushed his rogue lock of brown curly hair from his forehead and gave me a warm smile. "I'm still open to adoption."

But I wasn't ready to give up on having Sam's baby. "Let's see what the doctor says."

"Okay." He stuffed the last bite of the pancakes into his mouth.

How he had such an appetite with our future in the balance baffled me. Fortunately, Eli interrupted us with a bark, and I didn't get to ask. The dog's eyes held an expectant look. Sophie stared at me from her empty food bowl, then did a little dance.

"I'll feed the dogs." I escaped to the pantry, happy to avoid any conversation about adoption until after the afternoon appointment. Sam had been supportive through everything but, lately, I sensed him getting impatient with me.

By the time I'd fed the dogs, he had finished his coffee. He prepared to go to his office, then hesitated. "Busy day ahead. A client has a clock he needs appraised. It's a beauty; a Seth Thomas that's at least a hundred years old."

I had little enthusiasm for his clock project. "Great."

Sam noticed. "Are you okay?"

"Like I said, I'm scared and excited all at once."

"Are you still worried about the desk and the lights flashing from its crystal during your last case? Come on, Rae. The doctor said getting off your meds caused unusual side effects."

"No. I'm over that." I'd moved on from the desk and its accompanying events, but I harbored doubts about my ability to become a mother.

Sam's eyes darkened and his lips drew tight.

"Cripes, you're still hung up on that epigenetics book, aren't you?"

"No." A wave of guilt spread through me as I lied.

I should have been worry-free, but now I'd convinced myself I'd inherited an epigenetic tag from my missing father. My parents argued every day before he abandoned us. This childhood trauma caused a physical change in me. Somehow, this tag may have created a conduit for messages from my clients' dead ancestors. Or worse still, it could have altered my reproductive system. Made me unable to carry a baby to full term. Even though I'd promised no more secrets, I'd kept my fears from Sam.

"Then, what is it?" Sam's jaw clenched. His eyes remained hard.

"Remember the DNA results from the O'Leary woman we learned about while visiting that pub in New Jersey? I resubmitted my DNA profile and she came back as my relative. We're from the same branch of the family tree. It's possible we have the same father."

Sam scowled. "You mentioned that before. Have you told Caitlin?"

"The timing hasn't been right." The truth—my sister wasn't interested in finding our father. "By the way, Austin called. He has another case."

"Not like the last one, I hope."

I forced a laugh. "He says no. Says it'll be easy for me. It's an inheritance case. They need to track down a beneficiary. He's emailing me the details. I haven't agreed to take it yet."

"Good." Sam hugged me. "There's no reason to rush into it."

"That's what I thought. I figured I'd wait to hear what the doctor says later today."

In reality, I'd decided that taking the case would be a nice diversion from my fertility issues. Stressing over getting pregnant wasn't a good way to live. Besides, I knew someone with similar issues who'd decided to adopt. A few months after the adoption, she became pregnant and delivered a beautiful little girl.

* * *

At two-thirty, Sam and I drove to our appointment with my gynecologist. The doctor had tested us both and was ready to give us his prognosis. After that, we'd consider our next steps toward starting a family.

Sam smiled at me. "Nervous?"

"I'm beyond that. I'm ready for whatever he tells us." I swallowed the lump in my throat. I'd cried myself sick more than once. It didn't help. That morning, I'd put on my big girl pants and lectured myself. I would deal with the news, whatever it was.

We opened the door to an empty waiting room when we arrived. We'd taken his last appointment of the day.

His receptionist slid open a glass window. "He's on schedule and will be right with you."

I thumbed through my online issue of *Better Homes & Gardens* while we waited. I'd just started reading "How to Reduce Clutter" when the doctor appeared.

"Come right in." He motioned us into his office. "How are you folks today?"

"Good so far," Sam replied.

"I hope to make your day even better with good news for both of you." The doctor rolled his chair up close and grinned.

I let out a breath I didn't realize I'd been holding.

Sam's face relaxed.

"I can't find a thing wrong with either of you. Your recent stillbirth could be a fluke. Sometimes things don't develop the way they should, so Mother Nature takes over. I see no reason why you can't try to have another baby."

Sam took my hand.

"Is there anything I should do to keep healthy? I mean other than eating a balanced diet. Vitamins? Drink green tea?"

The doctor laughed. "Vitamins can't hurt, but I don't know about green tea." We discussed what I should expect if I got pregnant. "And I'd like to see you the minute you suspect. I'll run tests to track your body chemistry."

Sam and I stood in unison.

"You'll be hearing from me," I said. "And I hope soon."

Sam grinned when the doctor raised his eyebrows. Motherhood might be in my future after all.

Chapter Three

A ustin's email arrived the next morning, but it didn't answer all my questions. Before I'd agree to take the case, I wanted to know more about the time limit he mentioned in our previous conversation. I'd never encountered that kind of restriction.

Both corgis laid at my feet as I waited for Austin to answer my call. Eli, our tri-colored corgi, chewed on a piece of Velcro he'd removed from a toy. When I reached down to grab it so he wouldn't choke, he played keep away. He made a victory dash to his favorite chair, then dropped the fabric onto the floor. I grabbed the scrap just as Austin connected.

"Good morning, RaeJean. Calling to accept the case?" Austin teased.

"You know me better than that. I have more questions."

He chuckled. "Yes, I do. Shoot."

"I'm curious about such a short deadline to find the relative." I'd heard of several years, but never one. Sometimes, it took a lot longer to sort out a large estate.

"The private investigator didn't get very far. He said half the population in New Zealand had the same first and last name as the beneficiary." I'd faced this issue in previous cases. In one instance, I'd found twenty women with the same name in the same city. "That's not what I'm asking. I'm wondering why the will was written to assure this particular relative would inherit Jill's estate, and as you said on the phone, none of her other family members."

Austin cleared his throat as if preparing to unveil the crown jewels. "Jill Hamilton's maternal great-uncle practiced law in New York for years and set up the initial trust. I'll give you his name if you accept the case. Maybe we can start with him and gain access to his case files."

"Should I know the ancestral family?" I recalled an article in the newspaper about her relative being a partner at Murbeck, but the paper didn't reveal the partner's name.

"You would if you lived in Manhattan and mingled with old money." He paused. "Usually, a trust is bulletproof. But, here in New York, several of the Hamilton relatives are already contesting the terms of the will. With big money involved, all sorts of issues arise. A single person, her adoptive father William Hamilton, was the only family member who knew her bloodline. He put language in the provisions of the trust to locate a close relative believed to be living in New Zealand.

"If the New Zealand beneficiary isn't alive, then *per stirpes* his children by birth or adoption will inherit the estate. Otherwise, we liquidate the entire property and turn over the proceeds to Columbia University for a scholarship fund." Austin hesitated. "And, of course, this case must be concluded within the next six months. But I'm sure you'll find the person quickly. That's why I want you on the case."

"In my brief conversation with Ms. Hamilton in Central Park, she mentioned her adoption from there. If I trace both her and the beneficiary back to New Zealand, I should find out how she and the beneficiary were related. It might be tight, but I think it's feasible.

"The limited timeframe is the main reason why I called. What about my compensation? Do I get paid if the time expires without success? I can't work for free."

Austin laughed. "Don't worry. You'll get paid. If you don't locate him by the cutoff date, you'll receive your typical fees for time spent."

I thought about the offer. The case may well be a slam-dunk. Doubts crept in as I realized my research would no doubt require a trip to New Zealand. A prolonged travel at the moment might not be a good idea.

"I'm not sure I'm up to this right now." Austin knew Sam and I wanted a family. After our recent news, a stressful case might mess up my biorhythms.

"Don't decide yet. Let's discuss your compensation."

I relaxed in my chair and examined my nails. "What kind of fee are we talking about?"

"Your standard rate up to six months, plus an additional bonus of three percent of the estate value for closing the case within the time constraint. We have the most recent estimated value from five years ago. At that time, between bank accounts, investments, and real estate, the estimated property value amounted to forty million dollars."

I sat upright as I did the math, then almost fell out of my chair. Sophie barked.

"One point two million dollars?" It was triple my salary as a full-time forensic genealogist. As I contemplated the fee, my high-risk antennae lifted. Warning! Nobody offered that kind of bonus unless you were Colleen Fitzpatrick or CeCe Moore.

"Roughly. Of course, we'll reappraise the estate before the final payment."

"Phew. That's a big enticement, but what else do you know beyond the missing relative who once lived in New Zealand?"

"Not much. I've already checked our archives. The adoption specifics remain sealed, except to Jill's father, long since dead, who had privileged access. I have a redacted copy of the official paperwork. The Hamiltons adopted Jill from Saint Saviour's Home in Christchurch, Southland, New Zealand. The trust documents list a maternal blood relative. However, I can't release the beneficiary's name until you sign an agreement."

"Another *Mission Impossible* case. Will your email disappear if I say no?" I laughed. "Let me have a couple of days to think about it. A high reward suggests a high risk of failure. Why else would the family agree to pay so much?"

I drew a breath. *One point two million dollars!*

"I'm not sure about the risk involved. I know you're sensitive about this since the last case, but if her parents tried to erase the child's ancestral trail, they had the money to do a first-rate job. Jill's parents belonged to two well-known New York families. I suspect no coincidence when they adopted this specific child from New Zealand. The adoptive parents had to know one or both of her biological parents..." Austin's voice trailed off at the end of the sentence.

"Why do you say that?" Austin must have been anticipating problems.

"Old money, the document redactions, and the secrecy surrounding the files."

"I'll get back to you in a day or two." Darn. Another case wrapped in secrets and coverups. The principal question in my last case ended up being the tip of the iceberg of a much larger mystery. It's possible I'd be facing the same situation with this one.

"That's fine. The meter doesn't start until you sign an agreement. The firm needs the best forensic geneal-ogist and you've proven more than once that you're who we want."

"Thanks. But I still want to talk with Sam." My head spun at the prospect of earning over a million dollars for one case. If I wrapped it up quickly, I'd coast for a couple of years, maybe sort out our starting-a-family issues.

"No problem. I'd like an answer in a few days, if possible." Austin disconnected.

I stared at my phone. My hands shook, but maybe I needed to consider it.

Unable to focus, I looked down at the dogs. "How about a treat, you guys?"

Both corgis leaped to their feet, then raced to the door, barking a duet before I stood.

* * *

I'd rustled up a peanut butter and jelly sandwich, tea, and a handful of M&M's when Sam waltzed into the kitchen carrying his Darth Vader mug. "You look like you've just swallowed a hard-boiled egg."

"Not just any egg—a golden egg."

"Huh?"

"A one point two million dollar bonus if I solve a case on a tight deadline."

"You're kidding!" Sam set his Vader cup in the sink.

"No, I'm serious. A percentage of the estate as well as my usual fee structure." My heart pumped harder at the thought.

"Holy crap. What's the case about?"

"Austin Bradley wants me to find a man from New Zealand who might be related to the Hamilton woman who died in Central Park." Thinking of Jill saddened me. I reached down and patted Eli. Sophie stuck her nose between my arm and his head.

"You mentioned she came from there as a child."

"Apparently, Jill had a relative in New Zealand who will inherit a boatload of money if I find him."

"How big of a boatload?" Sam raised his eyebrows.

"The mother lode—forty million dollars minus fees."

"Did you tell him you'd take the case?"

"I said I needed to talk to you first. Isn't that what we agreed?"

Sam pulled me into his arms. "Uh huh. I didn't realize I'd married the next CeCe Moore. One point two million dollars!"

"Don't get excited. Moore has solved over fifty cold cases since 2018. I'm not in her league. Plus, she's a TV celebrity." I backed away from him. "Doesn't that seem like a lot of money to locate a relative?"

"It does, but who's to argue if they're willing to pay?" Sam's eyes twinkled at the thought.

"There must be more to it than just finding someone. You know the old saying about high risk, high reward." I stuffed a handful of M&M's into my mouth.

"True. But you're the best."

I fist-bumped Sam's arm. "Austin said that, too. Don't you start. Flattery only goes so far."

Sam grinned. "It doesn't hurt to try."

"One other thing. I have six months to solve the case." A twinge of self-doubt rippled up my spine.

Sam raised his eyebrows. "If you don't, then what?"

"Then, Columbia University gets the entire estate, and the firm pays my normal fees."

"Cool. We either hit the jackpot, or you'll be working for the usual amount." Sam wrapped me in his arms again.

"I guess if you put it that way, why not?"

We kissed, and I leaned back and looked up at him.

He caressed my chin with his thumb. "What do you think? You going to take it?"

"Yes. If you'll come with me to New Zealand."

Chapter Four

I called Austin to arrange a meeting. Before I'd even said I'd accept the case, he was all business. "I've prepared an agreement, assuming you'd sign. You can either come to New York or receive it by email. Either way, we require a notarized copy with two witnesses."

"That's presumptuous of you. I would need to read the contract, and I haven't said I'd accept."

"Oh, but RaeJean, you will. It's an offer you can't refuse once you hear the case details."

"You sound like the Godfather."

He laughed. It turned out some lawyers had a sense of humor.

"What details?"

"Sorry, the trustee requires a signed document before I disclose specifics of the case."

"Would you be available if I came into the city on Monday?"

I had more questions for Austin that were best asked in person. The mystery surrounding this project held me in its grip. Out of curiosity, I'd check for Jill Hamilton's adoptive ancestors today and see who surfaced.

"That would be perfect," he said. Austin had a client conference Monday morning, so we arranged to meet after lunch.

I disconnected and purchased train tickets to the city. Then, I spent the rest of the day researching the New York Hamilton family. I didn't find anything about Jill's natural parents.

* * *

On Sunday night, Sam and I retired to the living room for our after-dinner drink, a *Lustau Vermut Rojo* over ice with a slice of orange peel. The spiced vermouth had become one of my favorites after receiving a gift bottle from Caitlin and Greg that they'd brought back from a vacation in Spain. My sister and Sam's best friend had become inseparable.

Halfway through the wine, Sam looked at his watch. "Why don't you call Caitlin about the DNA results? Get it over with. She'll be in bed soon."

"Not yet," I groused. It was my family, not his.

He held his hands up. "Hey, don't get prickly. It was just a suggestion."

I'd done it again. Taken out my frustrations on Sam. "Sorry. I've been procrastinating."

"Why? Caitlin's your sister, but she's also your best friend."

"Second best. You're my best."

He reached out and drew me close. The top of my head slipped under his chin. To be truthful, I didn't quite reach his chin. I melted into him, and he nuzzled my wild red hair.

"Besides me, I meant." He leaned in and kissed me.

"You're right. I need to call her." I looked at my phone on the table, but I froze like Lot's wife, unable to take the step.

Sam jumped to his feet and collected my phone. "Here. Go call your sister. You'll feel better if you get this off your chest. Eliminate the distraction. You need to concentrate on your next case."

Sam handed me the phone and I trudged to the library. The pitter-patter of dog feet assured me I'd have a peanut gallery while sharing my discovery with my sister. Once comfortable on the couch, I grabbed the printout of the DNA search results. I'd left it there for two weeks, planning each day to make the call. Sophie and Eli curled up at my feet between the coffee table and the couch. After several deep breaths, I pressed Caitlin's number.

"Hey, Cub. What's up?" Caitlin had tagged me with the nickname ten years ago when she became a newspaper journalist.

"Checking in. I'm considering another case about a missing heir."

"That should be interesting. Anyone I might know?"

"Eli's previous owner. Apparently, she came from New Zealand and left her fortune to a male relative. I don't have all the details yet. I haven't decided if I'll take it."

"Is that why you called?" Caitlin asked. "Really?"

My hands began to shake. I cleared my throat.

"Well, what is it? Are you and Sam doing okay?" she asked.

It took a few seconds to find my voice. "We're fine. I have some news."

"You're pregnant again!" Caitlin whooped.

"No. Not that." I almost didn't continue.

"Sorry. I've been expecting to hear that from you, that's all. Then, why are you calling me on a Sunday night?"

"Remember I told you about that bartender at O'Leary's Pub in New Jersey?"

"Yeah, what about him?" Caitlin's voice had dropped to a growl.

"Well, his sister, Aileen, had her DNA tested, so I resubmitted mine to see if we might be related." My jaw tensed. "I—we—are related to her."

Caitlin didn't respond at first. When she did, her voice trembled. "How related? Distant cousins from the Mayflower?"

"Possibly a half-sister, half-brother. Maybe first cousins."

"Jeez Louise." She paused, then hissed, "That miserable rat. I knew it."

I waited to see if she would tell me about our father, but she clammed up.

When she spoke, her voice had elevated. "Are they younger than us? He probably deserted us for them."

"Don't jump to conclusions. I said it's possible they are half-siblings or first cousins. I haven't pursued it any further. We've talked about how the Irish population is an endogamous group, lots of inbreeding. I'll need to go to the gene level for a closer look. I only know what I've told you. I hoped you'd point me in a direction, maybe tell me what you know about Dad."

"What I know? I know he's a jerk who left us without a goodbye." She ranted for the next five minutes.

Finally, I interrupted. "I've always felt that you knew something you never told me."

"Nope. Nothing worth repeating."

I didn't believe her.

"What are you going to do?"

"Research first. See what I can find online about Kevin and Aileen O'Leary of Jersey City. Beyond that, I don't know."

"Are you going to tell them we're related?" Caitlin paused. "I'd be careful about that."

"No idea. But I'll let you know what I find out before I talk to them again."

"Good. People don't always react as expected with that kind of news."

"That's for sure."

"To tell you the truth, I wish you'd called to tell me you are pregnant," Caitlin huffed. "Nothing good will come of finding that sack-of-Irish-potatoes-father of ours. He's part of our past. We don't even know if he's still alive."

"Maybe I can find out." Our conversation recalled counsel I'd received from Zeke Rogers, an old friend I made on a previous case. *The past has a way of seeping up through the soil and revealing itself.*

"Well, don't bother to tell me if he is. I don't ever want to see him again."

"Caitlin, he *is* our father. He may be sorry for what he did." Maybe being so young I didn't see his bad side. Caitlin shielded me from a lot of family trauma by taking me to the public library when war broke out at home.

"Sorry? Him? He's sorry alright. A sorry piece of work." She remained silent for a moment. I heard her breathing. "I've got to go, Cub. Call me when you have good news."

"Caitlin?"

She'd disconnected.

Chapter Five

Early Monday morning, I caught the express train and arrived at Penn Station ninety minutes later. During the ride, I began Grisham's book about a law school scam as a distraction after my previous evening's conversation with Caitlin. Reading the book didn't improve my opinion of lawyers, although I had to admit Austin remained an exception. Time would tell if his track record would hold.

When I entered Austin's office, I half expected to see Zeke Rogers, a person from my last case, sitting on the leather couch in the reception area. The same Walt Kuhn print, *A White Clown*, hung above the sideboard opposite the couch where Austin kept the coffee pot and mugs. Today, he'd filled the infusion beverage dispenser with lemon slices, giving the water a buttery hue.

Austin's voice rumbled behind his inner office door.

I sat and waited for the clock to strike on the hour. It didn't quite make it before Austin peeked out the door. "RaeJean, good to see you. Come in. I have the contract ready. I've arranged for witnesses to join us."

"I'll read the contract before I sign. Not that I don't trust you, but it's my policy."

"I understand. You're already aware of the high points, so go ahead." He winked and handed me a thin agreement. Well, a mere twelve pages, which was thin as far as contracts went.

Austin busied himself while I read.

"I'm not comfortable with the last clause. I always keep my research confidential."

"You'll see why when I release the players' names."

I continued reading. By the time I'd finished, the witnesses had arrived.

"Olivia and Tim are interns from Columbia Law."

Olivia, a tall, slender brunette with a blunt bob, carried a record book and a notary stamp. Her nondescript gray suit conformed well to the male environment in the firm. Tim stood empty-handed. His black-haired Ivy League cut complemented his charcoal Hugo Boss suit and his black wing tips. Tim's smartly cut suit trumped Austin's slightly worn Brooks Brothers.

"What's the purpose of the last clause?" Pretty much a boilerplate contract, except for the penalty there. I'd read that section twice.

"It's to protect the family from negative exposure."

"Or to protect the law firm by blaming me if the word gets out."

Austin's eyebrows arched. "If you release the names and circumstances of the case and anything appears in print, you are liable."

The interns glanced at each other. Olivia shrugged.

Austin's eyes narrowed.

"Okay. Let me reread it. Maybe I'm overreacting." I reread the last page of the contract while Austin and the interns waited.

"Well?" Austin spoke first.

I stood and held out the contract. "I can't sign this as written. It says I'm culpable for *any and all leaks*. Why should I be held responsible for other people's mistakes? What about the law firm? It's more susceptible to a leak than I am."

"We have very strict protocols governing client privacy." A slow flush crept above his collar. "Hmph! Wait. What if I strike the phrase holding you solely responsible?"

"Propose away."

The suggested change alleviated my concerns. Still, something felt off. I never discussed work with anyone but the firm, except occasionally with Sam or Caitlin. However, when I thought about the fee, I acquiesced. That must be the risky reason for the bonus—get the case closed fast and keep it out of the press. "Okay. Strike the phrase and we have a deal."

Austin handed the agreement to one of the

students to modify. Once he dismissed them, he closed the door. "I don't want interruptions or eavesdropping. This case is very sensitive. Since you've agreed to the terms, signing is a formality. I'll tell you all about it."

I waited. Every project with a lawyer began this way. They would wax on about the sensitivity of the situation. I'd listen and nod. I cleared my throat, hoping he'd get started.

"Well, let's get to it. Jill Hamilton's uncle was Lorenzo Armstrong, a big-time New York lawyer who practiced in the early 1900s. He's the guy I alluded to earlier."

I'd researched the New York City Hamilton family. Now, I could complete the maternal side of the tree by researching the Armstrongs.

"The relative we need to find is Roy A. Beauchamp."

"Okay." The Beauchamp name didn't turn on a strobe light in my head. The name hadn't surfaced during my Hamilton research, so I assumed he was a maternal relative. "What's the *A* stand for?"

"We have no idea. We don't have a middle name. However, in New Zealand, Beauchamp is a well-known and respected name."

"Beauchamp." I'd attended high school with a Mark Beauchamp. His family moved to town in my freshman year of high school. Mark's father worked at the Frito-Lay plant in Baltimore. I doubted he had any relationship to the Beauchamp family from New Zealand, but one never knew.

"Yes. That's it."

"What do you mean, that's it?" I stood up. "I've agreed to a contract to find a person you had no luck finding using all your available resources. Do you have additional leads?"

"The private investigator reports. Plus, a special lead for you. One of our law partners, Morris Hadley, handled Jill Hamilton's adoption." Austin handed me a stack of file folders.

"Can I talk to him?"

"Unfortunately, no. He died sixty years ago."

My entire forehead lifted as I blurted out, "That's it?"

"Let me explain. Hadley's daughter lives in a senior living facility in Clifton, New Jersey, ninety minutes northwest of Manhattan. She's eighty-four years old."

"Why haven't you interviewed her?" I said, asking the obvious.

"She refuses to talk to us." Austin avoided eye contact.

"Why would she do that?" The daughter's refusal to talk wasn't reassuring.

"When Hadley died, our senior partners denied her access to her father's files, a legal and justified decision. The files belong to the firm, not the individual lawyers, but she didn't accept our explanation. She wanted to write his memoirs and demanded the files. Even took us to court and lost, of course."

"Hmm. Is the woman alert? And..." I tap danced around the sensitive question.

"Oh, she's clear-witted and savvy. That's why she won't see us. Her father drew up the original documents for the Hamilton Trust. We suspect she knows the name of Jill Hamilton's birth mother and maybe even her father."

"Why would you think that? It would be highly unusual for a father to divulge privileged information about a client to his daughter."

"One would think. But during the court proceedings, she said she planned to write about Jill Hamilton's adoption case, so we think she knows more than she should."

"If that's true, this shouldn't take long." *High risk, high reward* echoed in my head.

"That's what I thought, but she stonewalled our investigator. Your skills are a better fit for this case than ours. We read law books, not diaries and journals."

"That's why I'm here." I locked eyes with Austin.

He didn't flinch. "And we're confident you'll solve this case. Remember—"

"Don't start that again. I remember. I solved a one hundred eighty-year-old cold case. This case is six months old." I wrinkled my nose at him. "A piece of cake."

Austin grinned. "You're starting to get the picture."

"I'll give it a month. If I don't make progress, the contract states I can give a thirty-day notice. I can quit after two months."

Austin made a face. "You've never quit on me before."

I sighed. "And knowing myself, I wouldn't quit this one, either. But I had to say aloud that I have an out if I need one."

"Yes. You always have that option. But I sold you to the partners. I'm counting on you." Austin handed me a card with the address of the senior living facility and the woman's name. Joan Shannon resided at Horizon Senior Living in Clifton, New Jersey.

I thought about the octogenarian in my last case. Had I jumped into another frying pan?

"One more thing," Austin leaned forward. "Jill's home has not been touched since her death. We have instructions to keep it that way until we find or rule out an heir. Would you like to visit it since you're here?"

Stunned by my good fortune, I said, "Absolutely!"

He held up a key. "I blocked off my schedule for the remainder of the day, anticipating you'd be interested."

Austin picked up the phone and called for a limo.

Chapter Six

Once I'd signed the contract and Olivia notarized it, Austin and I left and met the limo in front of the office building. The chauffeur drove us north on FDR Drive past the Brooklyn Bridge and the United Nations building. At the Queensboro Bridge, he exited and wound over to Fifth Avenue. Vehicles jammed the street.

"I don't know how you can drive in this madness."

"I take the train unless work requires off hours." He paused. "On weekends, I unwind at our lake house in upstate New York."

The idea of a lake house made me smile. "I could suffer through owning one of those."

"It's therapeutic." Austin's quiet reverie spoke a thousand words.

As the limo edged to the curb, I recalled Jill Hamilton departing with her corgi, Eli, in tow the last time I'd seen her. A warm feeling spread through me.

I craned my neck and looked up at the hundred-year-old building. Hopefully, I'd find a lead to Roy A. Beauchamp buried among Jill's personal belongings. It always surprised me where people hid things.

"This is it." Austin reached for the door handle, but a doorman grasped it first. A concierge checked Austin's ID before allowing us to proceed to the manned elevator. "The Hamilton apartment, please."

At the eleventh floor, we exited the elevator car to a circular vestibule. A faint fragrance of flowers hung in the stale air. Light filtered through stained-glass windows backlit from an adjoining room. Rainbows danced on the magnificent marble floor. The stuffy air suggested no recent visitors.

Austin smiled down at me. "Decadent, isn't it? I love this Italian marble foyer. Jill would point out the eighteenth-century tiles at every visit." Austin swept his foot in an arc across a gorgeous swirled white and gray tile.

"Not bad." I played it cool. Then, peeking through an open door into an art gallery to my right, I recognized a Rembrandt, a Picasso, and a Caravaggio hanging among other paintings from lesser-known artists. "Good God, Austin. Those can't be originals!"

His eyes sparkled. "Oh, but they are. They are."

I followed him away from the gallery, down a hall that spilled into a sizable living room. An arrangement of beige leather furniture focused on a massive fireplace. Central Park loomed straight ahead, visible through the eight-over-eight, double-hung windows.

"Dog hair." A brown plaid dog bed by the fireplace sat next to an overflowing toy basket. My eyes filled as I thought of Eli losing his mistress. "Poor Eli. He must miss his luxurious home."

I noted a stack of hardbound museum catalogs on a coffee table as we passed into a library lined with floor-to-ceiling built-ins. Mahogany bookcases sat atop waist-high barrister cabinets. A ladder leaned against a rail in a corner. "This is where I'd spend my time."

"Where do we begin?" Austin scanned the room.

His question surprised me. I had no intention of letting anyone help. "I search by myself."

Austin's eyes widened. "Really? How long will it take?"

"Hours, or maybe days. Depends on what I find." I never rushed a home search or accepted help unless my genealogist friend, Claire, offered. We'd worked on more than one case together.

"That won't work. I'm too busy to wait while you leaf through hundreds or thousands of books."

I scanned the room and did a quick calculation. "At least three thousand, I'd guess."

Austin retrieved his phone. "I'll get an intern to join you."

"I'm trustworthy." I didn't want an observer when handling Jill's personal things. I needed to get into her head. Share her feelings. See her world.

"I believe you, but I can't chance it. I learned years ago, where there's a *will*, there's room for a lawsuit." Austin returned to the living room. I heard him speaking with his secretary. "Thirty minutes. Great. I'll see her then."

I checked Jill's desk while I waited. Her appointment calendar laid open to her last day. I flipped through it and found an upcoming doctor's appointment. A small address book sat next to it. The remaining uncovered desktop sparkled.

"Our intern, Olivia, will be over shortly." Austin strolled toward the dining room. "Let's do a quick walk-through while I'm here."

"By the way, Jill has an upcoming appointment," I told Austin.

"I'll have Olivia check Miss Hamilton's planner and cancel anything pending."

"Does she have a housekeeper? If so, I'd like to interview her."

"Yes. Mrs. O'Sullivan. I can't see the harm if she agrees."

"Why wouldn't she?" This surprised me.

"You have quite a bit to learn about the New York elite." Austin stared out a window. "They don't share, and neither does their hired help if they want to keep their jobs."

"Including you?" I drew in a breath. What did he mean by that?

"First, I'm not part of the elite. And second, I answer to my clients. So, I share what they allow me to share."

"Got it." My neck heated.

Austin smiled. "We both have limits and penalties in our contracts."

We moved from the library into a tastefully furnished dining room with a sovereign set that seated ten. The inside partition of the dining room curved and shared the stained-glass panel enclosing the foyer. A full-length marble sideboard beneath four outside windows matched the entry floor. A scattering of expensive serving pieces broke up the monotony of the stone surface.

From there, we entered a modern kitchen equipped with a walk-in refrigerator and matching appliances. A moldy odor permeated the room. A half-filled Cuisinart coffee maker held a gooey brown liquid, formerly coffee. A healthy nest of green mold climbed the sides of the glass pot. Whoever turned off the burner had failed to dump the contents.

Austin emptied the pot, then refilled it with hot water. "Looks like we should get the housekeeper in case there are other surprises."

While he attended to his housework, I examined a corner breakfast nook. The worn leather bench suggested Jill preferred dining here. A six-month-old Saturday issue of *The Gray Lady* sat on the table open to the Arts section. Jill had completed the *Times* crossword and noted eighteen minutes in the margin, impressive for what was considered the most difficult daily puzzle, with an average solution time of at least thirty minutes.

"Ready?" Austin stood by the door leading to the gallery.

We'd made a complete circle after the gallery, entering into the foyer. Besides the three paintings I'd seen earlier, a Norman Rockwell sketch from a 1950s magazine cover and a Winslow Homer hung on the opposite wall beside a Kuhn, *The Blue Clown, 1931*. Something about it rang a bell. I jotted myself a note to check later.

Upstairs, we found four bedrooms and three baths. Outdated but neat, the rooms had a dust layer that dulled the finish of plastic drop cloths covering the beds.

"Last room." Austin waited in the stairwell while I entered the main bedroom.

Located above the living room, it shared the downstairs footprint, including a fireplace on its south wall. A clean dog bed sat by this fireplace, too. Based on a dog ramp and the brown hair clinging to the white duvet, I suspected Eli slept with his owner.

This room provided an even better view of Central Park, including the water in the Jacqueline Onassis Reservoir. A partial bottle of Estee Lauder's Private Collection Tuberose Gardenia sat on the vanity. Gardenias! The scent in the foyer.

A *whoosh* from the elevator sounded downstairs.

"Olivia's here," Austin called from the stairwell. "Hold the door! I'm leaving."

Austin and I met the young intern as she emerged

from the cab. "Nothing leaves this unit without my permission."

"Yes, sir." Her smug look puzzled me.

"But I may find items I'll want to check more closely." I scowled.

"Olivia will have copies made or take pictures, if necessary. But nothing original leaves."

"Okay, but I'll need photographs or photocopies of everything—inside, outside, front, and back. Otherwise, I can't do a thorough analysis."

Austin frowned. "We can discuss individual items, but nothing leaves without my approval." Once in the elevator, Austin nodded to the attendant and the elevator doors closed in my face.

"Where do we begin?" Olivia asked as she led us toward the living room.

"There's no *we*. I'll search each room, starting with the living room. You may watch, if you must." Austin's restrictive conditions irked me, and I'd taken it out on Olivia. "Sorry."

She shrugged, plopped in a chair, and pulled out a book from her backpack.

I leafed through museum catalogs on the coffee table and found a short grocery list. Nothing more.

Next, we moved to the library. "This room could take a couple of days. I'll have to check every book for letters or notes."

"Every book?" Olivia rolled her eyes. "Does Mr. Bradley know this?"

"Yes." My patience floundered. "You'd be surprised where I've found notes."

"And I'm to watch you look for a potential *surprise* note?" Her head wagged with each word.

"Not unless you want to. I'd rather you weren't here at all." I swallowed. If Sam were here, he'd reprimand me for being rude, so I added, "Nothing personal, but I work better alone."

"I'll study in the living room. I have an exam in two days." She headed for the door and echoed my reply over her shoulder. "Nothing personal."

I scanned the room for Jill's favorite items. She would have them within easy reach. Likely on the first few shelves of the bookcase, or the top shelf inside the lower cabinets. Nothing jumped out at me.

Next, I put on gloves, grabbed a cloth, and then drew the ladder to one end. I climbed rung by rung until I reached the top shelf. I'd check everything, starting at the ceiling and working my way down. Book by book, I flipped through the pages. Heavy dust on their top edges indicated they hadn't been touched in years.

By four o'clock, I'd barely made a dent.

Olivia peeked in. "Any luck?"

"Not yet. I won't finish today."

"I'll notify Mr. Bradley."

While she spoke with Austin, I found Mrs. O'Sullivan's information in the address book and scribbled her number on my notepad. Based on Jill's nearly empty calendar, I surmised she didn't entertain many visitors. With her limited socialization, Jill and her housekeeper may have become close friends.

"Mr. Bradley says you can return as often as you need, but not without someone from the office. He'll need your schedule to make sure he has people available."

"Okay." I groaned at the thought of my investigation being hampered by the availability of chaperones.

"He's a lawyer. He doesn't trust anyone." She arched an eyebrow.

"I'm only here for the day. I'm catching the train home tonight." I glanced down at the bumper-to-bumper traffic on the street below. "I dread the commute."

"I'll have the limo driver drop you where you can catch the express."

I felt a little guilty about my reactions to Olivia when I heard her instructions to the limo driver to make sure I made it safely into the train station. She sounded sincere in her concern.

By the time we reached the ground floor, the limo had arrived.

No leads today. Hopefully, my next visit would produce results. I followed my gut a lot. And my gut said something in the townhome linked Jill to Roy Beauchamp. I just had to find it.

Chapter Seven

On the train back to Philly, it dawned on me I hadn't asked Austin if Jill Hamilton had died of natural causes. "Darn!" I texted him the question.

I arrived home at our usual cocktail hour.

Sophie and Eli raced along the fence, herding my car into its parking spot.

The two dogs had bonded once Eli realized Sophie ruled. She'd shown him the ropes the first week. Now, they both chased the backyard wildlife and raced around the pool together when the automatic cleaner started.

Sam waved from the deck, saluting me with a half-full glass of wine.

I grabbed a glass in the kitchen on my way outside to join him.

"So, how'd it go?"

"Fine. I signed the contract once Austin made a

few changes. I'm keeping my options open should I decide to drop this case in a month. Oh, and I found our next home." I fluttered my eyelashes at him.

"What do you mean? Are we moving?"

"Just kidding. I spent a couple of hours in the deceased woman's apartment." I described the town-home and its contents. "I doubt the original art comes with it."

"Did you find anything useful?"

"Not yet. The library alone will take several days. Austin won't let me search it without a person from the firm there with me." I sipped my wine. "There isn't much for leads unless I find something at the townhome."

"What did Austin provide?" After ten years of marriage, Sam knew a forensic genealogist's process as well as I did. He'd listen to me categorize the data and blurt out the missing documents. Usually, I identified all of them, but sometimes he'd come up with something I missed.

"He gave me the name of the dead lawyer who drew up the conditions of the trust. Apparently, his elderly daughter resides in a senior living facility in Clifton, New Jersey. Austin thinks she knows something but won't share it with the lawyers at Murbeck. Hostile relations."

"And she'll share it with you?"

"I'm not sure. I told Austin I'd give him a month. If I hadn't made progress by then, I wanted out of the contract, and he agreed."

"That's fair."

"That's what he said." I paused for a moment. "I also know the name of the relative mentioned in the trust—Roy A. Beauchamp. According to Austin, their best investigator didn't find him."

"Beauchamp sounds French."

"Could be."

We spent the next half hour on the deck with the dogs. Sam checked his phone while I contemplated the case. There had to be a clue in Jill's apartment. Not to mention, something about the Kuhn painting still bothered me.

* * *

The next morning, I buried myself in Austin's files and outlined my report sections. At this point, I had no hint of Roy A. Beauchamp's whereabouts or his relationship to Jill other than he was more than likely a maternal relative. As I suspected, Austin's files contained readily available and mostly useless information.

An initial approach for this case floated around in my head, but for it to work, I needed to find the link between Jill Hamilton and Roy Beauchamp. I created a case file on my laptop and typed random thoughts. Unfortunately, what I knew about Roy Beauchamp wouldn't fill a fountain pen.

"Hmm. Let's see. The investigator thinks Beauchamp may have immigrated to the United States in 1944 through Canada. Where did that come from?

He has no proof." I mumbled as I grabbed an index card to start a pile for Roy.

Eli stood and shook himself as if my mumbling meant a trip to the backyard.

"Sorry, boy, this is how I work. You'd better get used to me talking to myself."

He stared at me with his big brown eyes, jumped into the chair by the window, circled a few times, and then plopped down to gaze out at the backyard.

"You might spot a squirrel out there." The words had barely left my lips when Sophie jumped up and barked. I'd used the magic word.

"Relax, girl, there's nothing out there." I patted her until she resettled at my feet.

"Roy A. Beauchamp. Who are you?" Someone whom Jill's parents cared about and wanted to provide for if Jill died. Or, at least they cared enough about his relationship with Jill to provide for him. Why? Maybe they didn't want other Hamilton relatives to get the windfall. They'd had the trust prepared as if they didn't expect Jill would bear children.

By lunchtime, I'd cataloged the information from Austin and outlined a work plan for most sections of my report. First, I'd create ancestral trees for the adoptive parents using online genealogy databases. That would show me the missing links that might require travel since Beauchamp came from New Zealand.

Jill's adoptive father, William, descended from Alexander Hamilton through Alexander's youngest son, Phillip. Alexander's grandson, Captain Louis

Hamilton, had enlisted in the cavalry at age seventeen. During his service, he had secretly married a woman who became pregnant. Unfortunately, before the woman gave birth, the grandson lost his life at age twenty-four during one of Custer's unprovoked attacks on a peaceful Cheyenne village.

The mother, unable to provide for the baby, left him with her relatives, who named him William and raised him as their own. At fifteen, William learned of his Hamilton heritage from his adoptive parents. To prove his lineage, he collected a copy of his birth record. Then, he sought out a Hamilton uncle, who, being of the same mind as other Hamiltons, welcomed William into the family and provided for his education. William legally changed his name to Hamilton before he met Isabelle Armstrong.

Jill's adoptive mother, Isabelle, hailed from the Armstrongs of New York City. Her great-uncle Lorenzo Armstrong practiced law in the early 1900s. As an investor in sugar, his name appeared regularly in the newspapers. Together with law partner John S. Keith, he financed sugar operations in the West Indies. Hoping for substantial profits at harvest, the partners established a rudimentary commodities market where they loaned money to the Caribbean farmers to finance their crop planting.

"Look at this! Armstrong and Keith handled Dorothy Arnold's disappearance before the police involvement."

Eli raised his head, looked at me, then resettled.

Jill had mentioned Dorothy Arnold that day in Central Park. Had it been the ramblings of an old woman, or was Dorothy important?

I emailed a draft of a work schedule to Austin. He responded immediately. *Looks fine. Also, Jill died of congestive heart failure.*

I'd return to New York on Monday, sign my contract, and continue searching Jill's townhouse. Hopefully, I'd find something to point me in the right direction.

Chapter Eight

The law firm's limo collected me at Penn Station. Olivia occupied the seat facing forward, with her briefcase and books covering the rest of the seat, telegraphing her opinion of my status. So, I sat with my back to the driver and watched her stare out the window for the entire ride to Jill's townhouse.

The same doorman greeted us and admitted us to the building. Once in Jill's quarters, Olivia disappeared into the living room without a word, thank goodness. Her hovering disrupted my concentration.

My search began on the top floor of her townhouse, working from the top down to the main level. The library would take the longest. After my brief survey on Monday afternoon, I decided to leave it for last. Crossing off items gave me the illusion of progress.

Even though the multiple guest bedrooms showed no signs of use, I searched each of them as if it held an important clue. I removed drawers to check for secret letters taped to the backs and bottoms, and even laid on the floor to peer under the beds, using my penlight to search for something adhered to the bottom of the bed.

When I looked into her closets, I found that Jill had filled them with pressed and folded clothes stored in garment bags by season. I did the same thing, a throwback from my childhood when I didn't have my own closet. Another practice we shared, along with owning corgis.

I didn't find a thing.

The master bedroom exuded warmth with the scent of gardenias. A dust bunny of dog hair under the bed. A cluttered dressing table. A worn upholstered chair. I seated myself at the table and peered into the mirror for a moment before continuing my search.

A hairbrush with a matching comb angled in its bristles held strands of fine white hair. Bobby pins and clips spilled from a ceramic box next to the brush. Loose hair strands bobbed when I lifted the set to examine it. I'd check with Austin about a DNA test. Still, I collected the hair for safe measure. I never left a clue behind.

"Find anything?" Olivia had slipped into the room unnoticed.

Startled, I said a little too loudly without turning around, "No! Please check with Austin to see if they tested Ms. Hamilton's DNA."

Olivia's chin rubbed my shoulder as she peered at the items on the dresser. "Sure."

I tried to ignore her invasion, but my body stiffened. "Excuse me?"

Olivia stepped back. "What?"

"I'd prefer you not get so close." My neck warmed.

Olivia's eyes widened. "Touchy, aren't we?" She turned and stomped from the room.

Glad to get rid of her, I completed my inspection of Jill's dressing table. Next, I examined the closets flanking the fireplace. I checked pockets, sleeves, tags, and hems. A shelf in one closet held a hatbox marked New Zealand. Jill kept a step stool tucked under the bottom shelf. As I lifted the hatbox, a puff of dust made me sneeze. A vacant spot next to it had a dust-free rectangular silhouette. Someone had removed an object recently. The maid, Mrs. O'Sullivan, might know more about it.

The hatbox contained articles of children's clothing and a well-loved antique doll. Worn and tattered, like the stuffed toy in *The Velveteen Rabbit*. Its lace bib barely clung together. When I lifted the doll, her glass eyes rolled open and met mine. The creamy coconut-and-peaches scent of gardenias wafted from the box. A tingle danced on the nape of my neck as I situated the doll onto the bed.

Like with my antique desk from a past case, the doll attracted me. A desire to possess her swept over me. The longer I examined her, the greater my yearning became to own her. Her glass eyes inexplicably calmed me. Mesmerized, I stepped back.

Thoughts of the used Barbie dolls from my father passed through my head.

Once the tingling subsided, I lifted the doll from the bed and checked for labels. Effenbee had molded their name onto the back of her neck. When I righted the toy, her eyes rolled open. My neck tingled again as the gardenia scent intensified.

The doll's eyes seemed to trigger a physical reaction. But had it, or was it Barbie being dredged up from my childhood creating a weird paranormal link?

Either way, I felt something strange and this time, my system was free of antidepressants. Plus, my hormones had stabilized. I'd reconciled my past. That left me as the common denominator. I doubted that I was a medium. But I wouldn't rule out me being crazy. Or that I had a genetic mutation that linked me to objects from the past. That mutation could best explain my sensations.

I placed her back in the box and returned it to the closet shelf. Arms and legs shaking, I left the bedroom convinced I hadn't missed a clue, and lightheaded from my reaction to the doll.

Jill had hung professional photos of her corgis on the wall along the stairs. I admired each one as I descended. Eli appeared in the last photo at the bottom. He gazed up lovingly at Jill, who sat on the same bench where we had met in Central Park. The candid print caused a lump in my throat. I planned to ask Austin for that picture.

When I returned to the library, the aroma of pizza

accosted me and wiped out the sweet scent of gardenias that had lingered from the doll.

Olivia emerged from the kitchen and waved a slice at me. "Interested?" she asked as she stuffed it in her mouth.

"No, thanks. I brought my lunch. Besides, I'm headed to Ms. Hamilton's art gallery."

"Afraid you'll get pizza sauce on the artwork?" She chuckled, then grew serious. "You can't touch anything in there. Austin made that clear."

"I won't touch anything." I passed through the kitchen, and opened the pocket doors to the gallery, leaving Olivia by herself. I knew about the artwork restrictions. Austin had set the rules at our last visit.

Jill had equipped each piece of art with security sensors. A chair in front of Walt Kuhn's *The Blue Clown* suggested it was a favorite of hers. It was becoming my favorite, too.

The pocket door at the opposite end of the gallery that led into the foyer slid open and Olivia emerged. Hesitating in front of the Kuhn, she licked her fingers as she leaned in for a closer look. Her eyes narrowed as if the painting puzzled her.

I controlled my impulse to tell her not to touch it. "Nice, isn't it?"

"It's okay if you like clown paintings." She scrunched her face, then moved to the next painting.

"I do." Her interest in the Kuhn revived my niggle about it. "Please check with Austin to see if he hired a professional to catalog the paintings. Be sure the back sides are photographed."

"There can't be much worth seeing on the backs." Olivia made a face.

"You'd be surprised where I've found hidden letters, photos, documents, and even coded messages."

She shrugged as she passed me and entered the foyer to the living room where I heard her talking on her phone, presumably to Austin. Putting her to work might discourage her from draping over my shoulder. I shuddered at the memory of her breath on my cheek.

I lingered over Jill's art collection, procrastinating a full-fledged attack on the library. The huge number of books overwhelmed me, so I sat in a stuffed reading chair and called Mrs. O'Sullivan. She answered at once and agreed to meet the next day at Jill's. Apparently, she hadn't pledged secrecy to the Hamiltons.

"I should be the one to clean the flat. Jill wouldn't want strangers touching her things."

"I take it she was a very private woman." Mrs. O'Sullivan's mention of Jill's feelings about her personal things caused an uncomfortable guilt that dampened my enthusiasm.

"Aye. That she was." Mrs. O'Sullivan paused. "I'll check with the lawyer before I come."

"Sounds good. I'll be here until after four o'clock today."

We disconnected and I exited the gallery through the door that led to the kitchen. Between the kitchen and the gallery, the architect had tucked a pantry and a half bath on one side of the hallway.

A quick scan of the barebones bathroom revealed nothing.

The pantry held a few collectible cookbooks that looked unused and a small recipe file of yellowed index cards. I fanned through them. Nothing.

I moved on to the kitchen and ate my lunch. I'd packed myself tea, a peanut butter and jelly sandwich, and a bag of M&M's. Hopefully, the lingering aroma of pepperoni wouldn't spoil the peanut butter flavor.

Olivia walked in midway through my meal.

I held up my sandwich. "Want half?"

Olivia stared at me like I had two heads. "I just ate a whole pizza."

"Right. I won't take long. I know you've got to study."

Her face belied what I interpreted as disgust as she left the room. Her voice floated in the stairwell. But she'd already spoken with Austin, so who was she talking to now?

When she returned, she wore a satisfied expression. "All set. Murbeck will take care of the artwork. Do you mind if I join you for tea?" She rummaged through the cabinets, moving around the tins of tea bags. "I prefer pekoe."

We didn't have much in common to talk about except Austin, and that wasn't going to happen. She planned a career as a prosecutor. That is, if she passed the bar. Even though I'd only been out of school for ten years, I'd forgotten how tedious students could be when they're struggling through their major exams. All they talked about was the material they were studying. That's why they formed such lasting bonds with their classmates. Nobody else tolerated them during this time. Sam and I bored my poor mother the same way. She'd sit and smile at us as we rambled on.

When our conversation in the kitchen stalled, I decided it was time to return to my task in the library.

Jill's desk, the dominant furnishing in the room, beckoned to me. Not like my antique desk, but with a mournful ease. Austin had given me permission to search its drawers. The organized surface held paperweights, pens, and pencils. A day planner spoke to Jill's fastidious nature. At least, until I opened the top right-hand drawer and discovered chaos. I wondered if maybe the mess reflected Jill's inner conflict.

Anxiety in my past clients caused by unknown parents manifested itself in similar ways. She'd wanted to learn the identity of her birth parents, yet her fear kept her in turmoil. Adopted children wanted to know why their parents abandoned them at a young age. I shared that feeling about my father. I blamed myself, even though as an adult, I knew better.

My phone vibrated, interrupting my search. Mrs. O'Sullivan confirmed her visit the next day.

Unmarked folders contained printouts describing places in New Zealand, Canada, France, Italy, and

Great Britain. A book published by the Charles River
Editors, *The Disappearance of Dorothy Arnold*, hid
beneath her files—the same woman Jill had mentioned
in Central Park. She had slipped a folded paper inside
its front cover with "Must Read" printed on it. She had
listed *Engaged Girl Sketches* by Blake, *The Bond* by
Boyce, and *Lorenzo in Taos* by Luhan.

I photographed the list for future reference, then
opened the Charles River paperback. Jill had highlighted a portion of Chapter Four where a theory
suggested that Dorothy Arnold had a rendezvous with
a man just prior to her disappearance. The author also
emphasized Dorothy had traveled the world with her
family. Further on, Jill had highlighted another police
statement indicating they believed Dorothy had run
away.

For some reason, Jill cared about Dorothy Arnold
and her travels. Was Dorothy's fate tied to this case
somehow? Would revealing what happened to her help
me locate the beneficiary?

It didn't matter because my contract didn't include
solving another century-old cold case.

I replaced the paperback. If Jill had copies of the
three books on the list, I'd ask to borrow them for
several weeks to properly review them. It was something I'd rather do at home. I'd also request the
contents of the top drawer be sent to my house, another
task that required time and concentration to learn what
Jill had discovered about Dorothy Arnold's disappearance.

Next, I pulled open the center drawer. It reflected organization. A neat pile of stamps, stacked envelopes, and writing paper in the rear. A front tray held a letter addressed to me.

I lifted it up and examined both sides. She hadn't affixed a stamp, so I suspected she had second thoughts about mailing it. I fought the urge to open it.

Just then, Olivia poked her head in and interrupted my search. "How's it going?"

"Fine." I hesitated, then waved the letter. "I found this addressed to me. Should I read it?"

"Why not? But you can't take it with you."

Jill hadn't sealed the envelope, so I pulled out the single sheet. She'd prepared a formal request, asking me to investigate her birth parents' family lineage. Apparently, she planned to write her memoirs and wanted to include her adoptive heritage. She added, *I've always had the desire to write but struggled to put the right words together. I think I inherited my longing to write from one of my blood relatives. A memoir should satisfy that need.* That's where the note stopped. No closing. No signature.

"She planned to hire me to trace her family trees."

Olivia turned to leave the room, stopped, and said over her shoulder, "Mr. Bradley should let you have the letter. I'll check."

"Thanks." I returned it to the envelope. A sadness settled over me as I thought about Jill and her solitary life. When she did decide to search for her roots, she died. I didn't want to die before I found my father. I'd never stop looking.

Distracted by the letter, I moved on to the far end of the bookcases. Shaking off my melancholy, I donned a pair of disposable gloves, shoved a rag in my pocket, shifted the ladder to the far end of the shelves, and climbed to the top. A heavy layer of dust had settled on a set of the classics. I left it for the cleaning crew. The next level down, I wiped each book with the rag as I checked it.

I'd completed two bookcases, excluding the bottom cabinets filled with boxes and old magazines, when Olivia cleared her throat several times. Her interruption ended my search.

"What's up?" I asked as I climbed down and joined her.

"It's almost five o'clock." She bit her lower lip. "Remember? I have an exam tomorrow. Are you almost done here?"

I brushed dust off my pants. "Not even close. But let's quit for the day."

"By the way, Mr. Bradley said you may have the letter."

Olivia called the limo driver. I packed up.

Being cooped up in the car with her again bothered me. Besides, after all that dust, I needed fresh air. "I'll walk the few blocks back to the House of the Redeemer."

Her face relaxed. "Be careful. Traffic's bad this time of day."

She hadn't exaggerated. Bumper-to-bumper traffic crawled along Fifth Avenue. Luckily, I didn't have to cross. I strolled along the east side of Central Park and arrived at The Retreat within a half hour.

After a day, I hadn't found much, except the doll. The hair on my arms lifted at the thought of her.

Chapter Nine

My physical reaction to the doll suggested I should contact a friend at the University of North Texas. Dr. Art Eisenstein and I had spent hours discussing my inexplicable link to my father. It was more than a desire to reconnect. I sensed we'd never disconnected spiritually.

Art had studied spiritualism, epigenetics, and consciousness of the mind. Maybe he could help me understand my connection to the desk and now the doll.

Once back at The Retreat, I wrote him a long email. I received an automatic response from his work mailbox. He'd retired a year ago, but my message had been forwarded to his personal account.

* * *

After splurging on a mango salad at Three Guys on Madison Avenue, I returned to the House of the Redeemer, where I stayed whenever visiting the city. Once inside, I wandered through the foyer into the 1600s library the Vanderbilts had relocated from an Italian duke's palace. An exquisite coat of arms decorated the two-story vaulted ceiling.

I wondered if Jill Armstrong had ever visited this place. What little I'd garnered from her townhouse suggested she'd have loved it.

When Sam and I had stayed here during a previous project for Austin, we discovered a charming hidden staircase behind closed doors. I made it a point to use them instead of the building's unreliable and stuffy elevator.

Once in my room, I pulled out my laptop and searched for the three books on Jill's "Must Read" list. I hoped she had them in her library so I could review her copies. She may have inserted notes explaining why she included them with her family research. Maybe I'd find something that would lead me to her ancestors.

Lorenzo in Taos by Mabel Dodge Luhan turned out to be a memoir by the author that contained letters between her and D. H. Lawrence. And Dorothy Arnold had purchased *Engaged Girl Sketches* the day she disappeared. Was that another link to Dorothy Arnold, or was it a book to satisfy Jill's literary interests? The remaining book was by Neith Boyce, an unfamiliar author. I'd need to research her and read her novel, *The Bond,* to determine if it was related to the case.

Tired and perplexed, I shut down my computer and called Sam.

"Any news about the clock?" I asked. I still felt guilty over my lack of enthusiasm the other day.

"Things are percolating. How about you? Solved the case yet?"

"No. And I didn't get far searching the library. I found a few interesting items including an unfinished note Jill had written to me. She wanted me to find her birth parents. I don't know if she changed her mind or ran out of time."

Sam was silent for a moment. "I bet she wanted to review what she'd discovered before she engaged you. Get her ducks in a row."

"Possibly. I assume all is quiet on the home front." I didn't want to bore him with details of my day any longer.

"Pretty much. The dogs are their usual pesky selves, but they're fine. I miss you every minute we're apart, so come home soon."

Sam's voice soothed me and made me feel loved. I missed him, too, but when I worked, I immersed myself without the luxury of thinking about him or home. Feeling guilty, I fired off a quick, "I love you."

We shared a few romantic words, then disconnected. I laid back on the pillow. I did miss him when I heard his voice, but it would be a lie to say I missed him every minute we were apart.

More guilt.

* * *

Olivia wasn't in the limo when the driver picked me up in the morning.

Austin's other intern, Tim, faced the rear, giving me a front view of our travel route. He wore another expensive suit in navy accented by a maroon and blue paisley tie. He played the lawyer role well.

"Morning," he said, glancing up from his textbook. Apparently, prime assignments for interns did not include babysitting a genealogist. His disinterest in me indicated he'd pulled the short straw.

"Good morning." He might not have been happy with his assignment, but he showed me respect, and I liked him for that. I relaxed and enjoyed the views as we crawled through morning traffic.

Once at the townhouse, I returned to the library. A search through this many books would require breaks to keep focused. Otherwise, I'd miss important margin notes or, worse, skip pages.

A quick scan across the lowest bookshelf proved just how rattled the letter addressed to me had made me yesterday. Jill's three *Must Read* books sat in easy reach, in plain sight, and I'd overlooked them. "Oh, for Pete's sake!"

When I pulled *Lorenzo in Taos* from the stack, Post-it notes stuck out between multiple pages. She had tagged references to Kathryn Mansfield and Neith

Boyce Hapgood, highlighting their names in yellow. I set the three books aside for further review.

By noon, two bookcases remained. I chose the one farthest from the desk next to a stuffed chair. It held catalogs of prints from the Met and two other art museums in town. The well-used tomes showed me her art preferences. Jill had turned down the page corners of some of the paintings.

She'd also kept a 2013 catalog from an exhibit with a Walt Kuhn identical to hers. The certificate of authenticity of her piece would confirm its identity. I was unsure how this would relate to the case, but my gut said it was important. I made a note to research the provenance of the Kuhn painting.

Tim, the young law student, stuck his head into the library. "How much longer?"

"I still have the lower cabinets. I won't finish today." I looked at my watch. "Plus, the housekeeper's due any minute for an interview. Why don't you check with Austin? Perhaps, he'll let you leave once the housekeeper is here. I won't be searching after she arrives."

Tim left, already punching numbers into his phone.

I composed an email to Austin, asking permission to take home the family research documents in Jill's desk drawer, plus the three books. It wouldn't hurt to try.

He replied immediately. *Sorry, nothing leaves the townhouse. But I'll have copies made.*

Before beginning to search the bookshelves, I made a cursory inspection of the lower cabinets to estimate when I might finish. One held stacks of old *New York Times* papers. Another harbored board games and writing supplies. Wildlife books, small boxes, and bric-a-brac filled the remaining six cabinets. No way would I be done by three o'clock to keep my appointment with Mrs. O'Sullivan.

Tim returned to the room, looking pleased. "Mr. Bradley said I could leave once the housekeeper arrived if you promised to stop your search."

I put my hand over my heart. "I promise."

Tim gave me a thumbs-up and returned to his studies.

I'd worked my way through half of one cabinet when a *ding* announced the elevator's arrival. A nasal and breathy female voice, which I surmised to be the housekeeper, bantered with the elevator operator. Their conversation sounded familiar, as though they'd known each other for years.

"She's in the library." Tim's voice echoed from the foyer.

Maybe Mrs. O'Sullivan would provide some solid answers.

Chapter Ten

"Gracious, young lady, are you doing my job, cleaning out those cabinets?"

I backed out of the lower cabinet and looked up from my sitting position on the floor. A pint-sized lady I guessed to be in her seventies smiled down at me. Silver and gray Dutch braids crowned her round head that sat atop a body shaped like a heavy punching bag.

"Mrs. O'Sullivan?" I couldn't help but smile.

"At your service." She leaned over and stared into the cabinet. "What a mess! I'll be cleaning that out."

"I'm searching for a clue. I hoped you'd help."

The shock she wore told me I'd been unclear. Her lips quivered. "Help with what? Was Jill murdered?"

"No. No! I didn't mean to alarm you." When I stood, I met the clear blue eyes of the tiny lady. "I'm trying to locate someone I suspect is Jill's biological relative."

"She didn't have blood relatives in New York. She was a wee tot when she sailed all the way from New Zealand to the States." Mrs. O'Sullivan's rounded eyes nearly swallowed me. "When the Hamiltons collected Jill, they took my Mam with 'em. Mam always said she got off one boat headed west from Erin Shore and boarded another heading in the same direction within six months. My Mam nannied Jill for fourteen years."

"You knew Jill for a long time."

"Most of my life." A gentle sadness masked her sorrow.

I peeked into the empty living room. "Would you like to sit in there?"

"Not so much. I prefer the kitchen. That's where I feel most at home. And lass, please call me Maggie."

Maggie slipped a bibbed apron over her cotton print dress and bustled around, clearly familiar with the kitchen. Within minutes, she produced a pot of tea and a snack. As she placed the plate of cookies on the table, her chafed hands shook. "These biscuits will thaw by the time the tea is steeped. We keep bags of 'em in the freezer for such emergencies."

I smiled at her calling my visit an emergency.

Maggie tucked a loose wisp of hair into a braid. "You want to know who Jill's birth parents were, right?"

"Yes, I do." For a moment, I thought I'd solve the case today over tea and biscuits.

"Well, me, too! What parent would abandon such

a little tot?" She shook her head. "I'd have given 'em a piece of my mind!"

My optimism faded. "Sounds like you enjoyed working for Miss Hamilton."

"An odd duck, that Jill, but I blamed her behavior on orphanage life in her formative years. Any unwanted babe like her would likely be a little touched by the fairies."

"Touched by fairies." I'd never heard the expression, but *odd duck* described the woman I'd met in Central Park.

"A moody tot, that Jill. She'd get mean and sometimes violent. As she grew older, she'd sense gloom coming on and would withdraw into herself for days. I'd hear her playing with her doll." Maggie shivered. "But she'd keep to her room. No doctor ever found anything wrong with her."

"Then, they believed her moodiness was worse than that of a normal child." I assumed so, otherwise they wouldn't have sought a professional opinion.

"Mr. Hamilton said Jill's birth mam suffered from the same darkness. That's how I found out he knew of her."

"Did Jill know her mother?" Somehow, I doubted she did, but it would help to know.

"She never spoke of her." She pursed her lips. "What kind of mam would give up their child?"

"The kind of mother who had no other alternative, I suspect." Unsure of the social climate in New

Zealand in 1926, I speculated that it was like the rest of the world, filled with uncertainty. Digging into the details surrounding the society of that time may reveal why Jill's mother abandoned her.

"It doesn't seem possible...manky business." Maggie's face froze in a deep scowl.

I paused to let her relax, then continued. "Did Jill mention her life at Saint Saviour's Orphanage in Christchurch?"

Maggie thought for a moment. "Ne'er a peep."

"Did you play together at the Hamilton's when you were children?"

"No. When I got older, I'd spend time at the Hamilton's, substituting when Mam couldn't work, so Mr. Hamilton offered me the job when Mam retired. He knew Jill and I got along." Maggie stared at her hands for a moment before she looked up. Her uncomfortable eyes betrayed her.

I worded the next question carefully, hoping she wouldn't shut down. "Were the Hamiltons aware of Jill's dark spells when they adopted her?"

"I'm pretty sure that's why they adopted her. Nobody else wanted a problem child, but Mr. Hamilton knew Jill's family." She whispered as her eyes glistened, "Being a Hamilton, he had a soft spot for orphaned babies, especially those born stained. You know—out of wedlock."

"I don't understand what being a Hamilton has to do with it." Actually, I suspected it had to do with

Alexander Hamilton being born *stained*, but I wanted Maggie's opinion.

"His great-grandfather suffered the shame of the stained. To prove his worth, the poor man became an overachiever." Maggie frowned at me. "I'm surprised you didn't know that about Alexander Hamilton."

I hadn't fooled her. "Actually, I did. I'd read about Hamilton's insecurities and to honor him, his family focused on orphaned children when carrying out their social duties."

"Yes. After Jill's adoption, her father, William, called New Zealand relatives to learn more about Jill's strange behavior. Mam told a story about how one day he disconnected and called for his wife, Miss Isabelle.

"When she entered the library, she found Mr. William slumped into a chair with his head in his hands." Maggie fiddled with her apron. Finally, she continued. "Miss Isabelle abruptly closed the door. Mam heard wailing, but the Hamiltons emerged from the library silent and never mentioned the conversation.

"Mam would repeat the behind-the-door story when I'd complain about Jill's moods. She'd say Jill had been scarred by an event at the orphanage."

"So sad." I took a deep breath. "Last question. Do you recall any journals or diaries belonging to Jill or her parents?"

Maggie thought for a moment, then she shook herself from head to toe. "No, miss. Just that manky doll she carried from New Zealand. Every now and then, she'd beg me to fetch Patsy for her. She would stare into those creepy eyes as if in a trance."

I jotted a few notes to let Maggie recover before I spoke. "I'm sure after all these years with Jill you'll receive a few of her personal items. There must be things you'd treasure."

"Not really. Jill took care of me. I'll not suffer." Her eyes filled. "I'd have kept the dog, but no pets are allowed at my place, and I don't want to be moving after all these years."

I reached across the table and grasped her hand. "Don't worry. Eli's living with me now. My husband and I adopted him when we read about Jill's death. I had met him and Jill in Central Park last year on a case. He charmed me and I couldn't stand the thought of him being...well, you know what happens if nobody adopts an orphaned dog."

She nodded and wiped her nose on her apron. "That's wonderful. Bless you, girl."

"What about the doll? It's one of Jill's treasures." I wanted to know more about Patsy.

"No way! If you ask me, the doll's possessed. Those eyes!" Maggie shuddered for the third time at the mere mention of it.

"Do you know who gave it to her?" I waited, hoping for a name.

Maggie shook her head. "Jill didn't know. She had it when the Hamiltons collected her at the orphanage. If they knew, they never told her, or she forgot."

"Being so young, she might not have remembered."

Finding the buyer would be a challenge, but I might be able to find where they purchased Patsy. That could lead me to a potential buyer and public records.

Maggie lifted the teapot. "More tea?"

I checked my watch, then shook my head. "It's getting late."

"I'd like to stay another half hour." She scanned the kitchen. "Clean up a bit."

"The police or Mr. Bradley gave you permission to be here alone, then?"

Maggie winked at me. "They didn't say I couldn't. Besides, I've been paid out 'til the end of the year. I still work here."

I grinned. "Okay, then. I'll count on you to lock up."

"I've locked up this place every day for the last forty-two years until seven months ago." She wiped another tear from her cheek. "I think I can do it one more time."

"Of course you can. By the way, I noticed the dustless outline of a box beside the one marked New Zealand where I found the doll. Do you know what happened to it?"

Maggie stiffened and stared at her hands. "No...no. No idea."

"Any idea what it contained?" She had lied and I knew it, but I didn't want to confront her today.

"Papers, mostly. Old letters and documents from her art collection." She thought for a minute. "I bet the appraiser took them to help value the art pieces."

"Maybe." Maggie wasn't a good liar, but I didn't press the point. She'd lost a friend and confidant. She needed time to recover. Maybe she'd tell me where it went at a later meeting. Besides, Austin wouldn't let anything leave the townhouse. If I spoke to him before Maggie told me where it went, I'd let him know I suspected Maggie took a box of something before Jill died. "I'm going to look at the doll one more time before I leave."

"Go ahead. I'll stay down here if it's all right with you." Maggie stood, collected the plate, and ate the few remaining biscuits while I headed upstairs.

The hairs on the nape of my neck lifted as I slid the box containing the doll off the shelf. The scent of gardenias drifted in the closet. Once again, when I lifted the doll and tipped her to open her eyes, our gazes locked.

Finally, Maggie called from the stairwell. "Are you okay up there? Do you need help?"

"I'm fine. I'll be right down." My head buzzed as I put the box away. I didn't know how long I stood there staring into those sparkling blue orbs.

Steadying myself with the handrail, I descended to the foyer.

Maggie and I stood waiting for the elevator. "Would it be convenient to meet me here if I have more questions?"

Maggie's eyes filled. "I'd like that a lot."

As the elevator doors closed, I heard her singing an old Bing Crosby song, *It's the Same Old Shillelagh*. I smiled. A memory of my dad popped into my head...he was singing the song while he pranced and waved a walking stick.

Chapter Eleven

The limo picked me up at the House of the Redeemer at nine o'clock sharp. Olivia wore the same drab gray pantsuit as she sat slouched in the front-facing seat. She ignored my greeting. I rode in silence with my back to the driver for the short trip to Jill's townhouse.

When the elevator door opened at Jill's foyer, I beelined to my favorite place in any house, the library. If I launched into my search, I could finish by the end of the day.

Olivia headed for the art gallery. "I need a cup of tea," she said as she strolled straight through to the kitchen, thankfully out of my hair.

I noticed spaces in several of the rows of books, gaps that matched the ones in the half-dozen volumes Jill had piled beside her reading chair.

"What made you interested in these books, Jill?" I lifted the first one and read the title aloud. *"The Life of*

Katherine Mansfield by Alpers." I opened it and began reading. *"Born Katherine Mansfield Beauchamp, she chose to write under a pen name..."*

"Yes! Mansfield used her middle name as a pen name!" I had found my first potential connection to the heir, Roy A. Beauchamp. Jill and Katherine might be related. This could be the relationship I needed to find him.

Katherine's story hooked me. I became immersed and before I knew it, I'd spent an hour reading her biography. I wouldn't finish my search if I continued to read, so I set it aside. I fanned the pages of the remaining books. They described the lives of several prominent turn-of-the-nineteenth-century writers who at first glance didn't appear to help me, but I'd dig deeper later. The final book, a Gertrude Stein volume, remained stiff as if it had never been opened.

It took me until one o'clock to finish the last bookcase. One lower cabinet remained.

"Time for a quick lunch." My stomach growled as I carried my insulated bag to the kitchen. I'd packed my favorites, a peanut butter and jelly sandwich, unsweetened tea, and a bag of M&M's labeled *Sharing size*. I got a kick out of the bag labeled as such. Who shared M&M's? The bag claimed to contain nine servings, so I ate nine handfuls between sandwich bites and counted it as nine separate servings to rationalize I hadn't overindulged.

* * *

At two o'clock, I returned to the library and attacked the last cabinet, one crammed full of photograph albums, with the most recent ones in front. One new scrapbook contained baby pictures of Eli when Jill first adopted him. I'd never met him as a puppy. I planned to ask Austin for these photos, too, if the heirs didn't want them. Assuming I found the heirs. After digging through dozens of boxes and collections, I had produced no additional leads.

While replacing the last box in the back of the cabinet, I noticed a small object stuffed in a back corner. Someone had stored a dilapidated album in a plastic bag. Paper flakes had settled in the bag's bottom.

Without warning, Olivia's stick-straight hair brushed my shoulder. Garlic breath warmed my cheek. "What do you have there?"

Once again, she'd invaded my personal space. On instinct, I scooted backward and sat cross-legged a few feet away. Olivia claimed Jill's chair.

"It's an old photo album." I placed the artifact on the rug and gingerly slid it from the bag. The silk string bound together the rotted leather covers. Tiny chips of yellowed paper fell like confetti whenever I moved it. The musty odor seeping from its pages warmed me with a fond memory of our local library archives.

"You won't get much from that." Olivia wrinkled her nose.

"You'd be surprised." I carefully laid open its front cover. A note written in cursive on the flyleaf said, *Isabelle Hamilton, 1931.* Jill's adoptive mother had kept a mother's brag book. Today, smartphones had replaced them, except for those grandmothers who weren't tech-savvy.

A black and white photo of a woman holding an unsmiling child slipped from the next page. The tiny girl clutched a familiar doll. She held Patsy, the doll with the crystalline eyes. The hair raised on the nape of my neck.

The toddler had to be Jill. Her size and serious look suggested the photo marked her adoption. "The woman must be Isabelle."

Olivia pressed in for a closer look. "You'll need a picture of Isabelle for comparison."

I paused, afraid to turn another page. "It's disintegrating with every touch, and I need to study the photos. I'd like to take it home where I have the proper handling tools like a book snake, a cradle, or some foam pads."

The smug look on her face gave away her answer. "That won't happen." She walked to the window as if to gain insight from a neighboring building. "Mr. Bradley reaffirmed his instructions just before I left the office. But he'll get copies of anything you want to study further." She turned to me and hooked a greasy strand of hair behind her ear. "Mr. Bradley said it's not about trust. The contemporary Hamilton family is litigious. They contested their Aunt Adelaide's will when she died. And they've already made noise about Jill's estate. He's protecting the firm."

The hairs on my neck bristled. It wasn't what she

said that rubbed me wrong. It was the tone she used, implying I might question Austin's motives.

"This album needs special handling. It needs a professional archivist—or someone like me with equivalent skills, not some high school geek at Office Depot."

"I'll pass that nugget on to Mr. Bradley."

"So, how long will it take for copies?" With a six-month deadline, I didn't want to wait.

"I don't know. A week or two."

I slipped the album back into the bag. "What about the artwork? When will I have those photos?"

Olivia's face stiffened. "I haven't arranged anything yet. It slipped my mind."

"You can't be serious."

"I have another life," Olivia snapped.

"Whatever," I grumbled. "It's getting late." I decided I might have to speak with Austin about this.

"That means we're done here, right?" Olivia's voice softened.

"Yes. I've checked everything I can until I get the copies." I emphasized the last three words.

"Great. Are you riding or walking?"

"I'll walk." We both needed space. Besides, I craved fresh air after spending hours in Jill's stale-smelling townhouse.

Olivia called for a limo ride as we headed for the elevator. We split up downstairs at the front door.

I grabbed take-out on my walk back to The Retreat. Sam would be calling, and I didn't want to be in a noisy restaurant.

* * *

"How's the case progressing?" Sam asked.

He grunted a few responses as I described finding the photos and the Mansfield biography. I sensed he had something else on his mind, but he let me finish my briefing.

"How did your day go?" I asked.

"Unbelievable. The clock Paul Logan asked about is a 1910 Seth Thomas worth fifteen hundred dollars!" Sam babbled on for the next twenty minutes before he realized he hadn't given me airtime to respond. "Sorry. I get pumped when I find an item this rare."

I laughed. "Yes, you do."

My heart melted hearing Sam this excited again. He'd felt responsible when I nearly died during a previous case. It had taken him a while to forgive himself. We talked for another five minutes before he begged off for an incoming call. "This could be the guy."

After our usual I-love-yous, we disconnected.

Staring out the window at the dark streets of Manhattan, I mulled over what I'd found at Jill's. The doll, the books, and the photo album. They weren't enough to link Jill to Roy Beauchamp, but I'd begin with them. I'd need to do a lot more research and even then, it might not take me where I needed to go.

Even though I could go home, Austin had mentioned a living relative of the lawyer who had handled Jill's adoption. His daughter lived in a New

Jersey seniors' community, ninety minutes away. She might have some useful information, a lead connecting some of the dots.

I checked my notes and found her name, Joan Shannon—Senior Horizons in Clinton, New Jersey. Their website provided a number to call. Maybe Austin was right. Maybe she'd be candid with me.

The receptionist transferred me to Joan immediately.

The robust woman's voice that answered surprised me. I stumbled through an explanation for my call without revealing any names except Roy Beauchamp from New Zealand, the man in question. If she knew about me working for Murbeck, she might not agree to meet.

She remained silent for a moment. "Where did you get my name?"

"Through research for a case I'm handling to locate Roy Beauchamp. His U.S. family belonged to New York's high society. I found your name mentioned on a regular basis in the Society Section of *The New York Times*, which suggested you might be familiar with some of the old guard." I sweated bullets, hopeful my voice didn't give away the lie.

"I knew most of the players until the last five years. I might be able to help, and it sounds like a fun walk down memory lane." She laughed.

"I'm in New York. Are you available tomorrow? It would save me a trip."

"Tomorrow's fine. My days all blur together. I'd

love a conversation about something besides medicine and achy joints. Meet a new face—one without wrinkles and liver spots." She chuckled again.

"Great. I should be there by noon." I couldn't wait to meet this woman. She sounded like a hoot and seemed genuinely interested in a visit.

Would she be interested enough to share what she knew? And did she know Jill Hamilton at all?

Chapter Twelve

Seeing the entrance to Senior Horizons in New Jersey brought back a childhood memory of a similar visit years ago. A typical four-year-old, I'd napped during the ride to Nonni's senior apartment and woke up cranky, fussing about missing cartoons that Saturday morning.

Mom wasn't in the mood to deal with me. I know now that she didn't want to be there any more than I did, but she felt guilty about her mother not receiving visitors. My nine-year-old sister, Caitlin, stepped in and grabbed my hand. She dragged me through the doors, maneuvered me through the lobby full of grandmothers in wheelchairs, and down a carpeted hall ladened with the scents of old people. Smells I now recognized as a disinfectant, unwashed bodies, and urine.

When Mom unlocked the door to Nonni's unit, a fragrance of mint and camphor filled the air, an odor that still reminded me of her to this day. Heavy drapes covered the one window in the living area. An alley kitchen, a combination living and dining area, a postage-stamp-sized bedroom, and a floor-to-ceiling tiled bathroom had been crammed into a space the size of our two-car garage. Nonni's overstuffed furniture clogged the room. Dim overhead lights cast shadows on the beige carpet with a worn path leading to the bathroom.

Caitlin and I sat at Nonni's feet while she patted our heads and chattered about the other residents. Mom didn't have patience for gossip, so we didn't stay long. She always regretted cutting our visit short that day. Nonni died unexpectedly a week later.

Funny how certain memories remained vivid after decades. I could still smell the Bengay.

The main entrance to Joan's community mirrored Nonni's building, except it resided in New Jersey. The door clicked and swung toward me as I reached for the handle. A shrunken elderly man in a wheelchair beamed at me. "Surprise! I'm going out to lunch."

I grinned and stepped back while a stylish woman navigated his chair through the exit.

She returned my smile. "Dad loves restaurants."

He smacked his lips. "Food's good here, but variety's the spice of life."

His smiling daughter kept moving.

I waved at the pair and said, "Enjoy your lunch, and have a nice day."

"You have a nice day, too! Don't order the meatloaf.

They put carrots in it." His scrunched face telegraphed his opinion of the practice.

"Thanks for the warning."

I entered the lobby to a pleasant surprise. Unlike Nonni's retirement home, this place had charm. A vaulted beadboard ceiling and a fieldstone fireplace greeted me. In front of the fireplace, leather furniture flanked a glass coffee table with hardcover picture books. The lobby décor didn't scream institution like Nonni's facility had. And the air smelled as fresh as the outdoors. My dread turned to intrigue.

A receptionist at the window asked if I needed help. "Are you RaeJean Hunter?"

"Yes. I called earlier. I'm here to visit Joan Shannon. We're having lunch."

"Joan's expecting you. She's at her usual table—the corner to the right of the fireplace."

I looked around to get my bearings.

"The dining room's straight ahead on your right."

"Thanks."

If I'd taken a moment, I'd have guessed its location. A slow stream of pedestrians, walkers, and electric wheelchairs clicked and whirred down the corridor like lemmings migrating to the sea. Heads of silver and white hair surrounded me as I weaved through the maze of furniture and medical equipment.

I reached out my hand. "Mrs. Shannon. I'm RaeJean Hunter. We spoke on the phone." Her smooth face hid her age. If it wasn't for the rice-paper-thin skin that clung to her cold fingers as we shook hands, I'd never have guessed she was in her eighties.

"Call me Joan. I've thought about your case since your call. I've made a few notes." She pointed to a folded paper on the table next to her. "I hope I can be of some help."

"I hope so, too." It remained to be seen just how much help she could offer since she only knew what little I'd confided on the phone, and the name of my client remained a secret. I didn't like being devious, but since Austin had indicated bad blood between Joan and Murbeck, I didn't mention him or his firm.

"Let's enjoy lunch before we get down to business." Joan waved to a waiter. "If we wait to order, the kitchen may run out of the special—chicken Alfredo. It's one of their best dishes. If you like chicken, I'd recommend it."

"Sounds good to me."

The waiter took our order and delivered water while we waited for our salads.

Joan folded her hands on the table in front of her. "So, you're a forensic genealogist."

Her opening surprised me. I hadn't mentioned my profession during our phone conversation. I'd kept my conversation focused on my search for an heir. I could have been a private investigator. "I am. How did you know?"

"I surfed the Internet after your call. Bloodline Forensics, a clever name. I may be old, but I'm not dead." She laughed. "I try to keep my mind active by staying current with technology. When I turned eighty, I challenged myself—set a goal to learn how to surf the world wide web. I struggled using these." She waved her twisted hands at me.

"Arthritis?"

She nodded. "I use a mouse if I must, but I love Siri. She and my Mac are my best friends." She paused. "We used to call your projects 'probate' or 'missing heir' cases. You said on the phone that a large inheritance could go to Columbia University if the heir isn't located."

She surprised me when she didn't ask who died. But she'd remembered everything I'd told her.

"Yes." I hesitated. "As I told you on the phone, I've been hired to find Roy Beauchamp. He's in line for a substantial inheritance. Usually, swarms of relatives clamor for their fair share, but this case is about an adopted woman's legacy with no immediate family."

Mrs. Shannon pursed her lips as she absorbed what I had said. Her eyes darkened.

I continued. "Without known siblings or children of her own, her adoptive father set up the trust before he died. He wanted it to go to one of her relatives, a relative the deceased never knew existed, a man named Roy Beauchamp. Have you heard of him?"

She shook her head. "I am familiar with the name Beauchamp, but not Roy. It's a prominent family name in New Zealand. I've traveled Down Under several times in my life. The Beauchamp name is common there."

"I've heard that." Austin had spouted a list of well-known political leaders and lawyers with the same name. "I'm sure you read about the woman found dead in Central Park a month ago."

"Yes. I saw her picture in *The Times*. I read it every morning. Some habits are hard to break. I don't know many of the New York society elite anymore. Everyone I knew either lives in a seniors' home or is six feet under. But that's life, isn't it?" Her lips thinned into a weak smile.

Trying to steer the conversation away from the depressing moment, I said, "This is a beautiful retirement facility."

"Or an upscale prison if you have no means to get out." She shook her head. "I'm sorry, but I loved living in the city. The staff tries to keep us busy, but I miss city life, the theater, ballet, and the symphony. In here, I'm just another old fossil."

"It doesn't sound like you're like everyone else. You read *The Times* and surf the Internet and have personal goals. Who else living here does that?"

She looked around. "You'd be surprised. Most of these old ladies set goals. Not the same type as me." Her eyes sparkled. "You see the old guy sitting by the door?"

I looked for the gentleman. "Yes?"

"He's a target. Half the women in this room have set a goal to snare him. He's gotten so gun-shy that he barks at anyone who even says hello. A big-time politician in Utica, he planned to climb the ladder to the state government, but never made it."

I choked back a laugh, not sure what to say. Fortunately, our lunch arrived. The chicken was scrumptious, and Joan did everything but lick the plate.

"Let's have dessert outside. I like to get my vitamin D naturally." She slipped the folded note into her sweater pocket as she left the table.

As I followed Mrs. Shannon to a patio adjacent to the dining area, I retrieved my list of questions from my pocket and eliminated the first few. I'd need to be direct with a shrewd woman like Joan, or I'd get nowhere.

Chapter Thirteen

We collected our ice cream topped with fresh fruit and moved to an umbrella table on the patio. The cool air nipped at my uncovered arms. I'd anticipated low temperatures in March in New Jersey, but I'd left my jacket in the car. My mind had been on the doll and the books I'd found that Jill had been reading.

"Will you be warm enough?" Joan pulled her sweater tight. "It's a brisk day."

"I'll be fine." I fumbled around in my purse for a minute before realizing I'd packed my mini recorder in my suitcase. "Darn."

"What's the matter, dear?"

"I forgot my recorder." I retrieved a small notebook and pen. "This will work."

Joan smiled. "Good job. Always have a backup plan."

"Exactly." I readied myself, then began. "As I said

earlier, I'm trying to locate Roy Beauchamp. He emigrated from New Zealand in 1944, right after the war. I thought you might be able to help because you knew the Hamilton family in New York City."

"New Zealand. Hmm. That's interesting."

I waited.

"As I said at the beginning, I don't know Roy." Joan stared at the patio floor for a moment, before answering. "But I knew of a Beauchamp family from New Zealand. Grandmother didn't speak of them often, but she did mention how her friend, Adelaide Hamilton, wired money on a regular basis. That would have been before Mother had me."

"Do you know the name of the Beauchamp who received the money?"

She retrieved the folded note from her pocket. "Here are the names of everyone I can think of who may help in your research."

I recognized Adelaide Hamilton's name immediately. "Is your grandmother's name on this list?"

"No. Why?" She clenched her jaw.

"I'd like to include her in my research."

Joan's eyes narrowed. "I'll answer your questions about her if you reach a point in your investigation where it might matter."

She had raised her guard for some reason. I let it lie and pursued information about one of the other women. Scanning her list, I saw that she had underlined one woman's name.

"You've underlined a woman named Charlotte Parks Samuels. Who was she?"

"Mary Arnold's mother."

At our chance meeting in Central Park, Jill had commented that we could be looking at the path of Dorothy Arnold's last walk. In my brief research into Dorothy, I'd read that Mary was Dorothy's mother's first name. "Any relation to Dorothy Arnold?"

"Good guess. Charlotte was Dorothy's grandmother." Her eyelids fluttered as she looked away. Her stiffened body language suggested she knew more than she shared.

Doubt crept in about my persuasive abilities with Joan. "Did you know Charlotte?"

"I'm old, but not that old." She rolled her eyes. "I knew about Dorothy. For many Decembers after Dorothy's disappearance, Mother visited Greenwood Cemetery in Brooklyn to place flowers on Mary Arnold and her mother Charlotte's grave. Mother felt bad that Mary died believing her daughter lived, but not knowing where. Mother said she'd whisper the location to Mary in her grave if anyone ever found Dorothy."

She closed her eyes, took a deep breath, then looked at me. "It's a sad story, you see. Dorothy wanted more out of life than being a society woman. She rebelled against her father's strict rules. Did things behind his back, like hanging out in Greenwich Village with writers and traveling to Boston with a boyfriend."

I scribbled *Greenwich Village, writers, Boston, a*

boyfriend. Leads to follow-up on. She'd given me a few more breadcrumbs. "Anything else?"

"In 1905, Dorothy traveled to Paris with her brother, John, before she left for college. She visited the Rue de Fleurus and met Gertrude Stein and her brother, Leo. Apparently, someone she met there promised her an audience with Katherine Mansfield in Brussels."

That explained Jill's reading choices. "And?"

"She went to Brussels but made her brother promise to keep her trip a secret. John kept his word about Dorothy's side trip until after she disappeared. That's where Grandmother and her friends believed she met someone who helped her disappear."

I'd check manifests of ships leaving from the East Coast to Europe during the period Dorothy and John might have traveled. Try to pinpoint their trip. Then, I'd check for writers from Greenwich Village visiting Europe at the same time. Particularly Brussels.

"Was that the end of Grandma's stories?"

"No. Like I said, those women talked about the disappearance for years. My family knew everyone involved in the case including John Keith, the Arnold's lawyer."

I checked her list and found Keith's name. Another person to research.

I made notes while Joan paused for a sip of water. She'd provided a link from Jill's parents to the law firm that handled Dorothy Arnold's disappearance.

"Mr. Keith's reputation became slightly tarnished

with his handling of the Arnold case, but lawyers watched each other's backs. They probably still do. I've always suspected he had strong feelings for Dorothy and that he had helped her."

My hopes of a quick solution faded the longer we talked. "These relationships are complicated."

"That's New York society. That's what I miss, and why I loved it so much. It's complicated. A challenge. But once you understand it, it becomes simple. Back then, everyone of note knew each other." She shook her head. "Not like today. The city has become unmanageable."

I checked the list for other well-known surnames. "And your grandmother fraternized with the Hamiltons."

She nodded. "She did."

"When I mentioned earlier about the woman found in Central Park, you said you'd read the article in *The Times*. Why didn't you say you knew Jill Hamilton? Have you been keeping this from me for a reason?"

Her eyes sparkled. "Of course. You're working for Murbeck, aren't you?"

She'd seen right through me, but I held the company line. "I can't disclose my client."

"I detest helping those rascals, but Isabelle Armstrong and Mother remained best friends until Isabelle died. She was such a dear lady. I knew about the trust, but Isabelle never disclosed the conditions. She adored Jill and wanted to ensure her future. I'd love to solve this mystery. Jill and I weren't close, but I loved her dogs. She always kept corgis." Joan's gaze drifted toward the umbrella shading us.

I scowled. And from the sounds, she'd confirmed the real mystery in this case, Dorothy Arnold's disappearance. "You've provided me with numerous options. Do you recommend anyone that I should research first?"

"Yes. Look into female friendships. Back in the early 1900s, people in New York's high society helped each other. They kept secrets. That is, if secrets can be kept." She laughed. "Maybe one of them kept a diary where she recorded the circumstances surrounding Jill's adoption."

Secrets—that's how my last case went, but I hoped for a direct path on this one. "Maybe. But finding private diaries depends a lot on luck. It's not easy."

"Not much that is meaningful in life comes easy. A lesson I learned long ago."

"True." I reflected on my own situation and our desire to have a family.

"The women I mentioned, my mother included, were progressive thinkers." She paused and stared at the sky. "They railed about how Congress freed the slaves but left women as nothing more than their husbands' chattel. They belittled their higher education, claiming it prepared them for nothing more than marriage—entertaining their husbands' guests. But Mother was brilliant. What might she have achieved with the benefit of an advanced education?"

"Probably a lot, if she's anything like you." I reached out and patted her arm.

A random thought spilled from Joan. "Dorothy's father wouldn't support her ambition to become a writer."

Her statement prompted a question. I started to ask, but she'd closed her eyes.

Her frail hand shook as she ran it through her hair. "I'm sorry, Ms. Hunter, but I suddenly feel very tired. I hope I've helped a little."

"You have. You gave me a list of friends. Where would you start?"

"Start with the wives of the Columbia University alumni." She winked. "Armstrong, Hamilton, and Arnold graduated from Columbia, King's College back then."

"Should I delve into the men's lives or their wives?"

"Both, dear. Things back then were like today, except now the Internet spreads gossip as fast as meatloaf on the menu travels through this institution. They put carrots in it!" She scrunched her nose. "An indiscreet affair back then became fodder for a proverbial grapevine. I guess things haven't changed that much."

I laughed. "No, they haven't. Why start with the women?"

She raised her eyebrows. "It's obvious! Women kept diaries and wrote personal letters to each other sharing gossip. Men focused on business."

"Right. If men kept journals, they wrote about their businesses or monetary successes." Although I'd found some gossip in letters between men, I generally found mostly task lists or expenditures. All business.

She hesitated for a moment. "Most of the women of society didn't contribute to the family income. They managed the household staff, so they could donate their time working for charitable groups. Try the Children's Aid Society. That's one of the oldest organizations in New York City. I believe you'll confirm the relationships I've mentioned. Several of the women on that list participated together as board members."

"I'll do that. Thank you for seeing me. You've been a great help."

"Something will pop into my head the minute you leave. My mind works that way now. I remember every word of Sinatra singing *Autumn in New York*, but I can't remember what I had for breakfast." She laughed and took my hand. "Come by to see me anytime. I love talking to someone who has all their faculties."

"I will. Once again, it's been my pleasure."

I left Clifton with several leads. I'd use my trip home to sort out my subsequent steps and lay out a plan.

Jill mentioned Dorothy Arnold, and Joan Shannon had brought up her name. Somehow, Dorothy Arnold fit into my current case.

Chapter Fourteen

Back at home in Wyncote, I searched the Internet for charitable groups in New York City in the 1800s. At Joan Shannon's suggestion, I studied the online records for the Children's Aid Society. Being one of the oldest organizations in the city, I anticipated New York's elite women would be members. Not surprising, the 1873 list of board members included mostly men. But I did find two of the four women Joan had mentioned on the board, Adelaide Hamilton and Charlotte Parks Samuels.

Once convinced I'd exhausted that lead, I reviewed the thin folder Austin had provided for Roy Beauchamp. The private investigator said Roy may have immigrated to the United States in 1944, but the PI hadn't recorded his source. I emailed Austin requesting it to secure the primary documents.

Austin replied immediately. *Sorry. You have every-*

thing I received from the PI. If you need further clarification, contact him.

I did exactly that, but I held little hope for answers. I couldn't be sure, but if shoddy work was to blame for the lack of information, then there was a chance he had minimal interest in anything but his fee. And, if that was the case, it would surprise me if he recorded where he found his information.

After sifting through ship manifests, I came up dry. None of the West Coast ports of entry listed a single male with the first name Roy. The tedious task of reviewing the hundreds of U.S. immigration manifests for that year lay ahead. I needed a break.

"Sophie and Eli, what do you think?"

Both dogs lifted their heads.

"Outdoors?" I didn't need to ask twice. I barely had the word out before Sophie sprang to her feet and dashed to the door with Eli nipping at her heels.

Dog feet clicked and thumped down the oak stairs, through the music room, into the kitchen, and halted at the French doors leading to our deck. Sam stood outside with his back to the house, phone to his ear. The dogs barreled into the back of his legs. He caught himself from falling into the porch railing.

He disconnected from his call and turned, grinning as he steadied himself. "How's the research going? Any luck finding Roy?"

"Not yet. I've read all the available ship manifests. Next, I'll tackle the immigration records. I half expected Roy to show up by now. Beauchamp might have traveled under an alias. Or the ship's captain never filed the trip manifest, or he lost it."

"Maybe he arrived as part of the crew."

"Most manifests list the crew members along with the passengers if they've worked their way to the States."

Sophie and Eli returned and stood by the door, panting and lapping at the bottom glass panels. I wasn't sure whether they enjoyed the dog slime they'd deposited earlier or if they were adding a new flavor.

"Are you guys ready for water?"

Sophie barked, and Eli wiggled his stub of a tail.

"I better get back to work. Let's go." They plowed through the door shoulder to shoulder, each wrestling to reach the water dispenser first.

* * *

Back at my desk, I logged on to the immigration database and began searching for Roy A. Beauchamp. Nothing. I bracketed 1944 by six months and resubmitted my search. Still nothing. Next, I searched for any male with "Roy" in the name. The search returned sixteen passengers with names of Leroy, Elroy, Delroy, Royal, and Conroy on various ships.

An immigrant named Conroy Parks arrived from New Zealand in 1944 through Eastport, Idaho, after arriving on the ship *Canberra* at the Port of Seattle. The others arrived from different countries not yet on my radar. I noted them but put the list aside. I'd focus on Conroy Parks since Aunt Adelaide sent money to New Zealand and Jill came from New Zealand.

Joan mentioned one woman with no relationship to a Hamilton or an Armstrong, Charlotte Parks Samuel, Dorothy Arnold's grandmother. Her surname of Parks before marriage matched Conroy Parks'. Not much to go on. I plugged "Conroy Parks" into a broad search on the Internet.

Within an hour, I'd narrowed my list to the Idaho Panhandle. A 1996 obituary from Bonners Ferry reported the death of Conroy Parks, a man born in 1916 in Dunedin, New Zealand. He had to be the immigrant. He left a wife, Rozine, two daughters, Virginie and Margaret, and a son, Lester, all still living.

Lester Parks resided in Bonners Ferry. Within minutes, I found his phone number listed in an online directory and called it. He answered on the second ring.

"I ain't buying nothin'," the man said.

"Please don't disconnect. I'm not selling anything. My name is RaeJean Hunter, and I'm looking for a relative of Conroy Parks." I spoke fast, hoping he would listen.

"Why should I talk to you?" The man growled under his breath.

"Don't worry. It's nothing bad. I'm trying to locate Mr. Parks for a relative." I knew better than to give out information about a potential inheritance. If I did, I'd create all sorts of problems. Once people thought they might have been left money, they would try anything to convince you they were that person.

"What relative?" Lester's voice softened.

"I'm not at liberty to disclose that yet. I require a positive identification that you're the correct person before I can share details."

"Well, I ain't the sharin' type neither, so you might as well forget it."

"Don't hang up. Listen." I explained a few details without revealing the gold at the end of the rainbow. "Do you have a relative named Charlotte Parks Samuels?"

"No idea. My daddy never talked 'bout relatives." He paused. "And I ain't 'bout to, neither. I gotta—"

"Lester. Wait a minute. You might have had an aunt who lived in New York City."

"What do you mean *had* an aunt? Did she die?"

"Yes. They found her body in Central Park." Lester sounded interested.

"I ain't surprised she croaked in the park. Probably got mugged. Ain't safe in big cities."

"Nobody mugged her. She died of natural causes at age ninety-two."

"What the heck was she doin' alone in the park at that age?" Lester snorted.

"Walking her dog. I met her there last summer when I worked on a different case. We talked for a few minutes because we both owned corgis."

"The Queen's dog. Never saw the charm in them stubby-legged wieners."

The hair rose on the back of my neck, but I resisted the urge to hang up. Instead, I pinched my leg. This could be an opportunity to get Lester to open up. "Do you have a dog, Lester?"

"Used to, but he died. Never owned anything but huskies. My last dog stole chickens until my neighbor followed him home one night with a shotgun. Said if I didn't tie up the dog, he'd fill old Rex full of buckshot. He wasn't lying. Rex left one night and never came back."

Too much information for me, but he'd opened up and relaxed a little. So, I asked one more question, hoping he would answer. "Mr. Parks, do you know if your father changed his name when he came to the United States in the forties?"

"Could have. When he'd get liquored up, he'd talk about the war. His buddies called him Arnie." Lester hesitated and added, "But I ain't sure why. He never explained."

I continued. "Your father's obituary indicated you have two sisters. Are they still living?"

"You ain't gonna get nothin' from them. Marjorie moved to Seattle years ago, and Ginny lives at the old family farm. She's a half-wit. Never leaves the place." Lester's voice softened. "But she's a good kid."

I cringed at him calling his sister such names. "Does Ginny have a phone?"

"Yup. A cellphone. But she don't answer unless she knows you."

I kept rolling out the questions. "Did your parents leave behind any diaries or letters?"

"Never seen none. But if there was papers, they'd be at the farm with Ginny."

"Would it be possible for me to meet her?"

"I'd have to go with. Ginny fires our old shotgun at strangers. Daddy and me taught her to protect herself. Almost scared a Bible salesman to death a few years back." Lester laughed. "He complained to the sheriff, but the sheriff just told him to stay clear of the place."

"I'd like to visit Bonners Ferry and review the town records. I'll buy lunch when I'm there, my treat." I'd beg Sam to accompany me on this trip. There was no way I was going to meet the Parks family alone.

"Can't buy me that easy. Unless..." Lester trailed off mid-sentence.

"Unless what?" He wanted to haggle.

"Unless it's a ribeye. Then, I'd never refuse." He laughed.

"You're on. Ribeye, it is." I smiled to myself, relieved his price for helping me was a steak.

"It's a short ride to the farm from town. I'll drive you up in my rig. Ginny ain't gonna shoot me. I'd whip her butt." He laughed again, this time louder.

I shook my head, knowing he'd probably never lay a hand on his little sister. "We'll decide who drives when I arrive. My husband may be with me." I'd learned my lesson from past cases about being too trusting.

"Ah, shucks. And I thought I had a date." He

paused to chuckle. "Just kiddin'. By the way, the farm's in, umm, Good Grief."

"Are you okay?" He sounded stressed.

"Just dandy. Teasin', that's all. Good Grief. Look it up. It's in the Kaniksu National Forest. My daddy settled there 'fore the government took it."

"I will. Thanks for your help. I'll call with my plans once they're set."

"I ain't goin' nowhere." Lester disconnected.

* * *

When I shared my plans with Sam, he jumped at the chance. "I'll visit local antique shops. Most of my best finds are from rural areas."

I'd been on the case a week, and I'd found a potential candidate in Idaho. My optimism improved. Based on a ship manifest, a man had arrived from New Zealand in 1944. His last name, Parks, formed a weak link to Charlotte Parks Samuels, a name mentioned by Joan Shannon. And I'd found a possible relative of the deceased Roy A. Beauchamp. I just might ride this pony home.

Because it occurred to me that Conroy Parks could be an alias for Roy Beauchamp.

Chapter Fifteen

I received a package from Austin that included copies of the contents of Jill's desk drawer where she'd kept information about her ancestors. He had also sent *The Disappearance of Dorothy Arnold* and *Lorenzo in Taos* with a note saying he'd lend me the two books. He doubted the family knew of them but asked me to return them as soon as I had finished reading them.

I organized Jill's documents from her desk by name, but Jill hadn't identified all the relationships. If the name wasn't a Hamilton or an Armstrong, I had no idea where they fit on a family tree other than which generation based on dates. Her partial family tree had holes. I set her work aside until I had time to collect additional information to determine the relationships.

* * *

A digital copy of the photo album arrived by email two days later. Apparently, Olivia had called in sick and delayed things. She probably had to study for an exam. The sick excuse had worked for me, having once been a student. Two days wouldn't make or break my case, but insufficient prep for an exam would ruin a promising career.

Per my instructions, Austin's assistant had removed each picture and copied their front and back in the same order as they appeared in the album. For safe-keeping, I copied the file to a memory stick before I sent Greg—Caitlin's boyfriend, my tech support guy, and Sam's best friend—a copy to add to the case data-base. He would run a facial recognition program, if needed.

Austin included a copy of the more explicit work agreement. After another thorough review, I concluded the complicated language confirmed what we'd already agreed upon. I *loved* lawyers. Never a shortage of legalese.

The most interesting photo in the album turned out to be the one I'd already seen that captured Jill sitting in her mother's lap. Based on Jill's size, my second look agreed with my first impression that the photo had to have been taken soon after she arrived from New Zealand. Isabelle wore a chenille robe and Jill had on a printed nightgown. I shivered at Jill's blank-eyed gaze. It reminded me of how I felt after having nightmares when my father left us. The unsmiling girl clutched a doll identical to the one I'd found in her closet. It had to be Patsy. The glass eyes dominated the photo. The tingling...

The doll provided the strongest clues in the case by initiating my reactions. The more I knew about her, the better chance I had of solving the mystery. Just like the desk in my last case.

I found several versions of the toy on the Internet. Effanbee Company of New York mass-produced the first one, called Patsy, in 1928. Where it was manufactured wouldn't be as important as where it was purchased. The point of sale could lead me to the person who gave it to her. According to the housekeeper, Jill carried the toy from New Zealand and slept with it for years. The housekeeper wasn't sure who gave it to her. I made a card with the information about Patsy and that she was likely purchased in New Zealand. I'd get back to this line of inquiry later.

Another photo of interest included Jill with a familiar-looking woman having a picnic in a rural setting with a farmhouse in the background. In the photo, Jill held her doll as she presented the woman with a bouquet of fresh flowers. I'd ask Greg to search for the identity of the woman. A penned signature on the back floored me: *Bernice Abbott, 1931, 1/3.*

As I stared at the photo, I realized I'd seen an Abbott photo collection at the Museum of the City of New York located on Fifth Avenue. I logged on to their website and sent an email asking for help identifying and authenticating a photograph. I didn't expect to hear back right away. I'd contacted them on other cases, and they always responded, but not for two or three days. Depending on what I had, they sometimes had the information at hand and didn't need a copy of the photo. I'd wait for their response.

After studying a digital shot I'd taken of the woman, I cropped the image and sent it to Greg to run his facial recognition program. Then, I made a list of items in the picture that might identify the year and location.

I stood and went to the window. Eli licked my hand as I contemplated my next steps. The adoptive parents' family trees hadn't revealed much. Until I uncovered more about Roy, I couldn't tell if the two ancestral trees would reveal a tie to his family in Australia.

Back at the computer, I stared at the crystal-eyed Patsy doll in the photo. My entire body quaked. I set aside the album. "Time for a break, guys."

The dogs jumped up and raced downstairs.

Sam had met a client for lunch, so I grabbed a peanut butter and jelly sandwich and a glass of milk. As an afterthought, I threw a handful of M&M's on the plate, then went out on the deck to eat.

The dogs did their usual yard survey, and I planned my trip to Bonners Ferry.

I packed after lunch. Unsure of the March weather in Idaho, I repacked twice until satisfied that I'd covered all eventualities. When I put together items for my briefcase, I included the book by the Charles River Editors about Dorothy Arnold. I'd read it on the plane.

Maybe by the time I returned from the trip, Greg would have the identity of the woman in the photograph with Jill.

Chapter Sixteen

At the Canine Fitness Camp the next afternoon, Sophie leaped from the car and ran to greet a familiar golden retriever. She'd stayed enough times to always have a few buddies there.

Poor Mr. Eli, on the other hand, crouched in his crate, afraid to move. "Come on, Eli. It's okay. You'll make friends." His maiden trip to canine paradise posed a challenge. He refused to exit his crate. I pulled his collar to drag him out, but he dug in. He needed a dog whisperer, and I wasn't qualified.

"Mrs. Hunter, is this your new dog?" A young dog sitter approached.

"It is, but he's not cooperating." I stepped back, stood with my hands on my hips, and surveyed the situation.

"Let me try." She reached into her pocket and retrieved a hotdog-shaped treat.

"Hi, Eli." She waved the treat in front of his nose. The sissy-pants corgi stood and leaned toward her outstretched arm, nibbled the tidbit from her fingers as she lured him out of the crate.

Visions of him in Central Park flashed through my head. His eyes had followed every movement of my Coney dog that day. This moment with Eli resurrected memories of Jill's pained gait as she limped away from the bench where we'd sat together, the park bench where they'd found her body.

* * *

Sam and I boarded our flight to Spokane, Washington, early Tuesday morning. I hated flying, so a fifty-minute layover in Denver provided a nice respite. We arrived in Spokane by one o'clock.

After getting our bags and rental car, Sam and I headed for Bonners Ferry, Idaho. With the time change, we arrived at four-thirty. Even if Lester Parks turned out to be the wrong guy, the scenic drive made the trip worthwhile. I gawked for the entire ride, repeating, "I can't believe the views!"

The rugged terrain along our route contained mountain ranges, lakes, and valleys with rock outcroppings creating their own collage. We crossed Lake Pend Oreille on the north end where it met Pend Oreille River.

"The map shows that water flows northward to the

Columbia River into Canada." I laughed. "I thought all rivers flowed south."

Sam grinned. "Most do. But the mountainous topography makes this region an exception."

We wound through the city of Bonners Ferry and crossed the Kootenai River. After several turns, we drove into a parking lot fronting a three-story brick elementary school building. I climbed out of the rental car and stretched while Sam collected our bags.

Repurposing a school as a bed and breakfast required ingenuity. The owner had hung red canopies over the windows to soften the institutional appearance. Shocking red entry doors sat beneath an awning supported by massive white corbels. Two large urns on the stoop burst with petunias. It wasn't home, but the owner had made it inviting for guests.

"I feel like I'm back in grade school, except for the red canopies," Sam said as we sauntered up the walk to the Northside School Bed and Breakfast.

"Their website said the place functioned as a school for eighty years until shuttered in ninety-two." The idea of sleeping in a schoolroom intrigued me.

"So, it sat empty for quite a while," Sam replied.

"I think about twenty years. Until a couple came up with the idea to convert it into a bed and breakfast."

"I hope they up-sized the furniture for adults." Sam's eyes widened.

I laughed. "The owners did more than that. If it's anything like the website photos, you're going to love it."

I'd booked the Romance Suite, the one room with a king bed.

"Nice." Sam set the luggage down and went to the window to check the view.

"I struggled deciding which room to choose." I fluttered my eyelashes.

"Tell me more." Sam grinned.

"This is the Romance Suite, but I almost chose the Principal's Office."

Sam pulled me close and whispered in my ear. "We won't get sent to the principal's office unless we're naughty."

"I'll bet you spent a lot of time there as a kid." I snuggled into his chest.

"You might be right." He nibbled my ear. "Let's walk to town for dinner and after that see how naughty we can be."

"Dinner then naughtiness sounds like a good plan." I grabbed a sweater and floated out the door, thinking about dessert.

We headed out for a drink and a light dinner. We asked the innkeeper for a recommendation. He suggested Kootenai River Brewing across the river. A craft beer and a burger sounded good. Neither of us wanted a big meal.

"Bar or a table, then?"

"The bar. We'll have a better chance of interacting with the locals if we sit there."

We found two empty stools next to a man I estimated to be in his sixties. He'd spiffed up with a clean blue plaid shirt, jeans, and a baseball cap. I shuddered after my recent history with hired thugs wearing ballcaps.

He greeted us with a smile. "Evenin'. You folks here on vacation?"

"No," Sam answered. "My wife's here on business, and I'm her escort."

"You sure got a pretty date." He winked at Sam.

Sam sat next to the man in the cap, and I sat next to a woman and her husband. The couple argued over an appetizer selection.

Finally, the bartender intervened. "Listen, folks, I can get you half-orders of each, if you like."

"Can you do that?" the woman asked.

"I can do whatever I want. I own this place." He grinned and turned to me. "What can I get for you, young lady?"

"A glass of Two-Tail Pale Ale and a brewer burger. How about you, Sam?"

"Just a minute." He broke away from his conversation with the guy next to him and ordered a brewer burger and a Grizzly IPA. Turning back to the man, Sam said, "Do you know the Parks family?"

"Everyone knows Crazy Ginny. She guards the family farm like it's Fort Knox."

I'd leaned over Sam to join the conversation. "You know Lester Parks?"

"Yup. Me and Lester fish together."

"Did you know his father?"

"We fished together sometimes. But he pretty

much kept to himself on the farm up in Good Grief. Rumors had it he had a sketchy past."

"A sketchy past?" I wondered what that meant.

"He wasn't a heavy drinker, but he liked to hang out with the guys. One night, he told one of them he came from a rich family in New Zealand. When Roy realized what he said, he threatened to kill the guy if he ever repeated the story."

"He must have repeated it because you know about it," Sam said.

The guy smiled, took off his baseball cap, and put it over his heart. "Found the guy's body in the river six months later."

"Which guy? Roy Parks?" I asked.

"No, the man he talked with about his rich family in New Zealand. The coroner ruled it an accidental drowning."

"No way!" I reacted without thinking. This case possibly involved murder.

He replaced his cap. "Yup. I always figured Roy Parks kept his word."

"Two brewer burgers." A middle-aged waitress slid our plates onto the bar.

"I better get home to the wife. She doesn't mind if I stop for one drink, but if it gets too late, all hell breaks loose when I walk in my front door." He stood and donned his cap. "Nice meeting you folks. Enjoy your visit."

I watched him leave and wondered if he knew more than he wanted to share.

After we finished our sandwiches, we strolled back to the inn holding hands. The Romance Suite awaited us.

Sam turned out the light and pulled me close. As I relaxed in his embrace, a train roared by and blew its whistle. We lost ourselves in each other's arms.

Instead of swirling in eternal bliss after we'd sated our passion, I fell asleep wondering about Roy Parks and the body found in the river.

Chapter Seventeen

While I visited the Bonners Ferry municipal offices, Sam roamed through several nearby antique shops. We'd made plans to meet at the library just before noon. Lester Parks had suggested lunch at the Chic-n-Chop as he liked their large portions of home-cooked food. After lunch, we planned a trip to his sister Ginny's house.

I found the records room in the Boundary County District Court and signed in as a certified genealogist. After a brief introduction to the file arrangement, the clerk left me on my own.

The county filed marriage licenses in boxes by decade. As I had hoped, the box labeled 1940 to 1949 held the document for Conroy Parks and his wife. The Kootenai tribal elders had approved Rozine Redbird's marriage at the tender age of fifteen. My stomach turned over. A skeleton in my closet rattled, reminding me of my situation at fifteen.

Next, I pulled out the census records. Roy Parks appeared on the voter registration rolls from 1950 to 1990, but nothing after that. The Beauchamp surname never surfaced.

At eleven-forty, I headed to meet Sam. He stood leaning against the car and bent over to kiss my cheek. "Right on time."

He wore his *I-found-a-treasure* grin as he glanced at the backseat several times. I resisted peeking for a few seconds just to tease him. When I looked, I saw two items wrapped in brown paper, one square and the other about five feet long and tapered. "Looks like you found the Holy Grail."

"A beauty! We have time. Let me show you before I put it in the trunk." He lifted the smaller item from the seat and carefully placed it on the trunk floor.

"A clock. Right?"

He laughed. "Yes. But not just any clock. Wait until you see it."

I watched as he unwrapped the piece.

"It's a German pinwheel clock. The long piece is its pendulum. I've never seen anything like it. Typically, a clockmaker wouldn't use wood because it expands and contracts with changes in temperature and humidity, but this craftsman cleverly inlaid a mirror on the pendulum to stabilize the wood."

"It's gorgeous. Must be expensive." Sam didn't spring for high-priced antiques unless he had a buyer in hand. But he might be feeling giddy with the thought of our bank balance once I earned the fee for the case. "You know, I have to solve the case to earn the big bucks. And how do you plan to get this home?"

"Don't worry. I'll have it professionally packaged and use priority shipping. And you'll be glad to know I sent a photo to my client, the one who is buying the Seth Thomas clock, and he's already offered twice what I paid for this one, but I told him I'd have to do some research before I'd set a price. Besides, I have confidence in you."

"What did you pay for it?" I didn't really care, but his eyes betrayed him. He wanted to share his boon.

"I put it on a credit card. Fifteen hundred dollars." His sheepish smile convinced me that he needed to know I cared about his passions, too.

"Fantastic! That sounds like a steal. And a good investment." Maybe I overplayed my enthusiasm, but I felt guilty since I'd been obsessing non-stop about my case. Sam didn't notice.

"I'm hoping," Sam said as he swaddled his treasure before placing both pieces in the trunk.

"Now, we get to meet Lester Parks. This should prove interesting." My description of Lester after our initial conversation had made Sam laugh.

"I can hardly wait," Sam said as he slid into the driver's seat.

In less than five minutes, we arrived at the Chic-N-Chop.

A lanky timeworn fellow stood by the wheelchair ramp at the entrance. He puffed out smoke rings and grinned while he watched us park. Oily strands of salt-

and-pepper hair wrapped around his ears and hung to his shoulders. To tidy up his appearance, he'd tucked his red flannel shirt into a beltless pair of lightly soiled jeans. He waved his dirty white cowboy hat as he stubbed out the half-smoked cigarette on the side of the building and threw the remains on the ground.

I noted where the butt landed. I'd collect it later if Lester refused to be swabbed for DNA testing.

"Had to be you." He grinned, exposing a gap where a front tooth should have been. "A pretty couple in a white rental car."

Sam shook Lester's hand. "Nice to meet you, Lester."

Lester nodded, then looked me up and down. "You sounded bigger on the phone."

"That's a new one!" I said once he stopped laughing. I likened myself to an armadillo, small but tough on the outside. His cute remark paled in comparison to other comments I'd received.

Inside the Chic-N-Chop, we found a corner booth where we could talk freely. But Lester didn't seem interested in us. Instead, he flirted with our waitress, who looked like she'd been around the block more than once. I guessed her to be his age, early sixties. They knew each other because she called him a dirty old man.

Sam looked at me, raising one eyebrow.

Lester ordered chicken fried steak.

"I thought we agreed you'd get a ribeye?"

Lester grinned. "I was pulling your leg. Wanted to

see what my help was worth to you. But I ain't about to fleece ya."

I didn't recognize a couple of the dishes by their description or photo, so I ordered a fried chicken basket to be safe.

"Mr. Parks, have you recalled anything new about your father since we talked?"

He shook his head. "Not really, except Dad was a good trout fisherman. As a kid, I remember he'd be gone an hour, maybe two, and we'd have fish for dinner." Parks smiled to himself, enjoying the memory. As an afterthought, he added, "And call me Les."

"Les, it is."

When the waitress arrived with our meals, Lester reached out and pinched her backside as she served us.

"Les, cut that out!" She nearly dumped my chicken into my lap. Sam steadied the basket just in time.

"You still got the moves," Lester said, continuing his crude flirting.

Sam winked at me.

"You'll get my best move if you don't quit it," she said, throwing a mock punch in his direction.

Lester guffawed, then dug into his lunch as if he'd been starved for a week.

* * *

Once we finished our meals, the waitress returned to clear the table.

Lester mopped his plate with a dinner roll, cleaned

the excess white gravy from his chicken fried steak, and then popped the roll into his mouth. Pointing at the plate, he said to the waitress, "You won't have to wash this one."

She rolled her eyes, grinned at me, then hurried away.

I deliberately ignored their interaction as I formulated my next question. "We met a fellow at the brewery last night who claimed he fished with your father. He said something about a suspicious drowning. Do you know anything about it?"

Lester's eyes narrowed. "I've lived in Bonners Ferry my whole life. 'Course I know about it. Everyone's heard the rumor. I bet that guy wore a blue plaid shirt, jeans, and a baseball cap."

I nodded.

"That's Frank Perkins. He's the troublemaker who started the rumor. And that's all it is. A rumor. It ain't true. My old man may have been a loner, but he wasn't no killer."

"But he made a threat." I hated to press Lester, but my gut said his father's real name figured into my case.

"Frank never tells the whole story. The way I hear it, Frank, my father, and the drowned guy got drunk together. The three dared each other to tell a personal secret. Nobody knows what the men said, but my old man called it baloney."

"How do you think the man drowned?" I locked eyes with Lester, and he never flinched.

"He got drunk. Drove down to Kootenai Falls. Fell

into the rapids at the big drop." Lester paused for a sip of coffee. "End of story."

"You mentioned your father being called Arnie by his friends."

"My old man never said why, but I always suspected that Arnold mighta been his real first name."

"Maybe it was his mother's maiden name." Around the turn of the nineteenth century, parents chose the mother's surname, as a first or middle name for boys and a middle name for girls.

Lester shrugged. "Could be. But I don't know nothin' about that."

We sat in silence for a few seconds. Lester squirmed and kept staring at the door.

"Les, are you okay?" I had more questions, but he acted ready to go.

"Yeah. But we better hit the road. Ginny's expectin' us."

"One more thing before we leave. I'd like to swab a sample from inside your mouth for a DNA test."

Lester didn't answer immediately. He stared out the window. After a minute of contemplation, he turned to face me. "Nope. I ain't givin' the government my genes."

"This doesn't have anything to do with the government, but it could be the deciding factor for an inheritance."

He shook his head. "Nope. Don't think I wanna do that swab thing."

"It doesn't hurt." I showed him a kit.

He stared at it. "I ain't agreeing to no swab. Government doesn't need my DNA on file. They might wanna clone me!" He threw back his head and laughed.

Sam laughed a little too loud along with him.

"I doubt it. Besides, the government won't get the results."

"That ain't what I hear. Those computers get hacked all the time."

I tried to convince him he'd be safe, but I finally gave up. Something bothered him and he wasn't about to submit to the test.

The waitress returned with our bill. Lester tipped his head toward Sam and winked at the waitress.

"Keep the change." Sam handed her several bills.

Lester stood. "You guys ready for a ride in the country?"

We wound our way through the now-crowded restaurant. Lester stretched and belched as he headed toward the rental car. I signaled for Sam to occupy him while I retrieved the cigarette butt.

"Les, you ride shotgun and navigate." Sam pointed to the front passenger seat.

I climbed in the back, slipped the butt into an evidence bag, and hid it in my purse.

Occupied by entertaining Sam, Lester never noticed.

Chapter Eighteen

The thirty-minute trip northeast on Highway 95 to Good Grief took us into the Kanisku National Forest. About halfway into the ride, we turned onto a narrow road, crossed the Moyie River, then turned onto an unkempt driveway that led to a small cabin.

"You guys stay in the car until I signal. Wouldn't want anything bad to happen." Lester climbed out and approached the entry. A bluetick coonhound, lying on the stoop, stood and wagged its tail.

The cabin was maybe eight hundred square feet and had a front door flanked by two grimy windows and a small add-on the size of a bathroom. A half dozen dead cars, an old RV, a tiny A-frame, and four outbuildings filled the rest of the clearing. Tall evergreen trees provided a natural barrier blocking the wind off the mountains.

Lester and the dog disappeared into the cabin. He

emerged a minute later, yelled, and waved his hat, signaling us to join him. "All clear."

A small woman close to my size stood behind him, staring as we approached the door. Her unmatched outfit had food stains down the front. An odor of dirty socks drifted out the open door.

Lester slung his arm around the small woman. "This is my sister, Ginny. Ginny, this is the lady I told you about who wants to know about our old man."

Ginny sized me up, then turned her attention to Sam. Her face softened as her eyes roved up and down his body, hesitating at his pelvic area and again at his mouth.

Sam reached out his hand. "I'm Sam Hunter. Nice to meet you, Ginny."

She blushed as she shook his hand.

I reached out. "I'm RaeJean Hunter. I'm working on a case to locate a man named Roy Beauchamp."

Ginny ignored my outstretched hand. "I don't know no Roy Beauchamp."

She entered the cabin first, followed by Lester, me, and Sam.

A well-used Winchester Model 12, 20-gauge shotgun leaned against the counter inside the door with a box of birdshot sitting next to it. I wouldn't have been able to identify it except that we had the same gun that my maternal grandfather had given us. He'd bought it from a neighbor back in the late 1940s, telling my mother no house should be without protection. None of us ever shot it.

The air inside the cabin choked me. My eyes watered from the heavy musk of old furniture, dirty dishes, and wet dogs. The white kitchen chairs had taken on a brown hue reminiscent of earwax. An insect-encrusted strip of flypaper hung over a table mounded with empty TV dinner cartons. The waste bin overflowed onto the linoleum floor. The floor grime had worked its way out from the walls, leaving a small center circle of identifiable color. My sneakers stuck with each step.

"Let's sit in the livin' room and visit." Lester pointed toward a furniture grouping with a putrid green couch, a brown hairy recliner, and a coffee table. He grabbed a kitchen chair and placed it close to Ginny, who'd claimed the recliner.

The hound had settled on the couch. Sam lured the dog off the furniture, wiped away a nest of hair, and sat down. I perched on the edge next to him. I wasn't overly fastidious, but I'd need a shower when I returned to the inn.

"The lady wonders if you ever found any of the old man's papers around here?"

Ginny thought for a minute. "Got a stack of newspapers."

"Maybe old newspapers would be helpful, but I had hoped for letters or diaries." I smiled and waited as she tapped her thigh while she thought.

Ginny put her hand to her head. "I put Mama's shoebox full of letters in the old shed when Daddy

128

died. Didn't read 'em. I ain't a good reader, and they was full of lawyer talk."

"Which shed?" Lester asked.

"The new one with the metal roof."

Lester rose to his feet. "I'll go look. You guys visit with Ginny. Maybe she'll remember something." He hurried out the door and across the open field toward the row of ramshackle outbuildings.

I followed him to the door and watched. None appeared new to me. So, I waited until he entered an end unit, then returned to the couch.

Sam cleared his throat. "Ginny, what do you do to keep busy out here?" By the looks of the place, I knew it wasn't housework or yard work.

"Shoot vermin. Daddy taught me to shoot. He said it's my job to keep 'way the critters."

"I hear from Les you're a good shot." Sam smiled at her.

"Yes, sir. I can hit a red squirrel in the noggin at fifty yards." She puffed up her chest. "Daddy said I's the best shot in the family 'cept him."

Lester came through the door carrying a dusty shoebox marked 12 wide. Mama must have had big feet.

"I found it." He brushed off a layer of dust and lifted the cover.

"Give it to me. Daddy gimme the farm." She gestured with a broad sweep of her arm. "Everything here."

Lester's face reddened. "He did."

One hand on her hip, Ginny jabbed her finger at her brother. "You and Margie—you git all the bank money."

Lester shook his head and acquiesced. "Okay. Here, take it."

Ginny grabbed the box and clutched it to her chest for a moment. Then, she flipped through the letters, turning each one over twice before refiling it.

"I'd love to look at the letters." I worried she might wear them out by fondling them.

Sam smiled at Ginny. "Rae just wants to read them. She won't take them."

She smiled at Sam, then her eyes darkened. "I don't know. What do you think, Les? Should we let the lady look at Daddy's letters?" Her fingers fluttered back and forth across the tops.

Lester watched her for a minute before he spoke. "Oh, for the love of God, give the lady the box. There ain't nothin' in it to be ashamed of."

Ginny handed me the container.

Six eyes stared intently as I removed each letter and read it. Lester didn't lie. Roy Parks had spent most of his life working and saving his money to care for Ginny.

One of the last papers I pulled from the box was an invoice for a 1934 deed poll filing with a new birth certificate attached to it for Conroy Parks. The request originated in Wellington, New Zealand.

"This is your father's birth certificate with an issue

date of 1934 attached to an invoice for a deed poll filing.

"What's a deed poll?" Ginny asked.

"It's a legal instrument used to change a person's name."

Ginny's eyes glazed over.

Sam added, "It means that your old name disappears forever."

Lester furrowed his brow. "Our old man was always Roy Parks to us. He turned eighteen that year and needed a birth certificate to join the military. Bet he lost the original. Didn't tell us much about his old man 'cept that his father raised him alone. Never mentioned his mama."

I retrieved my phone from my pocket. "I'd like to photograph these two documents."

Ginny jumped up and grabbed them from me. "You can't have pictures of Daddy's papers. He gave 'em to me." She clasped them to her body.

Lester stood up and put his arm around her. "Now, Ginny girl, Daddy wouldn't mind if the lady took pictures. How 'bout I buy you some of those baseball cupcakes you like at Selkirk Sweets?"

Ginny relaxed and stared at the invoice and birth certificate. "Okay. I guess it'd be all right. Cupcakes best be chocolate. Not that icky lemon." She scrunched her face.

Lester winked, took possession of the papers, and handed them to me. I snapped a couple of photos with my phone, returned them to their envelope, and slipped them back into the shoebox. The last two envelopes didn't contain anything of interest.

"It's time we headed back to Bonners Ferry. Nothin' else here for you." Lester moved toward the door.

I held up my hand. "One more thing."

"Gonna hit rush hour traffic," Lester teased.

Sam laughed. "So, we'll see four cars instead of one."

"That's about the size of it." Lester chuckled.

I pulled out a swab kit and turned to Ginny. "I'd like to swab your mouth for a DNA test to identify your ancestors. May I?"

Her face blanched as she looked toward Lester. "I dunno. Did you swab Les?"

"Hell no. I know who my parents were." Lester looked at me. "But it ain't gonna hurt, Ginny. And it could mean we get another inheritance."

Lester's willingness to allow Ginny's DNA test surprised me after his adamant protests regarding his own swab.

"Don't we got enough stuff now?" Ginny twisted a strand of her unkempt hair.

Lester smiled his toothless smile at his sister. "Never enough stuff, sis. Why don't you go ahead and let the lady swab?"

At that moment, I had a feeling Lester was holding something back. Maybe there was a secret the DNA analysis would expose.

"I guess." Ginny turned to me and opened her mouth wide enough to fit her mother's shoe in it.

I rubbed inside her cheek with the swab, then sealed it in a container. "All done. That's it."

Ginny smiled. "Didn't hurt."

"Told you so." Lester turned and continued to make his way out of the cabin.

"Time to go." I looked at Sam. I'd had enough and was anxious to shower.

Sam stood. "Sounds good. Nice to meet you, Ginny. Good luck with squirrel hunting."

Ginny gave him a big smile. He approached her as if getting ready for a hug, but he tapped her shoulder.

As we walked toward the car, a shotgun boom rattled the silence, echoing off the surrounding hills. As if by instinct, Sam and Lester dropped to the ground. I froze. A puff of dust and sod lifted off the ground in front of an old vehicle.

"I got him!" Ginny hooted, running from the cabin toward a rusted Ford truck.

"Jeepers, Ginny. You shoulda waited 'til we got outta here!" Lester shook a fist at her.

Sam stood, brushed off his pants, and climbed into the driver's seat of the rental car.

It was a quiet trip back to Bonners Ferry where we dropped Lester at the Chic 'N Chop.

"Thanks, Les. I'm not sure where this will lead, but you've been invaluable."

"My pleasure, Ms. Hu—RaeJean."

I collected Lester's hair from the headrest before I

joined Sam in the front seat. I didn't put my head back. I'd need to clean it first.

Sam and I returned to the inn.

After a scalding shower, I studied the documents. "The best way to find out if Roy changed his name to Roy Parks would be to contact the New Zealand government or talk to someone in the law firm whose invoice is attached to the deed poll."

"Will either of those parties release the information needed?"

"I don't know. It depends. The only place that would have the original name is the application form for a name change or in the lawyer's files. I'm not sure if they keep paper applications as far back as 1934."

I'd call the New Zealand Internal Affairs Office when I got home.

This was more than a hunch. I'd finally found a real lead.

Chapter Nineteen

O n our way out of town, I had Sam stop at the records department. I had found Lester's parents' marriage license as well as birth certificates for both Margie and Ginny at the local town clerk's office, but I hadn't found Lester's yet. I wondered if he had a reason to refuse a DNA test.

"I'd like a copy of Lester Parks' birth record, please."

The clerk stared at me for a moment. "We don't have Les's records. They are in his birth county west of here. Shoshone County offices are closed today."

I rolled my eyes.

The clerk took pity on me. "I can request a copy and mail it to you. You should have it within two weeks."

"Two weeks seems like a long time."

"They make copies on Wednesdays over there. You'll have to wait."

"You're kidding." I'd worked with small towns before, but this one took the cake.

"Wednesday is Lindsey's day to work. That's the way it is."

I left her my address and paid the fee and postage.

We returned to Spokane, turned in our rental car, and stayed at the Hilton Garden next to the airport to catch an early morning flight. I missed my dogs and wanted to place my request with the New Zealand law firm for documents related to Conroy Parks' name change and his immigration records into the United States.

* * *

No direct flights flew between Spokane and Wyncote, so I'd brought along plenty of reading material. The four-and-a-half-hour flight time took over six hours with stopovers.

I pulled out the book published by the Charles River Editors about Dorothy Arnold's disappearance and read it from front to back in a half hour. Then, I systematically compared their report to what I'd found online.

There were minor discrepancies—the timing of some events, and the sequence of when evidence was found differed, but overall, I cobbled together a picture of known facts, the players, and the places of significance. To keep it clear in my mind, I opened my laptop and wrote my own version of the mystery of Dorothy Arnold.

On December 12, 1910, an event changed the lives of the well-to-do Arnolds of New York. On that date, their daughter, Dorothy Harriet Camille Arnold, disappeared.

She appeared happy on that day, but it could have been an act.

She lived a good life, graduated from Bryn Mawr College, and had ties to influential people like Justice Rufus W. Peckham. Her father, Francis Arnold, was an important figure in New York City.

But secretly, Dorothy had wanted to be a writer. Her family lacked faith in Dorothy's skills and mocked her when magazines rejected her stories. Late in the investigation of her disappearance, the family's lawyer, John Keith, revealed that Dorothy had rented a post box to receive her rejections in private.

Some folks suggested that she had a mysterious man in her life, but it was John Keith who escorted her to events. Her known boyfriend, George Griscom Jr., might not have been her actual lover. Dorothy lied to her family, saying she was meeting a college girlfriend when she visited Boston with George. On her way home from that visit, she pawned a large amount of jewelry for sixty dollars, and nobody knew what she did with the money.

The day of her disappearance, she'd gone shopping to buy a dress for her sister's society debut. Concerned or maybe suspicious, her mother confronted Dorothy as she prepared to leave their apartment on Seventy-Ninth Street and offered to go with her. Dorothy convinced her mother to let her go alone.

Dorothy had twenty-five dollars for a dress, the remainder of thirty-six dollars she'd withdrawn from her account the previous day to go to lunch with friends, and possibly the sixty dollars of pawn money, so a total of one hundred and twenty-one dollars—four thousand dollars present value! She headed toward Fifth Avenue.

Cold weather and slippery streets made her long walk a challenge. Along the way, she charged candy and a book to her father's account and bumped into a few familiar faces. Friends and shop owners who spoke to her that day recalled how happy she appeared during their last known encounters.

One reporter had remarked, "She disappeared from one of the busiest streets on earth, at the sunniest hour of a brilliant afternoon, with thousands within sight and reach, men and women who knew her on every side, and officers of the law thickly strewn about her path."

On that first night, the family didn't worry, believing she had stayed with a friend. The next morning, they called John Keith. When he arrived at their apartment, he searched Dorothy's room. He reported that none of her belongings were missing. *But how would he know that?* He also found personal letters with foreign postmarks in her desk, two folders for transatlantic steamliners on the desk, and burned papers in the fireplace.

When a friend called the next day, Mary Arnold lied, saying Dorothy had retired to her room with a headache.

Rather than alert the authorities, they proceeded with a private investigation and put their faith in their attorney, John Keith, a man they considered a family friend. He spent several weeks searching hospitals, morgues, and prisons.

She and George Griscom had corresponded through letters while he was in Italy with his parents. He later provided those letters to her father, who shared them with Keith and the other people searching for her.

On January 30, 1911, the Evening Star printed a story that indicated a worker at a local steamship agency had contacted police after seeing Dorothy's photo in the paper. He told police that on December 12, 1910, she had come to his place of employment and inquired about cruises to the West Indies. This led to theories about her eloping with a man. *But why the West Indies?*

Based on Keith's recommendation, the Arnolds hired the Pinkerton Detective Agency. Pinkerton repeated some of Keith's efforts at hospitals and interviewed more of her friends, then widened the search as far as Washington, D.C., but didn't find her.

After six weeks, the Pinkerton agents gave up, so the Arnolds alerted the authorities and got the police involved. A nationwide search ensued. Dorothy's father, Francis, offered a thousand-dollar reward for information leading to his daughter's whereabouts.

Francis believed that Dorothy had been attacked in Central Park and her attacker threw her body into the park reservoir. After the spring thaw, the police searched its waters but didn't find anything. Francis clung to this theory just the same. He preferred her dead to the idea that she had run away.

In a media coverup, Francis Arnold reported that his wife remained in New Jersey recovering from the trauma when, in fact, she and their son, John, had traveled to Italy to meet with George Griscom. They threatened George, but he claimed he had no idea of Dorothy's whereabouts.

"All I can see ahead is a long road with no turning —Mother will always think there was an accident." A direct quote from Dorothy's earlier letter to George. *What accident? Her disappearance?*

After George returned home, several of Dorothy's friends claimed that he had gotten Dorothy pregnant, and then had refused to marry her. *How would they know this? And which friends, exactly?*

A year after Dorothy's disappearance, Francis received a postcard signed by Dorothy stating, "I am safe." The handwriting matched Dorothy's. But her father believed someone had played a cruel joke. At this point, the police had already categorized her as a runaway.

Two months after her disappearance on February

15, 1911, a hotel guest reported seeing the missing New York heiress accompanied by a young man slightly older than Dorothy, eating supper in the café of the Windsor Hotel in Mobile, Alabama. The guest checked pictures in the New York Sun and the New York World. The guest claimed that the woman spotted him, and he heard her say, "He may be a New York detective. We had better leave this place at once."

Another plausible but unproven theory included amnesia after slipping and hitting her head. I would let that theory rest until convinced I'd need to pursue it.

Questions arose about her family. *Could they have banished her from the country and used the search for a body as an elaborate ruse? Had she become so upset from their mocking that she staged her disappearance?*

During this time, and even well after her disappearance, reports of sightings filtered into the police. Most of the tips proved to be false.

A kidnapping story turned out to be a hoax.

A report of a fatal abortion turned up nothing.

In the years following her disappearance, Francis Arnold claimed to have spent somewhere between a hundred to two hundred and fifty thousand dollars looking for her.

The search continued with George Griscom Jr., who also spent money to bring her home. Skeptics believed he tried to cover up the fact that he'd killed her. *Maybe it was a coverup because he helped her run away!*

During a lecture in New York in April 1921,

eleven years after Dorothy disappeared, Captain John H. Ayers of the Bureau of Missing Persons claimed that Dorothy's fate had been known to the Bureau and her family for some time. He refused to elaborate and would not reveal what happened to Dorothy. The following day, he claimed he was misquoted and denied that Arnold's fate was known. *Can we believe this?*

Francis died in 1922, insisting his daughter died in 1910. He wrote in his will that he would leave nothing from his estate to Dorothy "for I am satisfied that she is not alive."

Her mother, Mary, died in 1928. She never lost hope that Dorothy remained alive somewhere. *Or she knew that Dorothy was living somewhere else.*

* * *

When the pilot announced we'd be landing in ten minutes, I saved my summary of the Dorothy Arnold mystery and stored my laptop under the seat. The exercise of putting things into my own words had raised as many questions as it had answered for me.

Two things bothered me. First, people Dorothy interacted with on her last day remarked on her high spirits and good mood. Second, evidence found after her disappearance suggested she led a double life—a structured and proper life around her parents—and an unfettered life with friends in Greenwich Village where she'd spent most of her time there leading up to her disappearance. Yet, none of the references mentioned any interviews within the writing community. I couldn't fathom why the authorities would leave out such an obvious group of Dorothy's friends.

"You look puzzled," Sam said.

"I am. I think Mary Arnold knew more about her daughter's disappearance than she dared to reveal. Up to the day she died, she never lost hope that Dorothy was still alive."

"Or she wouldn't accept that her daughter died."

"Possibly. Or she knew what happened to Dorothy."

I ran scenarios through my mind about what Mary Arnold might have known. I didn't settle on one thing, but other names came up, including John Keith, their lawyer.

The plane bounced several times during touchdown. White knuckled, I squeezed the seat arms.

Sam winked, then wrapped his hand around mine.

Chapter Twenty

After arriving home late in the evening, Sam unloaded the car while I got the mail. The mail person had stuffed a signature-required notice into our box for a delivery addressed to me.

I waved the green card at Sam. "Somebody sent me a package. Says I can call for delivery or pick it up at the post office."

"Where's it from?" Sam asked through a yawn.

I studied the address but didn't recognize it. "New York, but it isn't Austin's office."

"Who else would be sending you something?"

"No idea." Although tired from the trip, I laid awake until after midnight. The mysterious package from someone in New York preyed upon me.

* * *

I rose at five the next morning. Sam joined me a little after seven.

"You got up early," he said as he made himself a coffee.

"Couldn't sleep." I'd planned to compile my trip findings first, but I'd decided to visit the post office and pick up the package instead. "The counter at the post office opens at eight-thirty. I'm going to pick up the package."

"Your curiosity got the best of you." He leaned over and kissed the top of my head on his way to his chair. "Collecting the package early is a good idea. You won't be able to concentrate. Just like Christmas."

"It is. I can't imagine what it could be."

"Have patience. You'll know in an hour."

While Sam visited the front porch for the paper, I continued to mull over the case.

"You look deep in thought." He tossed the paper on the table.

"I know it's speculation at this point, but more than one fact indicates Roy Parks and Roy Beauchamp were the same person."

Sam rubbed his chin. "Could be. Roy Parks came from New Zealand. And he had documents for a name change."

"I don't know what to think of the yarn about the three drunk fishermen revealing secrets to each other. And the fact that Lester said his father's friends used to call him Arnie." I sipped my coffee.

"It could just be one of his stories. You know, my fish is bigger than yours." Sam laughed.

"I suppose." Stretched to the limit, I relaxed and listened to him chatter about his clock. "I assume you'll be knee-deep in an appraisal today."

He grinned and gave me a Groucho Marx eyebrow wiggle. "Not just any appraisal. I barely slept, too, thinking about that German pinwheel clock. It could be one of a kind. If it is, it's worth twenty or thirty times what I paid for it. It's scheduled to arrive tomorrow."

"It's about time you earned your keep." I punched his arm. "I can't be the wage earner in this family."

When Sam didn't smile, I immediately felt bad about teasing him. He earned his keep in so many other ways. I threw my arms around him and hugged him tight. "Just kidding. Don't take me so seriously. You're my everything."

"Guess I'm a little sensitive today." He brushed my cheek as he walked past me. "I'd better get going. Let's have lunch on the back porch later. It's going to be a sunny day."

"Sounds great. I'm off to the post office." I grabbed my purse and keys and left.

The trip to the Wyncote post office took all of five minutes. People filled the lobby. It took me longer to reach the clerk at the counter than the drive over. I'd never been to the post office this early. Apparently, I'd chosen a popular time to collect mail.

The clerk glanced at the card as I pushed it across

the counter. "I'll be right back, Ms. Hunter." He disappeared into the mail sorting area, returning with a rectangular package the size of an extra-large shoebox. "Here it is. Sign here."

After signing, I hustled outside to examine the box. The return address lacked a name. I tried to open it, but whoever sent it had used strong tape. I'd have to wait another five minutes until I got back home where I had the proper equipment to prevent ruining the contents.

Back in my kitchen, I rummaged through the one place everyone had in their house: the junk drawer. There, I found a utility knife. Both dogs sat at my feet, staring up as I slit the tape along the top seam. Since we started ordering their food and treats online, they expected every package to hold a treat. Sophie bristled and growled at the package, but Eli wagged his stubby tail.

"Sophie, please don't start that again," I said. She'd reacted the same way when I received an antique desk last year.

"Sam," I called. "I'm back. Come watch me open the package."

"Sure." His voice boomed in my ear. I jumped a mile. I hadn't heard him walk into the kitchen. He laughed. "I heard Sophie. Go ahead."

I peeled back the top flaps of the box. The smell of gardenias alerted me to the contents before I removed the bubble pack wrapped around Patsy. The sender had enclosed a note. I opened it and read it to myself.

Sam leaned over my shoulder. "What does it say?"

"Oh, sorry," I said. "It's from Jill's housekeeper, Maggie. "

RaeJean,

There is no way I'll keep this creepy doll even though the lawyer said Jill had left it to me. I don't want it. Since you showed interest in her, I decided to send Patsy to you. Otherwise, she's going in the trash.

And about that missing box. I didn't tell you because Jill swore me to secrecy, but she sent it home with me about seven months ago. It held old letters and papers she'd kept over the years.

Respectfully,

Maggie O'Sullivan

"I knew it! I didn't push Maggie even though I knew she was lying. I guessed right that she'd tell me when she was ready." Those letters and papers could be a gold mine. I planned to call Maggie right away and see if she'd meet me at Jill's townhouse with the box.

"Unbelievable," Sam shook his head. "Women and their secrets."

I bit my tongue at Sam's remark. I wanted to comment that men had secrets, too. Instead, I pulled Patsy from the box.

"It's a doll," Sam said. "She smells like flowers."

Relieved that he smelled it, too, I smiled. "Gardenias, to be exact. They must have been Jill's favorite flower. Her entire townhouse reeked of them."

As I removed the blue bubble pack from around Patsy, the tingling at the base of my skull commenced. Then, her eerie blue eyes made of crystal rolled open and peered at me. We connected. My body tensed.

"Creepy-looking toy, if you ask me," Sam said. "It reminds me of the Chucky doll in the horror movie. Remember? The killer dies and uses voodoo to put himself inside the doll."

"Maggie felt the same way about Patsy. She loathed her. When I mentioned her, Maggie got a weird look."

Sam drummed on the table, did a little voodoo dance, and ended with a wild jump as he shouted, "Who–ha!"

His antics relaxed me a little, but my hands shook like I'd overdosed on caffeine. "As soon as I smelled gardenias, I knew it had to be Patsy."

"So, now she has a name." Sam hesitated, sliding his arm around me. "Are you okay? You're white as a ghost."

I nodded. "You startled me with your wild fandango, that's all."

"Those eyes." Sam wrinkled his nose. "And the clothes are stained yellow."

"True. But please, Jill Hamilton loved this doll." The blue eyes penetrated my heart as I thought of the tiny girl traumatized and abandoned in an orphanage.

Instead of frightening me, the more I studied her, the more I relaxed.

"Right. I'm going back to work." Sam had had enough of Patsy and returned to his study.

I carried her upstairs to my office with the two dogs trailing me. Sophie nipped at my heels between growls, but Eli had renewed energy and sprang ahead like a puppy.

Now that I owned the doll, I decided to give her a thorough examination. A cinnamon-colored wig glued at the crown with fuzzy tufts fanned out to cover the head. Maybe when new, the hair hid the painted brown waves beneath, but after eighty years the tresses hung in clumps and exposed it. Patsy looked like she wore a toupee. I sniffed her body. "Smells like a stale biscuit and gardenias." I glanced down at Sophie. "We know all about smells, don't we, girl?"

She wagged her stub of a tail.

Safety pins held the clothing together where buttons had been lost. An embroidered bib had worn thin from the extra loving of a child's touch, like the fuzz on the rabbit in Margery Williams' story, *The Velveteen Rabbit*. A full-length organza dress covered a cotton slip and a 1940s-style onesie with bloomer bottoms.

Maggie must have attempted to clean Patsy's papier-mâché head and appendages. The cheeks and forehead shined, but grime spots remained around the ears, mouth, and nose. The flesh-colored paint had worn off the tips of the fingers and toes.

When I placed Patsy in my satin chair, Eli jumped up beside her and laid his head across her. When Sophie approached to sniff the doll, Eli bared his teeth, ferociously guarding his former owner's treasure.

I moved the doll to the top shelf of my desk. The desk's quartz tulip flickered after remaining dormant for months. The nape of my neck responded with tingles. The scent of gardenias intensified almost to the point of nausea. I returned Patsy to the chair and laid the doll on her back to close her eyes. Eli rejoined her the minute I did.

He whined. I thought maybe the doll reminded him of Jill, so I reached down and patted him. "It's all right, boy. Jill's in a happy place. You're our dog now."

He lifted his ears at Jill's name. His dark eyes bored into me.

"Time to get back to work, buddy."

He rested his head in the doll's lap and closed his eyes.

I returned to my desk and spent a few minutes organizing my notes from the trip. I still had more research to do before I'd be ready to compose a formal proof argument regarding Roy Beauchamp and Conroy Parks.

I opened up my laptop and checked my email. Dr. Eisenstein had responded to my inquiry. *RaeJean, I'm captivated by your story and would love to spend time with you. And hear more about the desk and the doll. Unfortunately, I'm in the middle of the wilderness, fishing with a buddy. I'll call when I return home. Art.*

Art's interest in my spiritual situation put my mind at ease. He didn't think I'd dropped a stitch, as my Italian grandma used to say. I replied that I looked forward to his call and a subsequent meeting. Sam would be pleased, too. He and Art hit it off at their first introduction.

I left my desk and walked to where Sophie lay in her coveted window seat. "Life can get complicated, Sophie. And mine is no exception."

She lifted her head, wagged her back end, then returned to her nap.

Eli remained in the chair with Patsy. "What do you think, fellow?"

He lifted one eyelid, then stretched his front legs.

"I see you agree with Sophie." I reached down and tapped his front paws. He snapped them beneath his torso. He loathed having his feet touched or his nails clipped. He cried like a baby when the groomer worked on him.

Back at my desk, I picked up the index card marked *Effanbee Doll*, added *Patsy*, and taped it to my whiteboard so I wouldn't lose it amongst the table clutter. Patsy...she was special in the same way as the desk had been in my last case.

Next, I set up the file for the proof argument detailing why Roy A. Beauchamp and Conroy Parks were likely the same person. My eyes returned to the doll for assurance. Then, I continued investigating Roy until I'd exhausted all the accessible sources. I'd have to wait for responses from my email requests for more answers.

With that done, I checked my email and then sent an inquiry to the New Zealand Department of Internal Affairs asking for information about Roy Parks and his potential name change. For my domestic cases, I'd telephone, but with the time differences and the heavy accents in New Zealand, I opted for electronic mail.

Once I sent off the email, I turned my attention to the law firm who'd handled the deed poll. Rousseau & MacVale had been around for a hundred forty-five years and had a thriving practice in Wellington in 1934.

On my first search, a long list of newspaper articles described a firm under investigation. Partners at Rousseau & MacVale faced allegations of sexual misconduct with female interns. I found their website and shot off an email to one of the partners not mentioned in the lawsuit. Hopefully, he'd respond to my inquiry about Roy Parks' deed poll.

Chapter Twenty-One

By noon, I'd finished outlining my proof argument and joined Sam for lunch. He'd made us both tuna salad sandwiches, my second favorite sandwich.

"I had a productive morning. How about you?" I asked as Sam took a big bite out of his overstuffed Kaiser roll.

"You go first." Sam covered his mouth while he spoke.

"I reached out to the law firm printed on the invoice for the deed poll and sent an email to the New Zealand Department of Internal Affairs. Plus, I drafted the proof argument establishing Conroy Parks as Roy A. Beauchamp."

"That's good. You don't have a lot longer to decide if you will continue the assignment."

"I know. A week. But at this rate, I avoid the decision by solving the case. My gut says Roy Parks and Roy Beauchamp are the same person."

"Guts don't count. Facts, Sherlock." Sam grinned.

Sam was right, but my instincts hadn't let me down in the past and they were all I had to go on right now.

We ate in silence for the next ten minutes.

Sam finished first. "You must be curious about the identity of Jill's biological parents."

"I am, a little. But identifying them is not in my contract." Sam saw through my veiled response. He knew me better than that. *Of course, I'm curious. Curious is my middle name.*

"You solved the Mary Rogers mystery, and you weren't hired to do that."

"That was different."

"How?"

"Once I realized Mary's plight, I had to put her soul to rest."

"You may have a similar scenario with Dorothy Arnold's disappearance."

"It might be the same, but I'm putting it aside for now." I looked at my hands. "Besides, what if Dorothy Arnold wanted the truth hidden? Why not let it rest?"

"Maybe it's not what she wanted. Maybe it's what her father wanted. Or maybe it's just a theory and something different happened."

Sam's observations made sense. And he knew me well. I wouldn't give up. "Okay. I'll work another week and see where it leads me." The vibes from Patsy returned—the tingling. Right then, I knew I wouldn't quit. Couldn't.

"That's the spirit. You could solve the case next week if you hear from New Zealand."

"We can always hope to bank bundles of money by the middle of May."

Sam pecked my cheek. "Not that it matters. That's not what drives either of us."

He was so right. We loved our togetherness. But most of all, neither of us walked away from a challenge.

* * *

When I checked my email after lunch, I found a response from the Museum of the City of New York. The archivist had replied and suggested I review Bernice Abbott's documented photo journey of changing New York to see if she mentioned the photograph I'd found in the album. Or possibly, the Grace M. Mayer collection. Apparently, Mayer kept correspondence and personal notes of her interviews with local artists.

I added the museum to my list of places to visit on my next trip to the city.

* * *

Art Eisenstein called me just before eight that evening. "Wow! What a surprise to hear from you, RaeJean. How are things in your world?"

"Great." No point in dragging up old topics. I hadn't seen Art since a case in 2015. "I heard you retired from teaching and now you're a fishing pro."

He laughed. "Not a chance. It's an escape. I'm busier now than when I taught at the Health Science Center."

"No kidding." I didn't know many retired people, but I had an image in my head of retirees like my Italian grandmother, sitting around drinking coffee with her cronies and talking about old men.

"People think because I am not teaching anymore, I have nothing to do." He laughed again. "I've got more cases than ever."

"I didn't realize you retired until your email bounced back with the message." I hesitated, wondering if I should impose on him about my situation with Patsy and the desk. His expertise lay in identifying bodies, but when we last spoke, he'd talked about new cutting-edge research in the DNA field. He'd alluded to some dicey concepts about spiritualism. I'd blown him off, not believing in ghosts at all. My strong position about spirits had weakened since the previous case.

"I'm intrigued by your description." He paused. "In two weeks, I'll be at a session at the Center for Spiritual Living in Paoli, Pennsylvania, and be staying at the Crowne Plaza Hotel Philadelphia in King of Prussia. Maybe we could meet then."

"Perfect. It's twenty miles west of me. You'll need to come to my house to see the desk."

I gave him my home address, and we arranged a visit in two weeks on a Wednesday.

Excited at the prospect of seeing Art again, I celebrated with a second glass of wine and a handful of M&M's.

* * *

Within three days, I received an answer back from The Department of Internal Affairs in New Zealand. The information I requested was unavailable. If it existed, it had been packed away years ago in a warehouse in Wellington amid thousands of other boxes from the 1930s. *Due to staffing limitations, we cannot help you at this time.*

"Great." Hopefully, if I made the trip, they'd allow me access to search.

Sophie lifted her head, and Eli yawned.

Conroy Parks changed his name for a reason. I now had copies of the new birth certificate and the invoice for a deed poll filing. Plus, Lester had commented that a drunken fisherman claimed Roy had a nickname back in New Zealand, *Arnie.*

By the end of the day, I'd still not heard from the New Zealand law firm. Although I hated the phone, I tried an international call. Using a time zone conversion chart online, I calculated it was nine on Friday morning in Wellington, a day ahead of us. I found their phone number on the website and made the call.

A sweet voice answered. "Rousseau & MacVale Law Offices, how may I assist you?"

"My name is RaeJean Hunter. I'm trying to locate a man named Roy Beauchamp."

"Is he related to George Beauchamp? He visited last week." She added, "Divorce."

Loose lips for a legal assistant. "That's just it. I don't know Roy's family. Roy lived in Wellington in the early 1900s."

"Not even! I wasn't born then." She giggled. "My grandma was still a kid."

I cringed. "I don't expect to find the man alive. I'm looking for his family. I have an invoice for a deed poll filing dated May 15, 1934. Do you have records that far back?"

"I don't know. I just started here a month ago. I would have to ask Mr. Shriver. He knows about everything."

"I'll hold." The conversation was painful.

"Oh, Mr. Shriver's in a meeting. I can't interrupt him. And then he's going to court."

"I'd appreciate it if Mr. Shriver would return my call."

"I'll leave him a message, but I won't guarantee that he'll call back. He's very busy. He's both a barrister and a solicitor. He goes to court and handles other cases outside of court. What's your number?"

I gave her my country code, area code, and telephone number.

"Are you in New Zealand?" She asked with sincere interest, not realizing I'd included a country code.

"No, I'm in the United States."

"Wow. Okay, I'll give the message to Mr. Shriver. Thank you for calling Rousseau & MacVale." The phone disconnected.

"Oh, brother." I doubted anything would come of the call.

I spent the rest of the afternoon pursuing the "friend leads" from Joan Shannon. The trees for the Arnold, Armstrong, Hamilton, and Morris families supported Joan's suggestion. When I matched up the timeframe for four generations before Jill's adoption, I confirmed four contemporaries in each family: Charlotte Parks Samuels, Sarah Armstrong, Adelaide Hamilton, and Helen Morris Hadley.

Unsure of the significance, I made cards for all four women. The Morris woman didn't fill me with excitement, but Charlotte Parks Samuels was Dorothy Arnold's grandmother. This had to be important. Roy Beauchamp changed his name to Conroy Parks. It didn't strike me as a coincidence.

As I prepared cards for the women, I realized they all connected directly or indirectly through the law firm known today as Murbeck, Austin Bradley's employer. Adelaide Hamilton, connected through her great-grandfather, Alexander. Helen Morris Hadley and Sarah Armstrong bore the men who became the original partners. This law firm made the news when Dorothy Arnold disappeared.

I lifted Patsy from the chair amid Eli's growls and stared into her eyes. A shiver preceded a rush of confidence. *I'm on the right path.* The four women formed a complex web that, according to Joan Shannon, connected to Jill Hamilton.

Chapter Twenty-Two

A noise woke me from a deep sleep. I flailed with my blanket and sheet as I tried to sit up in bed. "What's that sound?"

Sam rolled over. "It's your cellphone vibrating on the nightstand."

"It's midnight. Who would be calling at this hour?"

I grabbed the phone. The leading number flashing on the screen identified the country code as New Zealand. "It's the lawyer from New Zealand."

"Well, answer it," Sam groaned.

I slipped out of bed, reaching for my robe. "Hello?"

"Ms. Hunter, this is Carl Shriver from Rousseau & MacVale returning your call. I'm sorry for the late hour, but my schedule is topped off and this was my one open slot."

"Thanks for the call back. Don't worry about the time."

I closed the bedroom door behind me and headed

down the hall toward my office. "I'm searching for a man named Roy Beauchamp. It's not likely that he is still alive, but I need to find out if he has living relatives in your country."

Shriver's voice softened. "Why would you call our firm?"

"In 1934, Rousseau & MacVale acted as the filing agent for a deed poll request. I found your invoice attached to a birth certificate for Conroy Parks born in 1916 in Wellington, who changed his name in 1934, then emigrated to the States ten years later."

"And you say we issued the invoice?" Shriver sounded interested.

I held my breath for a moment, then repeated myself. "Yes. I'm looking for Roy Beauchamp, and I suspect he changed his name to Conroy Parks."

"Our firm doesn't keep records that far back, but the Beauchamp family is a big client. We have lockers full of their family records in our Wellington warehouse."

"I need someone to go through the 1934 case files to see if Roy Parks and Roy Beauchamp are the same person. Is that something your law firm can help with?"

"Not without permission from the family. What's his father's name?"

"That's the problem. I don't know either of Roy's parents' names."

Shriver cleared his throat. "Okay. Tell me what you do know."

"Conroy Parks emigrated to the United States in

1944 at age twenty-eight. He married a woman from Idaho, and they settled in a small town close to the Canadian border near Bonners Ferry. Oh, and he had a nickname, Arnie, when he lived in Wellington."

Shriver remained silent for a few seconds before he spoke. "I'll call you back next week. Something is tickling my memory, but I'm not quite sure what. I'll ponder it over the weekend and pop a few questions around the office on Monday. I may need permission from the family."

"Great. I'll wait to hear. If I don't answer, text me a convenient time for a return call."

Shriver disconnected. Wide awake, I contemplated the "tickling" in Shriver's memory. I heard Sophie scratching on the inside of the bedroom door, so I ran down the hall to let her out before she woke Sam.

"Is that you, Sherlock?" Sam sounded like he'd hidden his face in his pillow.

"Sorry. Sophie wanted out of the bedroom."

"Aren't you coming back to bed?"

"In a bit. I'm going to read for a while. The call wired me."

"Tell me about it in the morning."

"Will do." I doubted I'd sleep. I'd read a book to reset my mind and slow it down.

* * *

At midnight on Monday, my phone rang. Shriver had

texted earlier, so I'd stayed up reading to wait for the call.

"Mrs. Hunter, this is Carl Shriver from Rousseau & MacVale." He sounded excited.

"Yes, sir. Thank you for following up. Any luck?"

"Actually, yes. I stirred the pot and made calls to our Beauchamp clients. I believe I've found the relative you're seeking."

"What makes you think that?" I picked at the hem of my nightshirt, trying to refrain from shouting a big wahoo.

"The woman disconnected the instant I mentioned Roy Beauchamp." Shriver sniffed.

Great. Another hostile woman. "Interesting. Can you share which family?"

"Not yet. It might help if you tell me why you're looking for Roy Beauchamp."

I didn't have a good feeling about sharing the information. "All I can say is it's regarding an inheritance claim."

"I assume it's a big one. Those are the ones that require an investigator." Shriver cleared his throat. "And get ugly."

"Sizeable." He didn't need the exact figure. Plus, I wasn't sure of the exchange rate between U.S. dollars and New Zealand currency.

"That complicates things. Money turns relatives into monsters."

"Tell me about it. I've handled a lot of bequest

cases. Even as a disinterested party, I'd get dragged into the drama."

Shriver cleared his throat. "I'm not sure I know your profession. I assumed you were a private investigator."

"I'm a forensic genealogist. I investigate family bloodlines."

Shriver remained quiet for a minute or two, then asked, "How would you feel about visiting New Zealand?"

I'd already suspected I'd need to make the trip, but I wasn't sure why he would want to see me. I remained noncommittal. "I'm not sure. I'd have to discuss it with my partner."

"It's lovely this time of year. The leaves are beginning to color up. You could take a leaf-peeping tour." Shriver did his best to convince me it would be a good idea.

"A leaf-peeping tour?" I chuckled.

"You know, see the autumn foliage."

"Right, I forgot. Your seasons are opposite ours. I don't see the benefit of me traveling to New Zealand if it's something I can hire you to do."

Shriver made a clicking sound. "Maybe you could talk to an old woman. She won't talk to me. In fact, she won't accept any male visitors, especially barristers from our firm. We've had a bit of bad publicity of late."

Another old woman who wouldn't talk to lawyers. No surprise. Women tended to live longer than men, and they were the ones who knew the gossip. I waited for Shriver to continue.

"Her name is Beatrix Rousseau. Her father was the solicitor and barrister to the Beauchamp family, plus her mother was born a Beauchamp."

My heart jumped. "I'd like to call her."

"She doesn't take phone calls. Everything has to go through her solicitor. She's old and lives alone except for a live-in housekeeper on a property called Northwood, located in Swannanoa, North Canterbury. It's been in the Beauchamp family since the early 1900s."

"But you think if I travel there to meet her personally, she might talk to me." Sam and I had always wanted to visit the country. This was a great opportunity to mix business with pleasure and take a little side trip with my husband once I'd concluded my research. It'd be like a second honeymoon.

"I'll try to arrange it with her solicitor if you agree to come. I expect if she's in good health, she'll agree to a visit." Shriver didn't sound convincing.

"I'll need to discuss this with my partner." After my last case, Sam and I made a pact—no travel plans without first discussing it together. I didn't like the control aspect, but I appreciated his concerns, so I'd agreed. At least, for a little while.

"I'll wait to hear from you. If you decide to make the trip, contact me. I'll help with your arrangements once you're in my country. In the meantime, I'll make a preliminary call to her solicitor."

Sam needed to sleep, so I didn't wake him to fill him in on the latest about a possible Beauchamp cousin. I curled my legs under me, laid my head back on the chair, and stared out the window at the full moon. I had another name, Beatrix Rousseau, and her mother's name was Beauchamp.

Chapter Twenty-Three

I had *The Philadelphia Inquirer* spread out on the table when Sam entered the kitchen for breakfast. By seven o'clock, I had emptied the dishwasher, fed the dogs, taken them outdoors, and eaten my oatmeal.

Sam rubbed his eyes as if he was unable to believe what he saw. "You're up so early."

"I didn't sleep after the phone call."

He frowned. I'd had bouts of insomnia last year and resorted to a sleep aid for a few months after I lost our baby, and then after I stopped taking them, I had the shakes for days. That, on top of my stress from the case I'd been working, had concerned Sam.

"Don't worry. I'm fine. The call from Shriver wound me up. He suspects he's found a lead to Roy Beauchamp's family, but he's not positive."

"Why not?"

169

"Because the woman he called disconnected when he asked her about Roy."

"Seems to be a lot of hostility between women and lawyers. The woman in New York wouldn't talk to the lawyers, either."

"Yes. Joan Shannon didn't want anything to do with Murbeck."

"Did you get the name of the woman who wouldn't talk to him?"

"Beatrix Beauchamp Rousseau."

Sam poured a glass of juice and joined me at the table. "It's odd these old women won't talk to lawyers."

"A little. This case is all about women. I'm beginning to think there's a connection between Beatrix Rousseau and Joan Shannon. I spent half the night on the Internet trying to find a link. I need another cup of coffee. So far, all I've got is that both fathers practiced law."

"Did Shriver say anything else?" Sam dug into his bowl of shredded wheat and banana.

"No. Shriver's firm has provided legal services to the prominent Beauchamp families for years, including Sir Harold Beauchamp. I looked him up online. Here's a surprise. Sir Harold was Katherine Mansfield's father." A connection between Beatrix and Katherine flickered in my head.

"Katherine Mansfield, the famous New Zealand writer of short stories?"

"One and the same." My mouth hung open. Sam amazed me with his literary knowledge. "Jill had been reading *The Life of Kathryn Mansfield* along with several other books. Maybe she stumbled on to something."

"Mansfield sounds important." Sam chomped a bite from his toast.

"I'm sure she is. And perhaps that's why Beatrix Rousseau won't talk to anyone at the firm? She knows too much about the lawyers and their shenanigans." I hadn't upgraded my opinion of lawyers, especially the New Zealand firm under investigation. "Shriver suggested we visit Wellington. His firm has a warehouse full of records, including files from the Beauchamp family. Because they're short-staffed right now, he has no way to check the archives. He didn't say why, but I suspect it's related to an accusation of sexual harassment by one of their interns. He's requested permission for me to review the 1934 files, the year on the invoice for the deed poll. And..."

Sam stopped eating and looked at me. "And?"

I gave him my best smile. "And I think it's a good idea. Would you like to take a trip to the South Pacific?"

He set down his spoon. "How long of a trip?"

"I'm guessing at least three weeks. I have no idea how long it will take. Besides, we can plan extra days and hike. Kind of like a second honeymoon with Outward Bound. The country's known for its great trails."

Being an independent antique appraiser, Sam had

full control of his time. He loved to travel to new places.

Sam chewed and swallowed the rest of his toast. "Can you arrange it on short notice? Sounds like fun. I've wanted to visit the South Pacific ever since I saw *Flags of Our Fathers*. Heck of a story about raising the flag on Mount Suribachi on Iwo Jima."

I didn't respond. Instead, I opened my electronic calendar, and a reminder popped up. "Whoa, I have to call Austin. It's been a month today."

Sam winked. "Nothing to worry about. I doubt he has throngs of genealogists in line for the case."

I laughed. "Right. I'll check with Shriver to see what timeframe will work for him."

"Better check with the Canine Fitness Camp first. Three weeks is a long time." Sam went to the door and patted the dogs. "Do you guys need to go out?"

Two noses crammed into the crack as Sam swung open the door. Like *The Charge of the Light Brigade*, the dogs flew off the deck and raced toward the bird feeders.

* * *

By eight o'clock, I sat working on the Roy-Beauchamp-was-Conroy-Parks theory at my desk.

My initial search for Beatrix Rousseau, a Beauchamp relative mentioned by Shriver, came up empty. However, my Mansfield search unearthed a nugget. Mansfield's cousin, Elizabeth von Arnim, also a famous author, offered her younger cousin, Katherine Mansfield, refuge in Switzerland to recuperate from a serious illness. Von Arnim, born a Beauchamp, bore four daughters, one named Beatrix. Could she be the Beatrix mentioned by Shriver?

Now, I had Mansfield, von Armin, and Beatrix Rousseau, all Beauchamps of New Zealand and possibly related to Roy A. Beauchamp, also known as Conroy Parks. Plus, a new thread had formed around a writing community of international authors: Mansfield, who surfaced in Jill's library; von Arnim, the Beauchamp cousin; and the wannabe writer, Dorothy Arnold. Not to mention, the American writers from Greenwich Village.

It was the middle of the night in New Zealand when I messaged Shriver and inquired about dates. I wouldn't get an answer until the next day. Once it was a decent hour in New York City, I called Austin.

"Good morning, RaeJean. I hope you've decided to continue with the case."

"Yes, I have. I contacted a lawyer in New Zealand and have a lead on our man. I may travel to Wellington in another week. The solicitor, Carl Shriver, has been helpful and said he'd arrange my stay once I landed there."

"Shriver. That name's familiar. Which law firm?"

"Rousseau & MacVale."

I could hear Austin breathing. Finally, he spoke. "Oh."

"Do you know it?"

"I've heard of them. The firm is under investigation. Some of the partners allegedly participated in naughty business with their female interns. They've made the daily legal news."

"Why haven't I heard about it?"

"It's in the British newspapers."

"Ah. I don't read the British press. Why would you read foreign newspapers?"

"Our firm practices internationally. I keep abreast of the goings-on in the global community." He hesitated. "Rousseau & MacVale—Shriver's a partner. I don't recall his name on the list of suspected offenders."

"Since I've accepted the case, may I submit an expense claim? Also, would it be possible to get an advance for a trip to New Zealand? My husband plans to go with me. Of course, his expenses will come out of our personal account."

"No problem. Send over the numbers. I'll have a check cut right away." Austin hesitated. "And I'll make sure Shriver isn't an implicated partner. I wouldn't want you blindsided. Can't talk, I have a client waiting." Austin disconnected, and I headed for the kitchen. I needed a peanut butter and jelly sandwich fix. And maybe a small bag of M&M's. A tug at my waistband indicated a green light on the candy.

"You look pleased with yourself." Sam leaned against the counter with his *Kick-Ass* coffee mug in hand.

"I am. I've had a productive morning. I found another intriguing relationship."

"Geez. This melodrama has more characters than Tolstoy's *War and Peace*."

"I know. It's confusing even to me, and I have a scorecard."

"Who's the new player?" Sam asked.

"Elizabeth von Arnim."

He nodded. "*Love.*"

I rolled my eyes. "Don't tell me you've heard of her, too."

"British lit class." Sam sipped his coffee.

"I took the course, too, but I still had to look her up."

He tapped his head. "A memory like a steel trap."

I pecked his cheek as I passed his chair. "Back to work for me."

Elizabeth von Arnim and Katherine Mansfield... somehow, Roy fit into their lives.

I would just need to figure out how.

Chapter Twenty-Four

Eli dashed to the satin chair where I'd left Patsy and leaped onto it.

"Eli, no!"

Ignoring my command, he proceeded to burrow under Patsy. His action caused her to slide off onto the carpet and land in a sitting position next to the chair. For some reason, the eyes stuck closed.

I grabbed Eli by the scruff of the neck and pulled him off the chair. "Bad dog! You almost damaged poor Patsy." When I released him, he laid by the doll with his head across her legs. *He misses Jill.* My heart tugged, so I knelt and patted the sad boy. When he lifted his head, he jarred Patsy, causing her eyes to open. A tingle ran up the back of my head. *Jingshen.* Spirits. "I know, Patsy."

My mind replayed the day I met Jill. The sound of her voice echoed in my head as she mentioned Dorothy Arnold. I thought about how she had a book about

Dorothy in her library. What led her to the woman? Had Jill heard her parents discuss the disappearance?

"Think, RaeJean."

Eli licked my hand that I'd left resting on his side. I patted him again, then glanced at the doll one more time. Another tingle and a thought. *The Hamilton Family Trust.*

After fiddling with the Beauchamp family tree, splicing together what I found on the Internet, I had a skeleton of several generations, but no connection to Jill. I'd need to visit the New Zealand public records to flesh it out properly.

Why had William Hamilton provided for Roy A. Beauchamp? Was Roy important to him, or maybe Jill? Whatever it was, William wanted Roy or his bloodline heirs to inherit the Hamilton fortune.

Rechecking my notes from my conversation with Joan Shannon, I'd noted that the four women Joan Shannon mentioned, Adelaide Hamilton, Sarah Armstrong, Helen Morris Hadley, and Charlotte Parks Samuels, had remained friends for years. There had to be other ties that kept them together besides being members of New York's high society and volunteering with the Children's Aid Society. I analyzed the data I collected about them for other connections.

Both Sarah Armstrong and Helen Morris Hadley had husbands who were partners in the same firm. Less direct, Adelaide Hamilton's connection lay between her great grandfather's friendship with the New York Governor Morris Hadley, a founding partner of the law firm. Charlotte Parks Samuels linked when the law firm handled her granddaughter Dorothy's disappearance.

Were these women the keepers of a big secret? Jill's adoption out of New Zealand continued to niggle me. The circumstances surrounding it could be such a secret.

I'd already covered the Hamilton family history, specifically Alexander Hamilton's background. A background that instilled a social conscience for the welfare of orphans and homeless children. It didn't take much to discover his mother bore him and a brother out of wedlock. His father left home when Alexander was five. He lost his mother at age eleven.

Maybe Isabelle and William Hamilton shared the family affinity to help orphaned children and adopted Jill, but I struggled to understand why they didn't adopt one of the many orphaned children in New York City. They'd traveled all the way to New Zealand for a child. And an *odd duck* at that.

According to Joan Shannon, Adelaide Hamilton sent money to someone in New Zealand. Perhaps to Roy Beauchamp. I made a note to search New York City public records for anything Adelaide Hamilton may have filed. She might have left a breadcrumb trail back to New Zealand, and to Roy.

Plus, Jill's father took care to prevent anyone in the large Hamilton family from inheriting his estate. He'd created a trust guaranteeing that his overindulged cousins wouldn't get his money. The beneficiary made sense if Roy A. Beauchamp turned out to be Jill's father or uncle.

I reviewed my index cards for Charlotte Parks Samuels and Adelaide Hamilton. Both served on the Children's Aid Society Board of Directors in 1854 and knew each other. Friendships between the ancestral families of society tended to continue into the present generation. I'd ferreted out pages of data available on the Internet about the women without finding the missing link.

The answers could be in New Zealand.

Chapter Twenty-Five

It was time to delve into Dorothy Arnold's disappearance. She and Conroy Parks had to be connected, somehow.

Every account I read describing Dorothy's disappearance mentioned she aspired to become a published author. Apparently, she begged her father to lease an apartment for her in Greenwich Village. She believed by living among the writers, she would learn from them and be successful. There had to be a connection to the New York City writing community the police missed during their investigation. I pursued that lead, once again collecting reams of data.

According to reports, Dorothy spent a lot of time in The Village after she graduated from Bryn Mawr College in 1905. Enough time that she wanted to move there. She must have formed comfortable friendships with prominent writers and college alumni.

My online search into Bryn Mawr revealed it was a

hotbed for aspiring writers, activists, and suffragettes. During Dorothy's early adult life in Greenwich Village, she had associated with notable people, including a classmate who was great friends with Willa Cather, an editor at *McClure's* where Dorothy submitted her final story.

Dorothy spent her last Thanksgiving in Philadelphia with a former Bryn Mawr classmate, who described it as a strange visit. She stayed Wednesday night, received a package delivered on Thursday, the holiday, and then left the next morning. Neither the classmate nor Dorothy's mother expected such an abbreviated trip. Neither one knew what she'd received in the package, or why she left so soon. At least, that is what they claimed.

* * *

The Hotel Albert at 23 East Tenth Street, a meeting place frequented by writers and artists, had a reputation as a haven for progressive ideas. Staff at the hotel recognized photographs of Dorothy during the investigation. Apparently, she met and dined there regularly with the writing group.

Dorothy's secret life may have begun in that hotel.

These writers exposed her to a different set of moral values in both their writing and their social behavior, which may have prompted her to lie to her parents and spend a week in Boston with her male friend, George "Junior" Griscom.

Her father never provided the support she needed to develop her writing skills. In fact, he threatened to cut off her allowance if she moved out of their mansion on East Seventy-Ninth Street and teased her when she received magazine rejections. This blatant lack of family support drove Dorothy's writing activities underground.

A close friend admitted Dorothy faced a bleak writing future if she remained with her parents in New York. An excerpt from a letter she wrote to Griscom confirmed her misery. *"Failure stares me in the face. All I can see is a long road with no turning."* Taken out of context, it appeared she'd lost hope. Without the entire letter, it's not clear what she meant. Unfortunately, her family never released its full content.

As I wandered around my office, I was drawn to Patsy and lifted her up. As soon as our eyes met, my head tingled. *Jingshen.* The notion of Dorothy dining in Greenwich Village with some of the great artists and authors drifted through my mind.

Patsy had attempted to communicate. The tingling increased. "I'm on the right track."

Who did Dorothy meet in The Village? Was it someone who could and would help her orchestrate her own disappearance? Perhaps a friend who believed she needed a chance?

I jotted down a list of influential writers active between 1905 and 1910 when Dorothy spent time there. Neith Boyce stood out as one woman who fit the profile, and Jill had one of her books listed as a *Must Read*.

Neith Boyce, a journalist and writer for *The Commerce* at the turn of the century, moved from Los Angeles and settled in Greenwich Village in a boarding house. A single woman determined to make it on her own, Boyce bragged, "*I never cook. I eat at the local salons and restaurants.*" She considered herself a bachelorette and promoted independence by young men and women. In her writings, she argued for young men and women to experience periods of sexual or relational experimentation to avoid making serious mistakes in their lives.

According to her autobiography, Boyce had moved to Chelsea by the time Dorothy roamed Greenwich Village, but she returned to gather with friends in the publishing industry. She wrote about frequent meetups in Washington Square with successful and aspiring writers. Boyce also traveled to Europe regularly where she rubbed shoulders with writers, including D. H. Lawrence and Kathryn Mansfield.

Contemporaries of Neith described her as poised, polished, and articulate.

A woman like Neith Boyce would be a perfect role model for Dorothy. And based on Boyce flaunting her own independence, I had no doubt she would have encouraged Dorothy to move out of her parents' home.

Dorothy's affiliation with the Greenwich Village writers must have influenced her behavior. Her desire for her own apartment in The Village. Lying to her parents. Spending two weeks in Boston with George Griscom. Having a secret post office box. These actions implied a young woman seeking independence.

Plus, her friends said she seemed in good spirits that last day. Not suicidal. She had travel brochures in her room and letters with foreign stampings.

I looked down at Sophie and Eli, who'd curled up at my feet. "What do you think, guys? Did Dorothy run away to lead a new life?"

Sophie woofed. Eli yawned.

"I thought so." I leaned over and gave each of them a pat.

I kept coming back to the fact that her mother believed Dorothy still lived. Dorothy had to free herself from her father's Victorian-based control, but she would need help. Help from people who sympathized with her views.

I speculated that her help came from someone in the Greenwich Village writing community. But who?

Chapter Twenty-Six

Lester Parks' birth certificate arrived by Priority Mail several days earlier than expected. After I opened it, I retrieved his parents' marriage license from my file to compare dates.

"Interesting. His birth date showed him being born twenty-four weeks after the marriage." The normal pregnancy term was forty weeks. Lester had attended their wedding. Maybe that's why he refused the DNA test. He'd insisted he knew his parents.

Maybe he did, and maybe he didn't share the same father as his sisters.

I'd find out soon. I'd selected a lab with a fast turnaround time. DNA results from Lester's cigarette butt and hair, and Ginny's swab would be available in a couple of days.

* * *

Before I pursued the lead to New Zealand, I decided to call Austin one more time.

"What can I do for you today?" He sounded chipper.

"When I spoke to you the other day, I didn't have time to bring you up to date on the Hamilton case." I filled him in on my trip to Bonners Ferry and finding the deed poll with the invoice. "Hence the reason for the trip to New Zealand."

Austin grunted his approval.

"Why didn't I find anything from your firm's archives amongst the documents you gave me?" Since Jill was a Hamilton, I expected to find something in their files that might lead me to Roy Beauchamp. "You've kept historical records for other long-term clients. Is there anything unusual about William Hamilton's family?"

"We checked before we hired the private investigator. Nothing. But it's always possible we overlooked something. Paperwork sometimes gets misfiled. I'll have our archivist recheck. But that's going to take weeks. We're understaffed in the basement and dealing with a long list of requests."

"I assume you keep all of the records for each of the firm's partners. You said Joan Shannon wanted access to her father's papers, but the firm refused."

"Yes. The firm has archived all of Morris Hadley's papers. They've hired a well-known writer to compile the firm's history. Our firm has handled several important and sensitive cases over its hundred years of practice." Austin's voice faded with the word *sensitive*.

I straightened in my chair. "Sensitive's the same reason the senior partners refused to release the documents to Joan. Her father had handled Jill's adoption, which was deemed a sensitive case, wasn't it?"

Austin cleared his throat. "Look, I didn't agree with their final decision, but I had no say in the matter. My boss instructed me to deny her access. Nobody gave me a clear reason."

"Do you think they're covering up something?" I paused for a moment. "May I see Hadley's files?"

"I won't speculate about a coverup." Austin cleared his throat. "I'll check with the partners about the files. But so far, they've remained sealed."

He didn't need to say another word. He suspected a coverup, too. And he doubted I'd get to see the files.

"Anything else?" Austin's clipped voice indicated he wanted a change of topic.

"Not much. That's it for today."

We disconnected.

I didn't bother to tell him I suspected a connection to Dorothy Arnold. Without the supporting data regarding the Greenwich Village writers, the Bryn Mawr connections, my gut feelings, and the odd allure of the doll weren't going to support my theory.

If denied access to the files for the American end of the adoption transaction, Shriver might provide access to the archived files in New Zealand. Unless, of course, the coverup extended across the Pacific Ocean.

Chapter Twenty-Seven

Art Eisenstein drove into our driveway fifteen minutes early and parked next to our garage, in full view of the backyard. Fortunately, Sam and I had finished breakfast and had walked the dogs. He found us enjoying coffee on the deck.

I waved as he walked toward the steps. He didn't look a lot different than when I saw him four years ago. He always reminded me of David Schwimmer from the T.V. series *Friends* with an additional thirty pounds and thinning hair. The wide strap over his shoulder supported a large brown leather bag.

"Morning!" I called. "No trouble with my directions, I see."

"Piece of cake. It's a straight shot from King of Prussia." He patted the bag. "Brought you some *light* reading."

"Art, good to see you again." Sam reached out his hand. "You're looking good."

Art shrugged. "As good as any old, retired professor looks, I guess."

I caught a vibe when he shrugged. I also heard something worrisome in his tone. Maybe his early retirement hadn't been an option, but I didn't ask. "Let's move inside. As pleasant as it is on the deck, the wind is a bit chilly."

Sam excused himself and retreated to his office. I'd explained to him why I'd contacted Art. He didn't press about my reactions to the desk or the doll. Instead, he only commented that he hoped Art had answers.

We settled in the library, where Art unloaded his bag of tricks. "Based on your description of the mystifying connection, first to the desk and then to the doll, I've brought you a few books from my collection."

I watched as he piled half a dozen well-used books onto the table.

"That should keep you busy, Grasshopper." He grinned.

He'd dubbed me Grasshopper on one of our cases with the FBI. He said it should have been *Ant* because I pulled more than my weight. I thought Grasshopper had a better ring to it.

I scanned the stack. "I've already read Nessa Carey's book, *The Epigenetics Revolution*."

Art lifted his eyebrows as he repacked the Carey book. "Why am I not surprised?"

"You know me."

He nodded and continued. "Some of these books

discuss topics that are speculative, but isn't everything hypothetical until science proves it's so?"

"The earth is flat."

"The earth rotates around the moon," Art added.

"You can tell by the shape of his head he doesn't know anything." I laughed.

"Someday, man will fly." Art laughed, then said, "We could go on like this forever."

"Tell me what the deal is with the desk and the doll." He sat back, ready to listen.

"I think they help me with my cases." I spent the next fifteen minutes telling him about the desk in my last case, finding the note, and identifying the bones found at Connecticut College. "And now, there's this Patsy doll with glass eyes. She's doing the same thing, I'm sure of it."

Art stood. "Where is this desk and doll? I'd like to see them."

"In my office upstairs. Follow me."

We left the library. As we walked by Sam's office, both dogs shot out and charged up the stairs ahead of us.

Art laughed. "Bodyguards!"

"They protect me when I work." I reached down and patted Eli. "This little boy became an orphan when his mistress died in Central Park. We adopted him, and now finding his owner's heirs is my current case."

As soon as I opened the office door, both dogs

dashed to their spots. Sophie grabbed the window seat and Eli sat in the chair with Patsy.

"That's the doll, isn't it?" He walked over to Patsy and reached down. Before his hand got very close, Eli snarled and draped himself over the toy. Art's hand snapped back like a ball on a paddle. "Whoops. Territorial, I see."

"Eli! No!" I rushed to the chair and retrieved Patsy. "Sorry. We're still learning his quirks. He's protective of her. The doll belonged to his former owner."

I handed Art the doll. He rotated it, checking the clothing first. Sniffed it. When he tipped it on its back, the crystal eyes rolled open. "Creepy. Reminds me of—what's the name of that doll in the horror movie?"

"Chucky. The movie was *Child's Play.*"

"Right." He handed Patsy back to me and turned to my antique desk. "Is this it?"

"Yes."

We walked over to the small barrel-topped lady's secretary. "The inlaid quartz tulip on the hutch is the active piece," I said. "It flashes. The tulip gets warm when that happens."

Art touched the quartz flower. "Cool as a cucumber."

I smiled. "It's been relatively quiet since I solved the case."

"Interesting." He lifted the top. Opened each drawer. Peeked behind it. "Hmm."

My stomach growled. "Let's break for lunch. I made up sandwiches just in case."

"Great. I need a little time to compose my observations." Art furrowed his brow as he took one more look at the desk and the doll.

Once in the kitchen, Sam joined us.

"Sam and I will set out lunch while you compose."

Art wrote in a small spiral notebook while we worked.

After lunch, we returned to the library. Sam retreated to his office.

"So, what do you think?" I asked.

"The list of possibilities is long, including you're a liar." Art laughed. "But we know that isn't the case. There are no easy answers. I'd recommend given what you've shown me that you investigate spiritualism, neuroscience, and epigenetic tags. They all relate to your experiences." He winked. "Even though the majority of scientists disagree with the premises put forth in the most recent publications on the topics."

"What do you mean by the majority of scientists disagree?"

He signed. "Some scientists have a difficult time letting go of the scientific method. If you can't replicate it, it must not exist."

"It's what we were taught from an early age." Hesitating for a moment, I recalled the drill. "Observe, question, hypothesize, predict, test, repeat."

"That's it. It will take something remarkable, like a breakthrough in quantum physics, to change minds. Some scientists will never concede."

My mind wandered as Art talked. Sam required solid evidence. He'd be one of those holdouts. He never called me a liar, but he always looked for an explanation for my spiritual events.

Art continued. "Arthur Conan Doyle believed in spiritualism. Not that Doyle's belief makes it true, but communicating with the dead is a keystone of spiritualism. And spiritualism as a religion is gaining followers. Plus, Buddhists practice a form of meditation that is akin to the same beliefs."

I listened. My stomach fluttered at the prospect of a different, more expansive, reality.

"Don't berate yourself or underestimate the significance of your experiences. They are real to you."

"Are you saying maybe I am imagining things?" My shoulders slumped.

"Not at all. What I'm saying is that what you've experienced is unique, so it's not repeatable. Therefore, you can't share it with others. But that doesn't make it false." He pointed to Woollacott's book. "Read this first. She's done a remarkable job of linking our scientific knowledge of consciousness using credible examples. She talks about the brain filter and how meditators say they do their best thinking when in a semi-trance. It's nothing new. But what happens remains a mystery, and thus controversial until we can make the next breakthrough in science."

We talked more about consciousness, but in the end, we kept coming back to the same place. Unless we could repeat the experience, most scientists wouldn't believe us.

"Sam considers my experience a side effect from an antidepressant and trauma. He's a smart guy. Plus, he knows I'm not a liar or a faker." I shrugged. "If Sam won't believe me, nobody will."

"Not true. I believe you." Art cleared his throat. "You're on the cusp of repeatability. The Patsy doll is acting the same as the desk."

"True."

"Keep a journal with the doll. And try to recreate a list of the events with the desk as detailed as you can remember. Let's see if there is a pattern or parallel."

"I'll do that."

"And call me if you need a reality check. You may solve the great mystery—*What is consciousness?*"

I laughed. "Maybe. But I'd just be happy to solve the case."

Art checked his watch. "Hmm. Four o'clock. I'd better head out. My flight leaves at six-forty. I hate cutting it too close."

Sam joined us on the deck to bid him farewell. The dogs and I walked him to his car.

"Don't forget. Call me anytime," he said as he climbed into his car.

"I will. Thanks for everything." I watched as he drove out of our yard.

"Ready for wine?" Sam called out.

"Absolutely."

Intrigued by the concept of consciousness and awareness, I wondered if Art was right. Had I found repeatability with the Patsy doll?

Maybe I wasn't crazy after all.

Chapter Twenty-Eight

After my visit with Dr. Eisenstein, I became obsessed with the concept of consciousness and the functions of the mind. Based on his recommendation, I scrounged up a blank journal I'd bought for my day notes, wrote Patsy on its cover, and began a log of my experiences with her. Before I closed the journal, I wrote, *Superior awareness, mind playing tricks, extreme stress?* before I closed the journal. I slipped it between two books on my desk.

Instead of working on my case to find Conroy Parks, I drifted to Dorothy's disappearance. At twenty-five, single, aspiring to be a writer, and still living at home, she had to suffer with great anxiety and stress. Her behavior that day might predict whether she was predisposed to harm herself or if she just ran away.

I'd lean on an analysis technique I used on other cases when I reached a dead end and needed a new direction. The technique relied on categorizing helpful and harmful behavior with two types of an individual's focus, internal and external.

Internal behavior, based on feelings, was subjective without a living person to interview. But from behavior published in the newspapers and included in other reports, I speculated Dorothy's parents had raised her to keep up appearances regardless of her feelings. She attended functions with her family, sometimes escorted by John Keith, the family lawyer. She argued with her father but, in the end, appeared to accept his decisions. However, as a young woman in a time when women's rights made the headlines, did she accept, or did she just comply? Did she abandon her dream of becoming a published author?

I had an easier time with the external chart. I listed known events in Dorothy's life and categorized them as helpful or harmful. From this, I found a preponderance of evidence indicating that Dorothy had not acted on autopilot. Nor did she appear to be in a critical state where her actions suggested she'd harm herself or someone else. Nothing indicated desperation. Nothing pointed to her taking her own life. Even the letters George Griscom produced early in the investigation, although showing disappointment, did not send up a red flag for a suicide watch.

I suspected Dorothy had spent quite a bit of time thinking about her situation and had a plan to move forward, gain her independence, and become a writer. The more I thought about it, the more it made perfect sense.

Dorothy lived with her parents, who provided her with a generous allowance. I suspected she left home with more than thirty dollars that day. Dorothy's behavior showed her resourcefulness. She'd secured a private mailbox. It wasn't a stretch to think she had tucked away enough money to escape. Maybe she pawned more than the jewelry the police learned about.

She struggled for her own identity—independence under her father's watchful eye. Reportedly, everyone in the family ridiculed her writing. But she'd continued to do it until just before she disappeared. That wasn't the action of a quitter.

Her time spent in Greenwich Village after college introduced her to different lifestyles. Mingling with independent women showed Dorothy that if she left New York, she had a chance for self-actualization and a freedom she was denied at home.

Dorothy not only wrote but also read as evidenced by her book purchase on that final day. I'd read a copy of *Engaged Girl Sketches* by Emily Calvin Blake. Blake wrote anecdotal stories about young women becoming engaged. Each woman's story reflected her acceptance of a marriage proposal based on feelings evoked by the prospective husband.

The women's feelings ran the gamut from flattery to what they believed was true love. The book showed the spectrum of reasons to move forward or call off a wedding. Some believed her reading that specific book indicated Dorothy contemplated marriage to George. But she could have been experimenting with George.

Griscom claimed he planned to marry Dorothy. This claim surfaced after he'd been confronted in Italy by her brother, John. Supposedly, John manhandled Griscom, hoping he'd reveal Dorothy's whereabouts. Griscom claimed he had no idea where she went. He promised to help look for her when he returned to the States. Griscom followed up on his promise. He provided another smokescreen for Dorothy.

On that last day, Dorothy walked away confident, refusing her mother's help. Her friend described her as *being in good spirits* when they met outside the bookstore. She'd purchased candy and a book, but no dress for her sister's coming-out party.

This behavior didn't indicate a person setting out to harm themselves.

Evidence mounted. Dorothy ran away to start a new life. A different life—less humdrum and less predictable. A life allowing her to pursue her writing.

All I had left was to figure out the *where* and the *how*.

Chapter Twenty-Nine

The *where* and the *how* of Dorothy Arnold's escape from her father's tight rein would take some serious research unrelated to the current case of finding Roy Beauchamp. But I'd reached a point in my search for Roy where my only lead was in New Zealand. So, I spent the next few hours on the Internet looking for a trace of Dorothy Arnold after her disappearance.

The obvious next step meant following the same leads the lawyer John Keith, the Pinkerton Agency, and the FBI had followed.

The first thing I'd check would be public records, including census records. If Dorothy gave birth sometime in 1911 in the United States, I might find something because the U.S. Census started recording them in 1903. I was particularly interested in births in case George had actually gotten her pregnant during their fling.

A quick search revealed almost seven hundred thousand babies were born in the United States in the three-month window of when Dorothy might have delivered a baby in 1911. No way I'd comb through all those records. So, I narrowed it down to the major cities where reported sightings would have placed her. Still nothing. If she did give birth in any of these cities, she used an alias.

I needed a way to logically expand my search. This tail-chasing wore me down. A break might shake off the frustration. I wandered around my office. The sun outside gave me no clues. Eli stood and stretched. "We need a break," I said.

He wagged his docked tail, bowed, and chortled.

"I take that as a yes. Come on, you two." As I left the room, I grabbed Patsy. Her frock needed sunlight and fresh air. I had planned to set her in the sun for a few minutes each day to bleach the cotton, but I kept forgetting.

My head tingled the minute I touched the doll. By the time I reached my chair on the deck, I was anxious to put her down. Laying her flat on the table in direct sunlight, I retreated inside to brew a cup of tea. A leisurely drink would be about the right amount of time for Patsy's daily dose of sun.

Once back on the deck, my mind spun until I focused on writers of that era. Jill had Luhan's book, *Lorenzo in Taos*, on her list of books to read. I'd discovered the book contained letters between Luhan and D.

H. Lawrence. Well known in literature, I'd research him first.

I picked up Patsy to return to my office. When I looked into her eyes, my body relaxed. I knew with gut confidence that Lawrence played a role in Jill's life. But I didn't know what role, or how significant it was to my case.

My search combining the surnames Lawrence and Beauchamp returned a digital copy of a register in New Zealand's governmental archives showing that in 1922 Lawrence had signed into Seacliff Lunatic Asylum in that country. He'd visited a woman named Camille Beauchamp. Jill must have found this connection between Camille Beauchamp and D. H. Lawrence. She might have found the purpose of the visit in his letters to Luhan, something I would check later.

At this point, with still nothing more about Jill's ancestry except a relative named Roy A. Beauchamp, I searched for his name among all the online records available for New Zealand.

As expected, the lawyer involved did a yeoman's job of eliminating any trace of the young man. It probably didn't matter, because if his birth record still existed, the lawyer who filed the deed poll would have redacted any identifying data and reissued a new birth certificate. If Roy Beauchamp became Conroy Parks, I still had no concrete evidence, just a relentless gut feeling.

If both Jill and Roy came from New Zealand, I'd

lay money that's where Dorothy hid. And Roy shared the Parks surname with her grandmother. But Dorothy being Jill's mother didn't feel right. The birth in 1926 occurred sixteen years after Dorothy's disappearance. That would have made Dorothy forty-one. Back then, having a child at forty-one was possible, but unlikely. It didn't mean Dorothy didn't have children. It just indicated to me that Jill might not have been Dorothy's child.

I picked up Patsy again. The visit by Lawrence fled through my mind like a lightning bolt. Maybe it wasn't Lawrence himself who was important, but his visit to Camille Beauchamp at Seacliff. Were Camille and Roy Beauchamp siblings? And if so, could Dorothy Arnold have been their mother?

I closed my eyes and concentrated on the mental flash card. My head tingled. *Was the doll telling me Dorothy had fled to New Zealand? Had Lawrence and Dorothy met while she was still living in New York and aspiring to be a writer? Would this explain why he chose to visit Camille Beauchamp?*

The Hamiltons had adopted Jill from Saint Saviour's Orphanage in Christchurch where Jill lived until she was four years old. A section of Saint Saviour's provided refuge for unwed mothers as well as housed orphans. Was Camille the mother? Multiple sources reported a devastating fire destroyed all records at the orphanage in 1942, making my task even more impossible.

For the next few hours, I read every article available related to the 1920s orphanage system in New Zealand. An online pamphlet, *Reference Guide to Children's Homes in Otago and Southland*, published by the University of Otago, printed an interview with a woman who described her stay at Saint Mary's, a place like Saint Saviour's.

"We were the 'dirty girls.' Men and boys just wanted to sow their seed. But, if we became pregnant, we were instantly condemned. When I found myself pregnant at seventeen, I was sent to Saint Mary's home for unwed mothers in Dunedin. I had no choice in the matter. I'd shamed my parents. They kicked me out of our house. I had nowhere else to go.

"I arrived with the clothes on my back and was given a bed in a dormitory. I ate porridge crawling with weevils. All of us young mothers worked throughout our pregnancies—scouring, laundering, and bottling preserves.

"The matron was a terrifying figure. She wore soft shoes, and silently appeared and then screamed at me if my mop-strokes were not square. She ran the place like an army. The laundry was like a scene out of Dickens. Copper kettles and fires.

"Saint Mary's Home adjoined an orphanage. I remember seeing the children. They used to run and press their faces against the fence when I walked by, but we weren't allowed to interact with them.

"My baby was born after a drug-induced labor. When I awoke, she was not in my room. The matron had delivered her without calling a doctor. I was torn so

badly I later needed reconstructive surgery so I could have more children.

"I saw my daughter once. My arms ached to hold my little girl. I was not allowed to touch her. I stared. She was so beautiful. I tried to take a mental photograph.

"After the delivery, I begged for my daughter. Instead, I was taken to a lawyer and ordered to sign what I assumed were adoption papers. I wasn't allowed to read them, so I'm not sure exactly what I signed, but I was forced to put my hand on the Bible and promised never to look for her."

My throat ached. Tears formed as I recalled Maggie's behind-the-door story just before the Hamiltons adopted Jill.

Something terrible had happened to Jill at Saint Saviour's.

Chapter Thirty

I stomped back and forth in the kitchen, ranting to Sam about what I'd learned. "Seacliff Lunatic Asylum! I can't believe the name!"

"Calm down, Sherlock. That was a century ago. Times have changed."

"Have they, really? Or do they still say the same things behind closed doors?"

"Maybe, but change must start somewhere. By taking their conversations behind closed doors, they've at least admitted the label is politically incorrect."

"What about morally incorrect? It just makes me so furious. Women in New Zealand had their babies taken away without a choice." My rage ebbed as Sam reasoned with me.

"And you suspect that's what happened with Jill Hamilton. They took her from her mother at birth." His eyes narrowed.

"I don't know. I'm puzzled. I can't find a single

mention of Roy Beauchamp, but I found a marriage record where a George Beauchamp wedded a woman named H. Parks in 1912."

"Why does this particular marriage interest you?"

"Because Dorothy Arnold's full name was Dorothy Harriet *Camille* Arnold. It could be a coincidence, but I've found a *Camille* Parks Beauchamp listed as a daughter of H. Parks. Remember, I told you Dorothy's maternal grandmother was Sarah Parks." Joan Shannon had mentioned Sarah as a person of interest in my investigation.

Sam stared at me.

"Don't you see? Roy Beauchamp, Camille Beauchamp—Roy Parks!"

"You think Camille Beauchamp might be Roy's sister." Sam sat up.

"Yes. And that Dorothy eloped to New Zealand and had children there. Camille being one of them, who had Jill, making Dorothy Arnold Jill's grandmother." I stared at the floor.

Sam paused, then asked, "What does this have to do with Seacliff being a lunatic asylum?"

I cringed at Sam's reference. "I suspect, but don't have the evidence, that Camille had Jill while at Seacliff."

"In New Zealand at that time, families sent unwed mothers to institutions or asylums when unable to place them in mother-and-baby homes. Maybe that happened to Camille. Once delivered, the family would put the babies up for adoption and leave the mother to live out her life in the asylum to hide her sin from the public."

"God. That's awful." Sam touched my hand. "Are you okay, Rae? This case is dredging up sad memories. Remember, you cannot change the past."

I frowned. "I understand. I can't change my life. And I believe I made the right decision at fifteen, but it still hurts when I think about losing our son."

"It will always lurk in your past, but don't let it be more than a reminder of what we want and will have someday soon, I hope."

"You're right. Soon." I leaned over and kissed him. "Back to the salt mines!"

Sam stood and followed me out of the kitchen. "Me, too. More clocks."

I always checked my email first before diving into work. I had a message from the lab where I sent Ginny and Lester's samples. I'd have results within two weeks.

Receiving the lab notice reminded me I hadn't followed through on my father's research. A quick search of the Jersey City public records for Aileen or Kevin O'Leary revealed a slew of them. I needed more specific information, like a middle name, date of birth, father's name, or mother's name.

I glanced down at Sophie. "Why hadn't I asked for their father's name when I was there?"

She looked up and yawned.

"Right! Stupid!"

I visited the pub's Facebook page and inquired

through Messenger. Hopefully, someone would check their messages and be willing to provide me with answers.

That done, I dug around for more information about Seacliff. I needed to understand why Camille Beauchamp's family committed her to the asylum and learn more about her living conditions there.

It didn't take long to discover it wasn't good.

An online article from the Christchurch library described the patient's treatment as callous or even outright cruel. Janet Frame, a famous New Zealand writer, spent time there in the 1940s. She described other patients being beaten for bedwetting and said most patients dreamed of running away. She escaped a lobotomy when she won a literary prize, but others didn't fare as well. Women submitted to unsexing through an operation removing female reproductive organs.

Another article described an environment where outdoor activities, exercise, good nutrition, and productive work became a part of their therapy regime. For thirty years under a reformer, the asylum operated as a working farm. Camille would have been a patient during the same administration. I hoped she fared well.

Next, I searched birth records in 1926, using Camille Beauchamp as the mother. Nothing came up, so I widened the search to all girls born in the same year. Seacliff recorded the birth of a baby girl, mother was listed as a patient at the institution, name redacted. They named the child Virginie with no surname listed.

A handwritten note indicated the infant went to Saint Saviour's orphanage in Christchurch.

I'd never heard the name Virginie until I met Lester's sister, Ginny. "It sounds French."

Sophie looked up again from her spot at my feet. This time, she stood and relocated to a spot near the door. She'd obviously had enough of my interruptions.

"Sorry," I said as I returned to my research.

As it turned out, Beauchamp was both French and English. Maybe to disguise the baby's parents, they gave her a misleading name.

Coincidentally, the baby shared Jill Hamilton's birthday.

But I didn't believe in coincidences.

Chapter Thirty-One

We flew into Auckland and spent the night there. Auckland sits at the northern end of Northland, New Zealand, with the airport southwest of the main city on Manukau Harbor, an inlet from the Tasman Sea.

Exhausted from the thirteen-and-a-half-hour trip, we fell into bed after midnight only to be awakened at five to catch the first flight to Wellington.

The hum of the engines lulled me into a semiconscious state as I stared out the window.

Sam touched my hand. "Are you okay? You look worried."

I hesitated. "Do you think we'll ever have a family?"

He leaned his head back, gazing into my eyes. "I have no doubts."

His confidence surprised me. I straightened in my seat. "What makes you so sure?"

"Like we discussed, we can always adopt. Nothing written or unwritten says you must bear our child. At least, not in my rule book."

"I know, but I don't want to give up on having our own yet." It had been six weeks since our last doctor's visit. Everything looked fine. We agreed not to stress over me getting pregnant. If nothing happened in six months when the case contract ended, we'd consider alternatives. Until then, I'd keep my options open. But I wouldn't stop worrying.

He reached over and squeezed my hand. "I know, but let's investigate adoption. Make an informed decision."

I didn't respond. Sam released my hand and picked up his book.

After about fifteen minutes, I whispered, "We should." Still tired from the long flight, I closed my eyes. My thoughts drifted from adoption to Roy Parks' trail through the public records in New Zealand.

Sam's silence in the limo ride from the airport was unlike him. I wasn't in the right frame of mind to discuss it right now. I'd wait for our week alone at the end of the trip. We both needed time to unwind and reconnect.

* * *

The five-star bed and breakfast Shriver had booked for us sat a few blocks from the beach. Our self-contained room faced Wellington Harbor. Sam and I lost track of time before dinner, or we would have walked to the beach and watched the ferries.

Shriver collected us at six o'clock and drove us to the upscale Boulcott Street Bistro and Wine Bar. Both of us had a mild case of jet lag and not much of an appetite after the long trip. Besides, it was our body's time for breakfast, not dinner. I had eaten cold pizza for breakfast at home, but the thought of a breakfast of wine and calamari turned my stomach. We returned to our room within an hour.

"My assistant will escort you around tomorrow," Shriver said. "Good luck and enjoy our country."

After dropping my purse on the bed, I suggested we take that beach walk now. Muffled voices rippled across the water as couples strolled along the opposite shore.

"Interested in joining me at the archives tomorrow?" I asked, knowing Sam would decline.

He looked out at the water. "I think I'll scope out the ferry service. If we have time, I'd like to venture out on the water. Maybe take a boat tour."

"I figured as much. I'm not sure how long it will take me." I envied him. The forecast indicated a beautiful fall day with temperatures in the low seventies.

* * *

Shriver's assistant picked me up at eight-thirty on Monday morning. The repository manager had the files pulled and ready. They didn't look like they'd been out of storage in years. By nine, I was up to my eyeballs in old records.

Instead of an alphabetical categorization system by client name, each box had been labeled with a lawyer's name and year. Inside, they grouped the files by client. Without knowing the past partners, I'd have to check every banker's box until I found Beauchamp. The warehouse held tens of thousands of boxes. I estimated a thousand cartons had been stored within the time-frame of Roy's deed poll filing. I called Shriver to see if he knew who handled his case. He suggested I check out the boxes attributed to Rousseau.

It took three hours of moving cases around before I stumbled upon a box marked *Rousseau 1930s*. Shriver had guessed correctly. Rousseau handled the Beauchamp accounts in the 1930s. I found a file labeled *George-1934* where a New York lawyer and a junior partner had collaborated on a rebellious youth —*name redacted* to withhold his identity. The boy's father, George—*last name redacted*, had hired the firm to get the boy into the military. A letter indicated the son's charges included larceny, vandalism, and public disorder. The identity of this youth had been protected.

In that same year, the young man of eighteen —*name redacted*, filed a deed poll for a name change. My previous research indicated Conroy Parks joined the Navy that year. I photographed the documents, then refiled them.

As I replaced the file, I noticed a bare paperclip hanging on an adjacent unmarked folder with a 1944 label. The deed poll application must have been clipped to George's file. "So, George No-Last-Name, what had your recalcitrant son been up to those next ten years? Was he enlisted in the military?"

The top document in the 1944 folder acknowledged receipt of payment for an arranged marriage in the United States. Someone had stapled the backup papers, a birth certificate, honorary discharge papers from the Navy, and a health certification form to the receipt.

Morris Hadley, a New York lawyer, had signed as the legal guardian for a fifteen-year-old Indigenous woman—*name redacted,* and tribe not listed. Her agreement allowed the man free entry into the country with her consent to remain married until the man earned his citizenship through the naturalization process. Conroy Parks immigrated to the States to marry Lester Parks' mother, an Indigenous American, in 1944.

I called Shriver. "I found a deed poll filing and some other documents. The surname on everything had been redacted. What do you think?"

"If it was in a Rousseau Box with the Beauchamps, then the bloke had to be a Beauchamp."

"If your constabulary kept records, Roy Beauchamp's mischief may have been captured in one of their old cases." In the past, I'd found useful information in police files.

"They did. Police gazettes. I'll alert them you're on your way. The department isn't far from our warehouse. Your driver's waiting nearby. If you want, I'll send him over."

"Thanks, but I'd rather walk. The weather's great."

Shriver gave me directions and said it shouldn't take more than fifteen minutes.

When I stepped out of the building, I regretted having to work. The sun had warmed the early morning's crisp sea air. I released my hair from a ponytail and strolled along the street to the police headquarters, thinking about being on the water with every step.

At police records, a desk clerk greeted me. "*Kai ora*, Ms. Hunter. One of our clerks will assist you. But our records for minors are sealed."

"No exceptions? This kid caused trouble years ago."

His expression implied a chance at negotiation.

"His arrests happened under your territorial authority. The person's name could be recorded as Roy Beauchamp or maybe Conroy Parks. I'm convinced they're the same person."

A woman in her mid-to-late sixties joined us at the desk. She raised her eyebrows when the duty chief told her my research involved one of the Beauchamp kids.

As we walked from the front, she muttered under her breath. "Beauchamp? I doubt we kept a file for their kids. They got away with everything short of murder. That family thought their kids were the last sheep shorn. Still do."

"What do you mean by that?"

"Oh nothing, really. But they..." She covered her remark once she realized her mistake.

"Last sheep shorn?"

She laughed. "You know—too good for us commoners. I attended public school with a couple of Beauchamp blokes who got tossed out of private school."

It didn't take long to figure out the files had been removed. There was nothing in 1934 or 1935 for a Beauchamp prior to the name change. I strummed my fingers on the table as I contemplated my next move.

"Did you say Beauchamp changed his name?" the clerk asked.

"I think so. In the early 1940s, before he left the country. Why?"

"Let me check our online database. We've been loading old records. I'm not sure if we got that far back." She sat at a computer and tapped away at the keyboard. "Nothing."

The clerk pulled more boxes and we both flipped through the records looking for Parks or Beauchamp.

"I think I might have something." She held up a file. "A bail agreement approved through MacVale and signed by Rousseau. It's for Conroy Parks, arrested for larceny."

"Does it list the person who put up the money?"

She shook her head. "No. Maybe the law firm still has the records."

"Maybe." I dreaded returning to the warehouse.

I called Shriver and gave him the news about the bail endorsement. "I've already asked one of my paralegals to get copies of the birth certificates for George Beauchamp's children, so I can bring the documents to dinner tonight. I'll have them check for the bail endorsement, too."

"Great. Maybe there'll be something helpful on one of them." Shriver had insisted on taking us to dinner again. Not that I didn't appreciate his attentiveness, but I'd hoped to have my husband to myself. Sam had remained distant since our last conversation about starting a family.

"By the way, Beatrix Rousseau has agreed to meet with you. Her father, Solicitor Rousseau, handled the Beauchamp family's affairs. You're scheduled to see her the day after tomorrow. I'll arrange for the trip. You'll need an overnight stay. We can discuss this at dinner."

Halfway through the afternoon, I threw in the towel. My mind kept wandering to the upcoming meeting with Beatrix Rousseau. Without more to go on, searching for Roy felt as productive as counting M&M's, which I'd done more than once.

* * *

At dinner, Shriver and Sam discussed boat tours and ferry schedules while I sipped a cabernet Shriver had brought from a local winery. He said he preferred to pay the extra corkage fee and drink good wine. Sam also mentioned our plans to do some hiking at the end of our business trip before we returned to the States. We saved business conversation for after dinner.

Shriver chose an exceptional restaurant. We ate like we hadn't eaten in months.

Once finished, Shriver placed his napkin on his plate before reaching down into his case. "I have something that may help you. My assistant found Roy Beauchamp's original birth record. When he changed his name, they crossed out his birth name and wrote his assumed name above, *Conroy Parks*. Against regulations, they never secured a clean copy for their files." He handed me the document.

Elated, I grinned. "So, Roy Beauchamp and Conroy Parks *are* the same person."

Sam smiled. "So, we're done. Do we cancel the interview and extend our hiking trip?"

I shook my head. "Not yet. The certificate links Parks to George Beauchamp. But the mother isn't listed unless her name is *VETO,* and you know that's not a name. It's another way to hide her identity."

I could stop now that I'd found Roy A. Beauchamp and just wait for the DNA results for Lester and Ginny, but I wanted to identify Roy's mother. Besides, Shriver had already confirmed my meeting the next day with Beatrix Rousseau.

Shriver laughed. "For years, public records were allowed to be filed without either parent's name. You wouldn't believe how many male and female VETOs we have in our historical records.

"George Beauchamp had five children, two by his first wife and three by his second. We've found evidence that his first wife's name was Harriet. But no records include her surname at birth. George's second wife is from a well-known local family."

I checked the documents one more time. "I found a marriage record from 1912 where George Beauchamp married H. Parks, but nothing else in your public records."

"Did the record include his middle name or initial?" he asked.

I thought for a moment. "R, I believe."

"It was likely him. George always used an initial instead of his middle name." Shriver held back a smile. "His middle initial stood for Rose, a family name."

I had one more question for Shriver. "Who's the other child from the first marriage?"

"Roy's sister, Camille Beauchamp." Shriver inhaled. "She died at Seacliff in the fire. I can petition the court for her records, if you want."

"Absolutely. Dorothy had two middle names, Harriet and Camille." This was no fluke.

Tomorrow would be a long travel day to meet with Ms. Rousseau. First, we'd catch an early ferry out of Wellington to Picton and then drive to Christchurch where we'd spend the night. Shriver had scheduled a luncheon meeting at the request of the lady of the house and hired a driver to chauffeur us around the island. Our trip would take us down the east coast as far as Dunedin, south to Invercargill, then north to Queenstown.

After our visit with Beatrix Rousseau, I looked forward to the hike we'd planned as our second honeymoon. Once on the Routeburn Track, I'd have Sam to myself.

Chapter Thirty-Two

The ferry, the *Strait Feronia*, left at eight o'clock and glided over the harbor's calm waters toward Picton as we ate our bagged breakfast and enjoyed the view.

Sam brushed the scone crumbs from his pants as he spoke. "We'll be entering Cook Strait soon, where the first mate said it can get rough at low tide. They lost a ferry there once when it hit the rocks and sank. Fifty people drowned."

We joined a small group of sightseers on the front deck to watch as the captain maneuvered the ferry through the narrow opening. I pulled a sweatshirt from my bag. The cool breeze whipped my hair against my face, so I clipped it into a ponytail.

Sam leaned over and kissed my cheek. "You look like a teenager with your hair up."

The ferry ride across Cook Strait lived up to its reputation. Waves broke across the bow and sprayed a group of daring kids who laughed and screamed when drenched by the cold water. The ferry heaved, swayed, and surged in its fight to stay on course. If I'd been susceptible to seasickness, the roll, pitch, and yaw would have finished me. Fortunately, my inner ear reacted like stainless steel, as did Sam's. Other than splashes and wind, the trip ended without incident.

A man in a small crowd at the dock held up a sign with my name on it.

"*Kai ora*, Ms. Hunter. I'm Nigel, your driver."

Nigel loaded our bags into the trunk, or boot, as he called it. I kept my extra jacket as well as the sweatshirt. The ferry ride had chilled me to the bone. The daylong trip to Christchurch followed the coastal road. I loved to tour, but my research took priority. So, we drove straight through, stopping only long enough to have lunch in Blenheim, and then made a quick stop at Lake Grassmere salt works to view coral pink water.

Nigel pointed toward the coast. "Sea water is pumped into the shallow pool and then moved from lagoon to lagoon to increase its salinity. By the last pools, crystalized salt forms. Those sparkling white piles are salt."

"What makes the water so pink?" I asked.

"High salinity encourages a special form of algae to grow during warm weather. Once the temperature drops, it dies, and the water returns to clear with a hint of blue."

The next two and a half hours took us through a rugged section of the coast. When we reached

Waipara, the land leveled out and supported olive groves and vineyards. The last leg of the journey took us by the surfing beaches with their spectacular waves and clean sand. There were no swimmers or surfers to be seen.

In Christchurch, Nigel dropped us at a local bed and breakfast. "I'm staying nearby. Call if you need me before tomorrow morning." He handed me a business card with his number. "Otherwise, I'll pick you up at eight."

Between the long ride and being cold, I climbed into bed and passed out from exhaustion.

* * *

Our morning ride to Swannanoa to visit Beatrix Rousseau took thirty minutes. As Nigel drove us around the circular gravel drive, I thought of Tara in *Gone with the Wind*. The two-story mansion faced the street. Both floors included a wraparound porch with white rockers and glass tables.

"Unbelievable."

Sam used his phone to video the plantation grounds. "Magnificent."

Nigel waited by the car while we approached the house.

A young-looking housekeeper greeted us at the door. Weathered hands suggested otherwise. A stiff white apron covered her cotton print dress. A cap covered a tight bun at the nape of her neck and completed her starched look. "Mrs. Rousseau is waiting in the solarium."

She led us through the entry into a grand foyer where a set of winding stairs led to the upper level. The rose-colored solarium opened into a manicured rear garden still in full bloom.

Beatrix Rousseau perched on a Victorian claw-legged couch facing the patio. She stood when we entered the room. "Welcome, Mrs. Hunter. And this handsome man must be Mr. Hunter." Her smile lit the room. "Please make yourself comfortable."

Beatrix returned to the couch. She resembled a China doll, her feet dangling an inch above the floor. Sam seated himself near the window while I chose a seat opposite her.

"I understand you are trying to locate Roy Beauchamp."

"Yes. Mr. Shriver suggested I speak with you. Apparently, your father handled Roy's cases when he got into scrapes with the law."

"Roy and his sister rebelled against their parents. Roy scoffed at the law, and his sister..." she glanced out the window. "His sister fell into bohemian ways."

"Bohemian ways?"

"Yes. She left her parents no alternative but to send her to Seacliff." Beatrix shook her head. "Such promiscuous behavior and outright defiance."

"I've identified Camille and Roy's father as George Beauchamp, but have not been able to identify their mother."

"I believe she immigrated from the States. All very hush, hush."

I leaned forward. "Do you know her surname?"

Beatrix rubbed her chin. "No. My father called her Harriet. That's all I know."

"Do you have any photographs of her? Maybe a wedding picture?"

"Heavens no. A strange one, that woman." Beatrix tapped her head. "Never let anyone take her picture."

"When did she arrive in New Zealand? If I had a specific timeframe, I might find her on a passenger list."

Head tilted back and eyes closed, she thought for a moment before looking at me. "It might have been in 1910 or 1911."

"From my research, it appears George Beauchamp remarried and had a second family. What happened to Harriet?"

"It's like a Greek tragedy. First, the boy got into the stew. Then, the daughter went dodgy. Rumor has it, the children's behavior caused Harriet to sink into a deep depression." Beatrix shook her head. "Plus, she aspired to be a writer but received rejection after rejection at the same time as her kids went off the rails. She became inconsolable."

"What about George?"

"He tried, but George didn't believe in discipline. He'd rather buy the kids out of trouble."

"Is that when your father got involved?"

"My father always handled George's business undertakings. So, when Roy upped his antics to robberies and public misbehavior, George asked my father for help." Beatrix straightened, lifting her chin. "Father had Roy change his name and enlist in the navy. He got in by the skin of his teeth—and with Father's help, without a single crime on his record."

"What about the daughter, Camille?"

"Camille went loony. As I said, her father committed her to Seacliff, where she bedded most of the asylum's male patients. She ended up pregnant. When she had the little girl, they took the baby straight to the orphanage at Saint Saviour's in Christchurch, far enough away so that Camille never saw her."

"What happened to the baby after that?"

"No idea. Father never mentioned her again. He took Camille's failure personally like he'd somehow shirked his duty. Camille had something very wrong with her. Her mother, Harriet, had a weak mind and Camille inherited the same blood."

Sam scowled.

"What happened to Roy after he got out of the navy?"

"He left the country. I overheard Father discussing an arranged marriage in America."

"Did you ever hear Roy's new name?"

"No..." She closed her eyes for a moment. "Well, yes. Father mentioned Roy took his grandmother's maiden name, Parks." Beatrix grinned. "I snooped as a child. Listened at keyholes. Hid behind curtains."

"What happened to Harriet?"

"She lost touch with reality. George had no choice

but to admit her to Seacliff a few years after their daughter." Beatrix bowed her head. "She died in a fire there, too."

"Is that all you know about her?"

"Pretty much. Harriet didn't associate with the locals. She was an odd one—bad blood. Spent most of her marriage living in two upstairs rooms. The help said she rarely came down. They said she spent all her time writing."

"She never came down. Not even to attend family events?"

"Well, yes for some family events. I do recall a big to-do when George insisted Harriet travel with him to Europe to visit his cousin, a successful writer who lived in Germany. George hoped meeting other writers might help Harriet's depression."

"Elizabeth von Arnim?"

"No. Kathleen Beauchamp. You'd know her as Katherine Mansfield, her *nom de plume*."

"Then, Harriet knew Elizabeth, too."

"I'm sure she did. We always referred to Elizabeth by her nickname, May. Her parents named her Mary Annette before she became Countess von Arnim-Schlagenthin."

The aroma of sausage drifted through the room as the housekeeper carried a full tray of food past us and headed to the patio. "Lunch is ready, Madam."

"Enough of this, let's relocate to the patio and enjoy a light lunch of sausage rolls and salad. I hope you like sausage. I've become addicted to it." Beatrix slipped off the couch and hustled to the door. She moved with the grace of a young woman, not a nonagenarian. I hoped I'd be as well preserved as her at that age.

After my first bite, I had to keep myself from wolfing down the rolls. Sam's disappeared fast and he eyed mine, but I didn't share.

During lunch, Beatrix interrupted our conversation as if struck by lightning. "I just remembered. Seacliff was also the home of one of New Zealand's famous female writers."

"Janet Frame," Sam and I said in unison.

"Yes. You're right. But did you know Janet's mother worked in Katherine Mansfield's home? Janet's mother used to brag that she raised two writers."

"No, I didn't." Harriet Beauchamp and Janet Frame both stayed at Seacliff. And Frame knew Mansfield. Not one, but three women writers. Would this connection lead somewhere?

The name Harriet had become significant. I'd check the names of other travelers to see if it was listed.

Without jumping to a conclusion, I'd found enough evidence to form a weak hypothesis—Harriet Parks Beauchamp was Dorothy Arnold. I'd keep this to myself without further proof, but my gut said I was correct.

Chapter Thirty-Three

After lunch, Sam and I bid our farewells. Beatrix Rousseau waved from the lower porch as she rocked in a white wicker chair that swallowed her. We left Swannanoa and headed south to Dunedin.

Nigel and Sam chatted about the area and the sights as we sped along the highway.

Beatrix had explained how the former Saint Mary's Orphanage on Elliot Street had become the Child Protective Services (CPS) main office. "A better use for the property," she'd remarked.

I called ahead to make sure the office would be open when we arrived. Jill Hamilton had been adopted out of Saint Mary's. Perhaps, they'd have the old records with more information than Shriver found. The woman who answered the phone indicated they had boxes of case files being digitized.

"Here it is." Nigel pulled our SUV into a marked space.

"I shouldn't be too long. I'll text if I anticipate a delay."

* * *

The CPS director greeted me, then closed the door. "Mr. Shriver explained that you are handling an inheritance case and asked that I be frank."

I nodded and took a seat beside his desk.

The director sat and steepled his fingers. "If I understood him correctly, you're here interested in a New Zealand orphan adopted by an American family in 1930."

"Yes. I'm trying to locate a male relative. I believe he might be her uncle."

"First, you have to understand the majority of the children housed here in the 1930s were not orphans, but children from families with difficulties."

I nodded.

"Along with the rest of the world, we suffered a deep economic depression back then. It impacted everyone. Many folks couldn't feed their families. Abandoned wives and mothers or women with illegitimate children found it impossible to both work and provide proper care. Plus, we had children of convicts and alcoholics."

As I listened, I recalled a photograph I'd seen

online of a group of young girls standing in front of Saint Saviour's. Did Jill's sad face appear in the group?

"The church operated the orphanage and took it upon themselves to remove children from what they deemed immoral situations, like a child of a prostitute."

"They could do that?"

"The church wielded substantial power back then. Religious crusaders roamed the cities and investigated children's living situations. The church paid informants to pry and tattle. Representatives of the church removed the children from their homes. Truth be told, many responsible mothers turned to prostitution to earn money to feed their children.

"Of course, some parents neglected theirs." He paused and straightened a pile of papers on his desk before he continued. "Orphanages also accepted unmanageable children from parents or by court orders. Orphanages became a dumping ground. Some children stayed until parents solved their personal or financial problems, but most lived at the orphanage until adopted or they aged out of the system."

Camille Beauchamp's father had institutionalized her. Beatrix said the girl gave birth to a baby sent to Saint Saviour's. "The child I am researching was born at Seacliff."

"Quite a few newborns passed through this orphanage from various institutions and were adopted quickly. A few with physical problems remained here until age seventeen."

"And if they had physical problems, the orphanage still released them."

"Afraid so. During hard times, the orphanage needed the beds." The director averted his eyes.

"Is there a list of children's names I can review?"

"I'm sorry. We don't open our records to the public. Access is restricted to proven descendants or family members."

"But Shriver explained to you that I'm working on behalf of a family member." I'd used this argument successfully in the past.

The director stared out the window a moment, then pushed himself upright. "I suppose if this is for an inheritance case, I should try for an exception. I wouldn't want to stand in the way of a beneficiary receiving an inheritance. Let me see what I can do."

I retrieved my phone and sent Sam a text message. *I'll be a while.*

Sam replied. *Text me when you're done. Nigel's taking me to view the ocean.*

The director returned carrying two banker's boxes. He placed them on his desk. The boxes had been marked with dates in the late 1920s and early 1930s. "We haven't digitized these files yet."

"I'm looking for someone named Parks or Beauchamp."

His eyes widened. "Beauchamp."

"Yes. Or possibly Parks." I doubted Parks would be the baby's last name, but I didn't want to chance an oversight.

He pulled up the first file in his box. "You're looking for an adopted child."

"Yes. The Hamiltons from the United States adopted a four-year-old girl in 1930."

"The red line on the file indicates adopted children." He pointed to a faded instance across the top of the folder.

"Let's review those files first. Both boys and girls."

I flipped through the folders in one box while the director rummaged in the other. It took us twenty minutes to pull the adopted files. I'd skimmed through the first page of the eight files I'd pulled. Each one represented a girl. Names had been redacted on the front page.

The director had two piles. "Ten girls and..." The director counted his other pile. "Seven boys."

My stack contained one file twice as thick as the others. I fought the urge to pull it out of order, suspecting more paperwork for an out-of-country adoption like Jill's. When I finally opened it, the letterhead identified a U.S. law firm, Peterson & Hadley. The document from Morris Hadley informed the orphanage that the child arrived in the States and passed a required health exam.

"This is it, Jill's adoption file." The hairs on my arms lifted. I'd found her.

The director put aside his stack and joined me. "Let me walk you through the documents. I can save you time."

I hesitated, wondering if I should agree.

"If you're not comfortable with my help, go ahead by yourself. I'll answer any questions you have." He smiled. "I'm not trying to hide anything. I have no idea what's in the file. I've never seen it."

I relaxed. He seemed sincere and I'd appreciate help since I was looking at records from another country. "Let's look at it together and if I have a question, I'll ask."

The director turned over the first document, revealing a copy of a request by the Hamiltons to adopt the girl. The next document had been sealed in a legal-sized white envelope, dated December 1930, and stamped "Incident Report" with the notation that it would take a court order to be opened.

"May we break the seal? It's been ninety years."

"Yes. These files are sealed by the church, not the courts. Plus, the people mentioned in the incident would be dead by now."

I stood to stretch my legs while the director retrieved a letter knife and cut open the envelope. His face blanched as he read the report.

His look sent a chill down my spine.

"Ahh, this is not good." His hand shook as he handed me the report. "You may want to sit down."

"Okay." I took my seat. The first sentence turned my stomach.

(Redacted) entered the room and abducted the 4-year-old girl from her crib sometime between midnight and two in the morning of the 20th of November.

(*Redacted*) *took the toddler to the garden shed where he* (*redacted*).

The girl suffered irreparable damage (*redacted*) *when repeatedly* (*redacted*).

Sister Agnes reported the girl missing from her crib at five in the morning. The gardener found her alive and unconscious when he entered the shed as part of the search team...

I looked up from the paper in my hand. The director handed me a tissue to wipe the tears running down my cheeks. "I can't imagine the horror."

The director stared straight ahead. "I know. I had no idea. But let's look further."

I pushed the incident report toward him, not wanting to touch it again. He refiled it and looked at the next few items in the folder. "Correspondence between solicitor Rousseau, a Hadley, and the head of the orphanage. It's pre-adoption screening."

The next item looked official.

"What's that?"

"It's the girl's birth certificate. Her mother and father are listed as inmates at Seacliff."

I shuddered at the term used to describe them. "Any names?"

He shook his head. "No. But there is a file number listed at the bottom of the page. Hang on." He sat at his computer. "We digitized most of these files and I have unrestricted access."

I watched him type in the file number as I recovered from the horror.

"Here's something. G. Beauchamp requested the child's mother be confined to Seacliff. In the court confinement order, she was described as unmanageable."

"Camille," I said.

The director looked surprised.

"Camille Beauchamp, George Beauchamp's daughter." Now, I was almost certain she was Jill's mother. "Is the mother's name listed?"

"VETO." The director shrugged. "I'm not surprised. Likely some debutant gone astray. The 1920s in New Zealand reeked of crime and immoral behavior, a real Sodom and Gamora."

"New Zealand wasn't the only country experiencing moral decline at that time." I didn't elaborate, but historical accounts of the United States reported a significant loosening of moral behavior, too. Some historians blamed the radical trends on the Industrial Revolution, urbanization, and a new definition of sexuality. I had a momentary wave of guilt as I remembered my teens, and I didn't grow up in the 1920s.

"May I take a photo of the official birth record?"

"Of course, and I'll print out the mother's court-ordered confinement. Those documents are public records."

I texted Sam. *I'll be done in five.*

He sent a thumbs-up followed by, *Already out front.*

I helped the director replace the files and thanked him for his help. As he escorted me out of the building, we passed a room with a glass front. Several small Māori children played with toys. A toddler looked out at me as if searching for a familiar face. She returned to the toy when she didn't recognize me.

Sam waved at me as I exited the building. His smile washed away the sick feeling I'd harbored since reading the incident report. I reminded myself I couldn't change the past as my handsome husband greeted me with a kiss.

* * *

After a quiet dinner, we spent the night in Dunedin and set out at the crack of dawn the next morning for Queenstown, excited about our chance to enjoy the lushness of the New Zealand mountains. Our second honeymoon had begun!

"To the woods!" I shouted.

Sam grinned. "To the woods, Little Red Riding Hood."

Nigel started up the car and we drove south toward our next destination where we'd spend the afternoon and night before venturing into the wilderness of New Zealand Fiordland National Park.

Chapter Thirty-Four

Sam cat-whistled as he stepped out of the car. "Spectacular."

I craned my neck and stared up at the mountains.

Nigel grinned, then opened the trunk to remove our luggage. "You think the view is nice here, wait until you ride the gondola to Bob's Peak. Mr. Shriver took the liberty of purchasing tickets and made dinner reservations for a window seat at the Stratosfare Restaurant." Nigel handed Sam an envelope containing our gondola tickets.

"I'm heading back north. Enjoy tramping about our great country." Nigel gave us a quick salute as he climbed back in the car, and Sam and I waved as the back of the car disappeared.

"Nice guy," Sam said. "So, what do you want to do for the afternoon?"

"Walk. I don't think I could sit another minute."

"Wait here. I've got an idea." Sam spoke with the desk clerk for a couple of minutes. The clerk handed him a map and a pamphlet, which Sam tucked into his shirt pocket. "We can walk the streets and shop, or we can go over to the Queenstown Gardens." He pointed to a peninsula jutting out into Lake Wakatipu.

"The gardens sound nice." I wasn't much of a shopper. Besides, whatever I bought, I'd have to pack and carry home.

The panoramic views silenced us as we walked along the path by the lake. Some orange and gold trees suggested autumn would arrive soon. The water sparkled against the feet of the surrounding mountains. At the halfway point, we rested on a bench.

"I'm not tired, but I don't want to rush through the experience," I said.

Sam pulled out the pamphlet and read it while I watched a pair of blackbirds jockey for a perch on a tree branch.

"The legend says the lake formed when the body of a giant burned so long it created a great trough that filled with water when it rained."

"Okay. That's it?" I rolled my eyes.

"No, that's not all of it. It's a love story. A rich girl and a poor boy fall in love. She gets abducted by a giant and the boy rescues her so they can be married. Fearing the giant may return for her, the boy burns the giant and poof, a lake. Easy peasy."

I laughed. "I can identify with the abduction part, but not a burning giant." I joked about it now, but it wasn't funny at the time being trapped in an old train station for days. But that's another story.

"I'm sure you can." Sam didn't smile.

We sat in silence for a few minutes.

"We still have a few hours before dinner. Do you want to walk to the Kiwi Birdlife Park on the other side of town?" Sam asked.

Sitting had given my body enough time to notify my head that I was, in fact, tired. "I'll take a raincheck. A nap sounds like a better idea right now."

We finished the garden walk and returned to our room. I slept while Sam read about New Zealand.

* * *

The gondola ride took all of five minutes, but we had a car to ourselves. We located the restaurant and bar inside the terminal. Leaf peepers, as foliage tourists were called in New Zealand, traveled in herds around the walkways. A large group waited to be seated at the Stratosfare Restaurant where we had reservations in forty-five minutes.

Sam raised his eyebrows. "You think they'll be ready for us?"

A member of the staff overheard him. "Don't worry. This crowd will be in and out in no time. They ordered ahead."

"We'll be back in a half hour," Sam said.

We checked out the luge, then the hiking trails, and made it back to the Stratosfare as the foliage crowd

exited the dining area. Our seats provided an unob-
structed view of the entire valley.

"You must be close to solving the kinship puzzle."

I smiled. "Back to reality. Yes, I believe I am."

"And Roy Beauchamp and Conroy Parks are the
same guy. Right?"

I nodded. "I'm sure. What I'm still not sure of is if
Jill Hamilton and Virginie Beauchamp are the same
person. But I'm close to finding that one out, too."

"So, Lester Parks might be in line for a bundle of
money."

"Maybe. Maybe not. I doubt Roy Parks is Lester's
father. But if Roy adopted him, then things might work
out." I had a bad feeling about it, but I didn't want to
jump to a conclusion.

The sommelier arrived with the wine, a pinot noir
from a local winery. He poured the tasting into the
glass in front of Sam, who took a sip and then handed it
over to me. I noticed the sommelier's neck redden.

"We don't always like the same wine," Sam
explained.

"I apologize. I should have asked if you both
wanted a taste."

I smiled. "Apology accepted. The wine is perfect."

The meal competed with some of our favorite
restaurants at home. Sam cut his lamb with a fork. My
prawns gave Sid Booker a run for his money.

"Dessert?" our waiter asked.

"Crème brulee and another bottle of wine," Sam
said.

When the waiter left, I reached across the table and took my husband's hand. "I may be close to solving this case, but there's something going on I haven't shared with you."

"I know." Sam stared into my eyes. "I figured you'd tell me when you were ready."

"Actually, there are two things."

"Go ahead."

"There's something bothering me about Olivia, one of the law interns who works for Austin Bradley. I don't trust her."

"Why?"

"I don't really know. I can't put my finger on it. But I feel like she's most annoying when we're in the art gallery."

"The art gallery?"

"Yes."

The waiter interrupted with dessert and wine.

"The art gallery..." Sam rubbed his chin.

"Yes. I instructed her to have photos made of the front and back of every art piece and copies of their provenance, but she hasn't produced anything yet. And she snapped at me when I questioned her about it."

"Maybe she can't find someone to do it."

"I don't think that's it. She says she forgot." I paused for a moment. "I'm ready to talk with Austin directly. He may know why she's stalling."

"That's a good plan." Sam paused. "What's the other thing?"

"It's the hunches and insights. I'm still having them, but now, it's when I hold the doll."

Sam set down his spoon, leaving his dessert half-eaten. "Rae, this is serious."

"Maybe. But I've been trying to figure it out on my own." My shirt hem had cut off the circulation in my fingers as I twisted it round and round. "I think it's me. I'm the medium."

Sam's face slackened.

"Seriously. I think I have something within me that conducts information from the past."

Sam's lips thinned. "Oh, come on. That's impossible!"

"I'm not sure, but maybe something genetic from my father. Or...God knows what."

Sam looked away. "We'll get you help once we get home."

"I don't need help. I need answers." My face burned.

Sam lowered his head and sighed.

"You think I'm crazy, but it's because nobody really knows. Please try to understand. I'm not imagining anything. I get physical sensations that are followed by insights into the case. Information arrives and I know it's true."

His eyebrows lifted and his nose wrinkled as his lips formed a tight line. Then, he spoke without emotion. "Is that why you've refused to discuss a family? You aren't sure what kind of baby we might produce?"

"No, not that. I'm not sure what kind of mother I'd be if I don't understand what's happening to me."

"Like I said, we'll get help when we get back to the States." Sam picked up his spoon and wolfed down the rest of his dessert.

I sipped my wine.

When Sam finished, we took the gondola ride back to Queenstown. I'd spoiled the magic of the night, but I had to come clean with him.

Shriver had dropped the backpacks at the hotel so we could add our clothing or anything personal we wanted to carry. He left instructions to leave them at the desk once packed, so the shuttle driver could load up while we had our breakfast.

Sam showered while I stuffed clothes and essentials into the loaned backpack. He'd put two ultra-light emergency blankets in mine. I peeked into Sam's, and saw a ground cloth and a small first aid kit. He'd provided sleeping bags, too, which our driver had left in the van rather than load and unload them twice. While I debated packing a lightweight parka, Sam returned.

"Pack layers. It's that time of year." He wrapped me in his arms and lifted me off the floor. "You're a lot of trouble for such a small package."

I snuggled into his neck. "I know and I'm sorry. Maybe I can make it all worthwhile."

"Maybe you can," he said, dropping me onto the bed.

Once the heat of the moment wore off, we laid next

to each other without talking. No doubt, Sam wondered how he got himself into this crazy marriage.

While he snored next to me, I pondered my suspicions about Olivia and the Kuhn, my hunches about Jill and Conroy Parks. The closer I came to finding the link in Jill's ancestry, the more I suspected someone assisting with the case had something to hide. I suddenly sat up straight. "It has to be about the huge inheritance at stake."

"What does?" Sam raised his head, startled by my outburst.

"Someone I'm working with on this case is hiding something."

"Maybe. But who are your stakeholders?"

"The most obvious stakeholders who should want me to solve the case are the Roy A. Beauchamp family, also known as the Conroy Parks family. Then, there's the Hamilton family who won't get a cent if I solve this case. If I fail, the entire estate goes to the Columbia University Scholarship Fund, which means students in need won't get the financial assistance necessary to complete their degrees."

"Does someone at the university know the stipulations of the trust?"

"As far as I know, just Olivia and Tim, the two interns. Austin has tried to keep the trust provisions a secret. Unless, of course, Jill's father confided in someone. But evidence indicates he was the sole person who knew what was in the trust."

"What about a secretary? They provide a source for information."

"Everything passes through a secretary's hands," I recalled Shriver's secretary blurting out about the current George Beauchamp and his pending divorce.

"Or maybe Olivia is a spy. Perhaps, she's reporting back to someone at Columbia. You said she seemed suspicious."

"I said she annoyed me. And she acted suspiciously around the Kuhn painting. I'll check with Austin as soon as we're done with our hike."

Chapter Thirty-Five

The shuttle dropped us off at the entrance to Mount Aspiring National Park at nine. The place appeared deserted as we climbed out of the vehicle. Although off-season, the forecast indicated a pleasant weekend.

Sam grabbed my frame pack and handed it to me. "Here. This one's lighter. Plus, it's a prettier sleeping bag."

I stared at it, thinking it wasn't what I'd have expected from Shriver—gold, purple, black, and turquoise print. Sam's hunter green bag spoke Shriver. "That is pretty."

A Māori ranger emerged from the building. He smiled and reached out his hand to Sam. "*Kai ora...* hello. You're tramping about, or as some folks say, backpacking, this weekend?"

Sam grasped the man's hand. "Yes. We're hiking

from here to the Divide, planning to take a few side trails along the way."

"Americans," he noted. "You won't find many blokes on the track today. The big swarm has already passed through for the cheap rates. You're lucky. The weekend weather looks favorable." He spoke over his shoulder. "Follow me. We'll need you to sign the intentions log. We keep records of all visitors." The ranger led us inside to complete the contact information. "Just in case."

Sam filled out the appropriate forms. When he got to emergency contacts, he looked at me. "Who should I put here?"

"Shriver's the only person we know in New Zealand." Sam wrote down his name.

"Is your contact a local?" the ranger asked.

"He's a lawyer at Rousseau & MacVale in Wellington."

I pulled out my cellphone, looked up Shriver's number, and then handed the phone to Sam. He made a note next to Shriver's name before returning the form with our information to the ranger. "Thanks. All done."

"You won't need that." He nodded toward my phone. "No cell service out there."

I shrugged. "Habit. I take it everywhere."

He looked over the registration form, then tucked it onto his clipboard. "It's first come, first serve at the huts, but like I said, you shouldn't have any issues. There's a half-dozen experienced hikers a day ahead of you. It's unlikely you'll catch them. They're training for a big tramp in the spring. And watch the clouds. The forecast is favorable, but snowstorms pop up without warning in the mountains."

"We plan to take our time and enjoy the views." Sam winked at me.

"I'm assuming you're both in top-notch health."

"We hike and kayak back home. This shouldn't be any big deal," I assured him.

"One other thing. There's a feral hog sow and her litter roaming around in the beeches. They're noisy, so you won't miss them. Take a wide berth and you'll be fine."

After we thanked him for his help, we strolled to the trailhead where I met my first challenge, a swing bridge.

"Oh boy. I don't know about this." As I stepped onto its edge, a slight breeze caused it to sway. "Oh, no. I hope there aren't too many bridges like this."

Sam laughed. "You can do it. Don't look down if it bothers you."

His laughing pushed my competitive button. I steeled myself and, step by step, I inched across the moving structure. Halfway across, my tentative sideways glance resulted in weak knees. But by boring my eyes into the opposite bank, I managed the crossing. Sam followed with no hesitation.

The initial mile of the trail wound alongside the Routeburn, a small, crystal-clear river.

"The water originates from a tarn six miles above us." Sam pointed toward a rise.

"A tarn?" I'd never heard the word.

Sam grinned. "I'm not that smart. I read the brochure. A tarn's a crevice formed by the erosion of a glacier. The hollow collects water like the fishponds at the arboretum, except it is fed from the melting ice, not city water."

Once past Sugarloaf Stream, the incline steepened up a rise to Bridal Veil Waterfalls. Between the elevation and the exertion, my muscles began to give out. I huffed and puffed like a steam engine until we reached the attraction.

"You okay, Rae?" Sam scowled.

"I'm good, but the backs of my legs are telling me I should have trained for this."

Sam laughed. "I hear you. Twenty miles isn't far by our standards, but we don't hike hills this steep."

We rested and enjoyed a protein bar before continuing. When my legs ached with every step, I contemplated asking for a rest. I hated to give in and admit defeat, so I pushed on. Finally, we encountered another swing bridge that led us to open grassed flats.

"Another rest?" Sam asked.

"Good idea." I dropped to the ground, groaning, "I thought you'd never ask."

Sam squatted beside me and rubbed my calves.

"Thanks. I'll be fine. A few hundred yards of flatland will be good medicine."

The break relieved my leg pain long enough to climb through a stunning beech forest with distant views of the Humboldt Mountains.

"Can you hear it?" Sam yelled as we emerged from the gorge.

The Routeburn Falls Hut and the campsite weren't much farther. As we neared the site, the roar from the falls drowned out most other sounds. The hut sat on the edge of the bush line, close to the cascade.

"We made it." I smiled at Sam. "Can you believe the view?"

"The ranger was right. The hut's vacant." I shivered. As the sun dropped below the western horizon, the air cooled rapidly. I pulled my jacket from the pack.

"Let's go inside," Sam said.

During the Great Walks season, the huts came equipped with a ranger in residence. But May was off-season, so the comforts included bunks, mattresses, and solar-powered lighting. The water had been turned off, with pit toilets replacing the flushers. A water tank provided fresh drinking water.

"This is great. Like the Ritz compared to some of our campsites." I pushed on a mattress to test its hardness. "Not bad."

"Pick a spot," Sam said, throwing his pack on a bunk and beginning to unpack his gear. "Hungry?"

"You need to ask?"

Sam laughed. "I'll get water."

When planning the trip, I'd asked Shriver about

the hike. He agreed to provide our gear, including sleeping bags rated for thirty below zero. He said it might get cold in the higher elevations. Still heated from the climb, I couldn't imagine being cold.

I pulled at the zipper. "Oh, for Pete's sake." The zipper dropped off the track and fell to the floor.

"What's wrong?" Sam asked as he stepped through the door.

"I broke the zipper on my sleeping bag."

"Here, give it to me." Sam messed with it, unsuccessful in getting it back on the track. "Use mine. I'm always hot."

"I'm hot, too. But I'd feel safer knowing I can zip into my bag."

As we swapped bags, Sam grinned and wiggled his eyebrows. "This must be Shriver's wife's bag. Exciting!"

"Yes. I thought so, too."

I loved camping, but the thought of something crawling on me in the night kept me zipped in. I'd had a bad experience on a Girl Scout camping trip. The girls put a frog in my bed. It hopped and kicked when I moved my feet. My screaming nearly gave the leader a heart attack.

"No problem." Sam laid out the bag on his cot.

While eating dinner, we watched the last vestiges of daylight disappear over the lake.

"Ready for bed? We have a long day ahead of us tomorrow."

"I am. I'm bushed. Hopefully, I can lift my legs high enough to get in the bunk."

We both fell asleep listening to the dull roar of the falls.

Chapter Thirty-Six

"Are you up for seven miles today?" Sam asked, yawning.

"I'll make it." I bent and stretched my calves. At first, my legs refused to cooperate. Once the muscles warmed, they loosened.

When we stopped for lunch, Sam scratched at his calf through his pants.

"What's the matter with your leg?"

"I don't know, but it itches like crazy." He rolled up his pant leg. "Wow. Something bit my calf."

I caught sight of the raised red spot. "Cripes. What did that? Does it feel hot?"

"Not really. It just itches." He scratched with fury until it bled.

"Leave it alone. You'll just make it worse." I looked in the first aid kit for a bug bite stick. The kit had a few missing items, including antibiotic cream and something for insect bites. Nothing looked promising, so I poured water from my bottle onto a clean sock. "Here, press this on the welt. Maybe coolness will ease the itching."

Sam pressed the wet sock to his leg while I fixed lunch and poured drinks.

"Hungry?" I handed him a protein bar.

"Not really. Breakfast didn't sit well." His face had turned ashen.

"Eat the bar. It might settle your stomach." I gobbled mine while Sam nibbled at his.

After he'd eaten a quarter of it, he folded the wrapper over and handed it back. "Save it for later. I can't eat it right now."

"Well, at least drink something."

He drank slowly as if sipping a good wine. "Tastes great."

Once he'd finished his drink, I packed up and we continued along the trail. Sam, usually the trailblazer, lagged behind instead of leading the way. I kept checking to make sure he remained in sight. Finally, I stopped and waited for him to catch up.

"Babe, I don't know what's wrong, but I feel like shit." He sat on a rock. "I just need to rest. How far until the next shelter?"

I retrieved the map from my pouch. It was about a mile and a half and would take another hour at our normal pace, but this was anything but normal. "I'd guess one to two hours. You gonna make it?"

"Yup." He stood and shuffled ahead on the path.

Clouds covered the sun, and the temperature

began to drop. At an altitude of over four thousand feet, it didn't take much to cool the air. I studied the sky to the west. Large clouds worried me. The forecast said clear weather, but the ranger had warned us about snow squalls coming out of nowhere.

We climbed at a steady, but painfully slow pace, up the valley, through wetlands and tussock-covered flats, before sidling along the bluffs above Lake Harris to reach the highest point on the trail at Harris Saddle. I insisted Sam lead so I could keep an eye on him. Two hours would be optimistic at his current pace.

After Harris Saddle, the trail descended and traversed along the exposed Hollyford Face, with expansive views over the Darran Mountains. Sam didn't even look up. His gait had slowed to that of a turtle. Gravity became his friend. We made a slow and steady descent to the Lake Mackenzie Hut.

"Sam, can you move a little faster? I think there might be a squall headed our way."

"I'll try." He wobbled and weaved, but he managed to lengthen his stride. We covered the last half mile amid large snow flurries. Sam kept sticking out his tongue to catch the flakes. We made it into the hut and shrugged off our packs.

Sam sat on a cot. His eyelids drooped, with his eyes mere slits as he breathed heavily.

"Thirsty?" I handed him water.

"Parched." He shivered from the cold as water dribbled down his chin.

"Why don't you nap while I set up and fix dinner?"

Sam didn't argue. I helped him with his boots.

"Don't bother with your socks." I unrolled his sleeping bag on an empty cot. When I flipped open the bag, a strange-looking spider scurried out and jumped to the floor. The spherical black body with a prominent red stripe on the upper side reminded me of a picture I'd seen. A black widow.

"Oh, crap! I bet that's what bit you!"

My instinct was to stomp it into eternity. Instead, I grabbed Sam's hat and trapped the creature underneath, then emptied a plastic pill container. When I lifted the hat, the spider clung to the headband. I shook the specimen into the bottle for safekeeping for future identification. It landed on its back and exposed an hourglass-shaped reddish-orange streak on its underside.

"There better not be more of those suckers." I grabbed the bags and took them outside. Nothing fell out except my lost sock. The spider must have been a lone stowaway.

"All set." I placed Sam's bag on the cot again.

"Thanks. I'm beat." He crawled into his bag and fell asleep. He didn't wake for dinner, so I ate the remainder of his power bar, and then checked the weather. The snow continued to accumulate, and the wind had picked up. If Sam wasn't better in the morning, we might have to stay another day at the hut.

An hour after I fell asleep, a thumping sound woke me. Sam thrashed in his bed. I squirmed out of my bag and shuffled to his cot. His beet-red face felt hot and dry. I found the wet sock, rewet it, and draped it on his forehead. Pulling a chair over to his bed, I watched him. Every ten or fifteen minutes, I rewet the sock.

Around midnight, a pelting noise began on the roof. When I opened the door, expecting rain, I found sleet turning to heavy snow. When sufficient snow accumulated, I made snowpacks using my spare socks and our towels and laid them on Sam's head. Sweat poured off him. He moaned and coughed, but never woke.

Sometime in the night or early morning, I stumbled to my cot and fell into an exhausted sleep.

Chapter Thirty-Seven

At dawn, I awoke to an unfamiliar sound.

"Sam? What's that noise?" I looked toward his bunk. He lay prostrate.

I flew out of bed. "Dear Jesus! Sam! What's the matter?"

His eyes rolled back in his head. He made a gurgling noise and went limp. Next, he vomited what little food he had in his stomach, so I rolled him on his side to prevent him from choking.

"Sam...Sam..." I brushed his hair away from his eyes.

"Rae..." He groaned and opened his eyes to slits. "What happened?"

"You're alive. You're okay. You had a seizure." In college, I had a friend who'd collapsed into a grand mal during a history exam. Sam exhibited the same symptoms.

"Rest. You'll feel better in a few minutes." I wasn't

sure he would, but I didn't want to upset him. It took my friend the entire day to recover. "We should stay here for the rest of today if you don't feel well enough to hike. It's an eight-mile trek to the Divide."

"I'll be okay. I feel better since I emptied my stomach." Sam crawled out of bed and went to the door. "It's still snowing. Let's wait for it to stop."

I didn't argue. Another few hours of sleep would feel good.

By noon, the snow had abated, and we were both awake.

He sat up in his bed and swung his legs off the bunk. "God, I feel like crap."

He looked like crap, too, but I didn't mention it.

Sam grabbed at his right leg and rubbed it through his jeans. Then, he rolled up the pant leg. The welt on his calf had festered, with red lines radiating from the center.

"Let me see that." I felt the spot. "It's hot."

He struggled to his feet and wobbled to the door. When he grabbed at his crotch, I noticed he had an erection. He caught me staring at his manhood and shrugged. "I don't know why this is happening."

Normally, I'd be aroused myself, but with Sam so sick, sex was the furthest thing from my mind. "Why don't you stay in bed and rest? We can head out tomorrow. We have an extra day. There'll be a ranger at the Divide who can get us a ride back to Queenstown."

"Let me have a few minutes to eat and drink. I feel a little better. Food may make the difference." He ate two protein bars and drank a full bottle of water. Then, he paced around the shelter, testing his legs and balance. "I'm fine. Just a little tired."

"You look like hell." His face was pasty, and his breath would have offended a dog.

"I've got this!" He glared at me, so I backed off, but in my heart, I knew I shouldn't.

The weather outside the hut had improved. The snow stopped as quickly as it had started. The hillside sparkled as the sun peeked through a mass of threatening clouds.

I checked the map while Sam watched. "No other trails will get us off the mountain as fast as continuing on this route. Are you up for it?"

"I can do it."

"Rest while I roll up your bag and pack your things." I had my doubts, but I needed to get him back to civilization and medical attention.

He didn't argue. Instead, he retreated outside and plunked down onto the steps.

I stuffed most of his things in my pack to lighten his load, then closed the door of the hut behind me. "Ready?"

"Ready as I'll ever be." He rose with the grace of an old man.

We hadn't covered more than a half mile on the trail, maybe a half hour out, when Sam stopped and leaned on a rock. "Rae, I've got to rest." He threw off his pack and flopped to the ground. I watched, worried, but he didn't have a seizure. After another half hour and a long drink of water, he readied himself to move on.

Within twenty minutes, Sam contorted, fell to the ground, and experienced another seizure. I turned him on his side and stepped back to wait for the body spasms to cease. When he had fallen, he'd hit his head. Blood poured from a wound on his right temple. My heart pounded. I wanted to scream, but I tried not to panic. Sam didn't need to worry about me.

Get something to press on the wound. Remembering some of my first aid basics, I threw off my pack and pulled out a clean shirt. Head wounds were bloody. "It's okay, Sam. I'm wrapping your head. You bumped it when you fell."

I wasn't sure he heard me, but he relaxed and drifted into a deep sleep.

Unrolling both bags, I laid one on the ground under him. Even though he was burning up, he needed to stay warm. Sam still had his erection when I wrapped him with the second bag. Fear gripped me. He wasn't going to make the trek to the ranger station.

I watched him for an hour as he slept. He hadn't moved, but his chest rose and dropped with each labored breath, and he had a pulse. He needed a doctor, not my limited first aid skills.

"I've got to go for help," I mumbled. My heart ached at the thought of leaving him on the trail. I felt his head. His skin was on fire and his breathing had become shallow and raspy. "Sam, I have to go for help."

He didn't respond.

It would be dangerous to leave him exposed to the elements. He'd need protection from wildlife and the whims of the weather. I raced back to a fallen tree we'd passed earlier and collected branches to construct a primitive lean-to.

Struggling to drag Sam on his bag over to a large clump of brush a few feet away, I proceeded to cover him with the branches. Shriver had included a couple of bright orange ultra-light survival blankets and a ground cloth that I used to make a tent.

Why hadn't Shriver replenished the first aid kit? He'd thought of everything else.

The wind had picked up. A new bank of clouds pressed in from the west, threatening another squall. It was now or never.

Shouldering my pack, I kneeled next to Sam and whispered in his ear. "It's me. I'm going for help." Tears ran down my face as I kissed his forehead.

The trail in the direction of the Lake Howden Hut and the Divide was mostly downhill. At a good pace, the remaining five and a half miles might take me three or four hours if I was lucky.

I didn't look back, knowing I'd never leave if I did.

Chapter Thirty-Eight

The cold air pricked at my wet cheeks as I hiked away from Sam. My chest ached as the situation became clear. Leaving Sam to get to the Divide was the one alternative that made sense. Otherwise, he could die. Hesitating, I turned to go back but caught myself, then choked out an apology. "Sorry, Sam. I can't save you if I stay here."

Sobbing, I stumbled across a small snow-covered flat to the bush line with a gradual slope into an open area dotted with ribbonwood trees. Calmed by activity, I stopped to check my map. "The Orchard, another four miles to the next hut. Three or four hours to the Divide."

If I met someone, I'd ask them to go ahead for help, so I could return to Sam.

The snow remained pristine, except for a few small animal tracks and bird footprints. As I entered the beech forest, I heard a faint grunting and squealing.

We'd been warned of the feral hog sow and her litter roaming this area. According to the ranger, she guarded her piglets and tended to be aggressive if people got too close.

I stopped and listened to determine her direction. As the rustling and snorting sounds grew louder, my heart pounded so hard I thought the sow would hear it. Piglets scrambled around her as she sauntered toward me. A brazen little sprig darted ahead and halted within twenty yards. The little beast began squealing as if being killed when he spotted me. The sow lifted her head. She snorted, her eyes widened, turned dark, and then she charged.

In one movement, I shed my pack and shinnied up a beech tree. The backpack distracted the sow. She charged in, head-butted it, then ripped it open with her tusks. Clothing hung from an ear as she foraged for the protein bars at the bottom of the sack. Her litter played push-and-pull with a pair of dirty socks.

"Get out of here!" I screamed. "Take what you want! Scram! Get!" As the sun disappeared, clouds billowed off the distant water toward land. I was running out of time. Sam could freeze up there.

The sow looked up and grunted.

"Go! There's nothing left."

She snorted again and wandered off the trail, away from Sam and the Lake Howden Huts with her swarm of piglets scattered around and under her feet. I stayed in the tree until she disappeared. Hopefully, the protein bars satisfied her hunger. I didn't want to risk an injury by climbing down too soon.

After a long and agonizing fifteen minutes, I descended to the ground. Tatters remained of my favorite shirt, but other than smelling bad, the pack survived the battle. I scooped up the remnants of my clothing and the protein bar wrappers, stuffed them into the bag, and set out for the Divide, grabbing a thick stick from the side of the trail. Not that it would provide much protection if the sow should return, but it would help to stabilize my legs.

Throwing the pack onto my back, I pressed on. The wet snow acted like grease under my hiking boots, impeding my downhill progress. One more hut sat between me and help. As soon as I saw it, I started shouting. "Help! Help! Anybody here? Help."

The wind whistled past the building, drowning out most sounds. At the entry to the hut, I spotted footprints heading away from the shelter toward the Divide. I burst into the building and found sparse accommodations. A quick scan revealed it had been used recently, but it held nothing I might need for Sam. When I turned to leave, an old sign hanging inside the door rattled with my movement. The message said, *'Your life is a mirror. Life gives us not what we want. Life gives us who we are. - R. Sharma.'*

"Two miles to go. Come on, RaeJean. You can do it." To occupy my mind as I slogged along in the snow, I ruminated on the quote.

Sam had been patient with me over the last year

and a half, maybe longer. He deserved an answer, a family. I had to trust in myself and stop making excuses about why I wasn't ready.

What if Sam didn't survive? I choked on a sob. "God, please don't take him now. Life gives us who we are, and I'm that person, the one who saves you, Sam."

A squeal echoed through the trees from behind me. I tightened my grip on the stick and quickened my pace. "No pigs are going to slow me down. I'll make it to the Divide. It's my turn to be the strong one. I can do this."

Wet grass poked through in patches where the snow had melted. My legs ached as I walked past a side trail to Key Summit Track. Sam and I had planned to climb the trail to an alpine wetland. Guidebooks raved about the panoramic views over Fiordland's mountains and alpine lakes from the summit.

When I first sighted the building at the Divide, it was a dark blob. As I got closer, I spotted a ranger standing at the base of the trail. He waved.

Like a deranged woman, I ran, fell, and cried while covering the last hundred yards in record time. "Please help me. My husband is sick. He's having seizures, vomiting, and fever...and..." I broke down sobbing.

The ranger whisked me inside, wrapping me in a blanket. "Sit down. Tell me what happened."

"Sam got bit by something and had an allergic reaction." I wiped my nose on my sleeve as I retrieved the captured spider from my pocket. "I think this is the culprit. I found it in his sleeping bag."

The ranger furrowed his brow as he stared at the opaque pill bottle.

"Look." I opened the top and handed him the specimen.

"A redback." He shook his head. "How long ago did it bite him?"

"About thirty-six hours." I wiped at my face again. "Is he going to make it?"

"We'll do everything we can. Tell me where he is."

I described Sam's location the best I could. The ranger used his cellphone to call a hospital in Queenstown. He explained the situation. "Right. Okay. Yes. There's a flat area in front of the Lake Mackenzie hut. You can land a copter there and follow the tracks for about a half mile. His wife says you'll see a bright orange makeshift tent next to the trail. Right." He hung up and turned to me. His pupils had dilated, and I knew what that meant.

"Not good." My lips quivered, my nose ran, and tears ran down my cheeks.

He shook his head. "They're sending a medical copter right now. They don't have any anti-venom in Queenstown, but there is some at Mercy in Dunedin. They're going to meet another copter in Kingston who will bring in the serum along with a paramedic to administer it."

I jumped up and headed for the door. "I've got to get back to Sam."

"No. You stay right here. The chopper is on its way to your mate and will get there before you can. I'll call my buddy at Glacier Southern. He'll give you a copter ride to Kingston."

I listened as the ranger made the call.

"Make it as fast as you can. No worries. She needs to be there in two hours. It's an emergency." The ranger disconnected, nodding. "My buddy will be here to collect you in forty minutes. It won't take long to get to Kingston, where you'll hook up with CareFlight's medical copter and your mate."

I paced the yard outside at the Divide, stopping and listening for the sound of a copter. Forty minutes felt like forty years. But almost to the minute, I heard the familiar *chop, chop, chop* of the blades. A gust of wind nearly blew me over as the bird settled to the ground.

"Come on." A man waved at me from an open door. The ranger grabbed my arm and pulled me to the copter, boosting me inside and strapping me into the seat before joining me.

During the interminable ride to Kingston, I prayed Sam was still alive.

I saw the two copters sitting in the parking lot of what looked like an elementary school. "Is that them?" My voice cracked.

The ranger reached over and squeezed my hand. "That's the rescue team."

When we landed, the ranger jumped out and lifted me from the doorway. He led me toward a red and blue copter. Several men stood outside while two EMTs worked on Sam.

"Is he going to make it?" I searched their faces for hope. I didn't see any.

My knees buckled. I must have fainted because the next thing I knew, we had changed helicopters and the ranger from the park sat next to me.

"We're taking you to Mercy in Dunedin."

I nodded and swallowed the lump in my throat.

Chapter Thirty-Nine

A man dressed in scrubs filled the doorway of the waiting room. "Mrs. Hunter?"

I stood and walked over with what little strength I had left. "Yes."

"He's stabilized, but we won't know the outcome for at least another twenty-four to forty-eight hours. Do you have family nearby?"

I shook my head.

"Do you know anyone in the area?" the man asked.

I was about to shake my head when I realized I did. "I know Carl Shriver at Rousseau & MacVale Law Firm in Wellington."

"You may want to call him."

"Okay."

"You can stay here, but you need to rest and eat. The Wains is a reasonable stop. They have a casual restaurant with a bar." He furrowed his brow. "If you give me your phone number, I'll call you if there's any change in your husband's condition."

I gave him my number.

The ranger walked up behind me. He'd stayed with me the entire time, waiting for a report on Sam's condition. Tears rolled down my cheeks. My hands shook so badly that I dropped my phone. "I need to call Shriver."

"No worries, love. I'll make the call." The ranger disappeared for ten minutes. He smiled when he walked back into the room. "Mr. Shriver's boarding a plane and will be here this evening. He's taken care of booking you a room and is having your things flown in from Queenstown."

"Thank you."

A nurse entered the waiting room. "Mrs. Hunter, the doctor said you could see your husband for five minutes every hour. Follow me."

Sam looked like a lab experiment. He had tubes running in and out of every orifice.

"Sam, it's me. I'm here." I squeezed his hand, but he didn't respond.

"He's in a coma, love. He might hear you, but he can't respond," she whispered.

I held his hand for the allotted five minutes every hour and returned to the lounge until ten when Shriver arrived.

"Mrs. Hunter, I'm so sorry. What happened?" He held my hands.

"A redback spider bit him."

"A spider this time of year?" Shriver looked puzzled.

"Is that unusual?" My skin crawled.

"Very. First off, they're near extinct. Second, they hide as soon as it starts to get cold. Where did you find it?"

"In his sleeping bag. Actually, in my bag, but the zipper broke so Sam took mine and gave me his."

"I stored the bags in sealed containers. How could it have gotten there?"

"You tell me." I was beyond thinking by now.

"That's a puzzler."

"Ma'am, did you bring the sleeping bags with you?" the officer asked.

Shriver leaned in front of me toward the officer. "They're mine. Why?"

The officer frowned as he spoke. "The spider. It should be in hiding for the winter."

"It's what I told Ms. Hunter. I seal and store them in my attic at the end of every season."

"Have you ever seen redbacks around your place where you keep the bags?"

"Never." Shriver's eyes widened.

The officer turned to me. "Mrs. Hunter, did you leave the bags unattended at any point during your trip?"

I thought about it. "We took a shuttle from the inn to the base of the trail. The driver packed up our gear. That's the only time it left our possession."

"Who was the driver?"

I looked at Shriver.

He leaned toward me. "What did he look like?"

"The one thing I can remember is he wore cowboy boots."

Shriver looked at the officer. "Lachlan Bowers."

The officer stood. "Excuse me. I've got a call to make." He rushed from the room.

"Lachlan knows everyone in the area. If he saw any strangers hanging around, he'd remember them."

I nodded, unable to think about anything but Sam. "I need to check on my husband."

The nurse looked up from her paperwork when I slipped into the intensive care unit. Sam hadn't moved. When I touched his hand, it felt warmer than the last visit less than forty-five minutes ago. I dampened a face cloth and wiped his forehead, neck, and hands. He never flinched. When my five minutes were up, I kissed his hot cheek and walked out to the nurses' station.

"He's burning up. Have you taken his temperature recently?"

The nurse checked his chart. "Yes, a half hour ago. It's climbing. I'll check it again." She rushed into Sam's room.

I stood in the doorway and watched.

As soon as she read the thermometer, she grabbed the phone and paged for the doctor. Within minutes, the phone beside Sam's bed rang and the nurse picked it up. "Yes. It's creeping over forty degrees."

I did a rough conversion from Celsius to Fahrenheit in my head. Sam's temperature had reached a hundred and five degrees.

The nurse put down the phone and hurried to the sink in the room for cold water. "We need to cool him down. If I wet the towels, can you wrap him? Get his head and neck first."

"Of course." I grabbed a dripping towel from the sink and dashed to the bed.

He flailed and tried to rip off the towels.

"Sam, Sam, you're going to be okay. We just need to cool you down."

"The coolness may shock him, he's so hot."

Before we finished wrapping his entire body, he went into a seizure. The doctor walked into the room as Sam's body jerked out of control on the bed.

"Ma'am, please leave the room while we care for your husband."

"Let me stay. This isn't his first seizure. I handled two on the trail."

The doctor and nurse looked at each other. Finally, the doctor turned to me. "Sit in the chair over there. If things get worse, you'll have to leave."

I nodded and staggered to the chair.

Sam's seizure lasted about four minutes. They tipped him to his side to prevent choking from fluids from his stomach. He'd dehydrated to the point where he no longer looked like Sam.

"We're going to put him in an ice bath to bring down his temperature. It will take a while for the anti-venom to work."

Just then, Shriver appeared at the door. "RaeJean, you have a call. It's your sister."

"Go take your phone call. Your husband has stabilized." The doctor waved a hand and shooed me from the room. I followed Shriver out to the nurses' station.

"Rae?"

I broke down at the sound of Caitlin's voice.

"C'mon, Cub. Pull yourself together. I'm on my way."

I managed to take a deep breath and control myself long enough to learn Shriver had called Austin, who then called Greg and Caitlin. Within an hour, they had booked tickets from Philadelphia, leaving at midnight. They would be in New Zealand in twenty-two hours.

"I'll tell Sam you're coming," I said.

"You do that. Let me speak to Mr. Shriver," Caitlin said.

I handed the phone to the lawyer and headed back toward Sam's room. The nurse met me halfway there. "Sorry. Not now. The doctor's working on him."

"What do you mean he's working on him?" My legs crumbled for the second time in less than twelve hours. I landed on the corridor floor.

Chapter Forty

"Hey Cub, it's me, Caitlin."

I heard the familiar voice and forced my eyes open. "Caitlin. Oh, thank God, you're here." I felt tears run down the sides of my face, but too weary to cry, I murmured, "It's Sam...Sam...oh, dear God..."

Caitlin patted my arm and in a calm voice said, "We just got in."

Greg's eyes were bloodshot as he peeked over her shoulder.

"Hi, Greg. It's been a bad night."

"I'd say," he replied.

"What happened to me? Why am I in bed? What time is it?" I bolted upright, feeling a little woozy.

"They sedated you after you passed out in the corridor outside Sam's room." Greg checked his watch. "It's eight o'clock at night."

"They dosed you for a normal female adult. It

knocked you out." Caitlin smiled. "They should have used the children's chart since you are cub-size."

"Sam." My heart dropped to my knees. "Is he..."

"He's holding his own," Greg answered.

"Relax," Caitlin said. "Sam's condition has stabilized. The doctors are cautiously optimistic he'll pull through. They said he's a fighter."

At that, I started to cry again.

"Cub..." Caitlin wrapped me in her arms. "Come on now. Don't you give up."

That made me angry. "Me, give up? Never." She knew how to push my buttons. I started swinging my legs off the bed and my johnny gown fell to my waist. "Where are my clothes? I need to see Sam."

"I'll be in the hall if you need me." Red-faced, Greg backed out the door.

"Hang on. They're over there. I'll get them." Caitlin rustled around in a closet and pulled out a folded pile. I grabbed my jeans and pulled them on, hopping around on one foot, and then the other. As soon as I was dressed, Caitlin and I headed for intensive care.

"Where are you going?" Caitlin asked.

"To Sam's room."

"They moved him to a private room. It's this way." Caitlin led me down a hallway and into a bright room filled with natural light. Sam lay curled in a fetal position on the bed. A nurse puttered.

"He's still sleeping, but his temperature has dropped to a hundred." The nurse smiled. "I've stayed with him all night. He didn't have another seizure."

"Sam, it's me, Rae." He didn't move.

"The doctor sedated him. He got violent last night."

"Runs in the family," Caitlin said.

I frowned at her. "When do you think he'll be awake?"

"You never know, but I doubt he will stir for at least twenty-four hours. We gave him a strong sedative."

I looked at Caitlin. "Want to find something to eat?"

"I thought you'd never ask. Greg and I haven't had anything decent since San Francisco."

Shriver had returned to the hotel to sleep once Caitlin and Greg had arrived.

The three of us found a small local eatery. I took a few bites of a sandwich, unable to swallow much. When Greg and Caitlin finished theirs, we returned to Mercy to check on Sam, then went to the hotel to get some rest.

* * *

The night at the hotel felt like an eternity. The next day, we took turns visiting Sam for five minutes every hour. At one point, Caitlin and I left the hospital and took a short walk.

"Are you ladies interested in art?" the nurse at the

station asked as we walked by.

"We are," Caitlin said. "Why?"

"Our new oncology wing has fabulous artwork selected by our CEO. He's a proponent of art therapy. If you'd like, I'll call and have them let you in to view what's on display."

I looked at Caitlin. "It sounds interesting, but I need the fresh air."

"Oh, don't worry. You can admire the artwork and exit to the outside at the end of the corridor. It's a nice walk back to our entrance. The gardens are wearing their autumn colors."

"Let's do it, Rae. Greg will text us if there are any changes with Sam."

We walked the corridor and enjoyed the art. The natural lighting, the paintings, and the light-colored walls cheered me up for the few minutes I spent there. We lingered in a garden outside the Manaaki Cancer Care Center, then began our stroll back to the main hospital when Caitlin received a text from Greg.

"The doctor wants to see you," Caitlin said.

It took us less than ten minutes to find our way back to the lounge outside Sam's ward. I saw Greg standing next to Sam's doctor.

"What is it?" Panic gripped me.

Greg put his arm around Caitlin and whispered something in her ear. She nodded.

"Let's all sit. I'll explain what's going on with your husband."

I collapsed on the couch, and the doctor sat next to me.

"Your husband has started to come out of the coma."

I nodded.

"His reflexes have been impacted by the high fever and the venom from the spider, but we don't believe it is permanent."

"Okay."

"He'll need rehab and therapy, but he should recover."

The doctor continued talking, but relief had deafened me. "When can I see him?"

"You'll need to stay on the five-minutes-an-hour visiting schedule for the remainder of today. Maybe by morning, he will have regained consciousness. Once he does, the more time you spend with him, the quicker his memory will clear."

* * *

Shriver came in late that morning. He had a strange look on his face as he stared at me.

"What's up?" I didn't have a good feeling, but I knew it wasn't about Sam.

"The police asked me to identify the gear I lent you. The wild-colored sleeping bag is not one of mine. I have no idea where it came from." His concerned look frightened me.

"What do the police think?"

"Somehow, you ended up with the wrong gear. Or someone swapped out my bag for one with the spider. They're checking with the shuttle driver."

Who and why would someone target me or Sam? "If they were targeting me, how would they know I'd pick the colorful bag?"

"If I were to guess, because it looks more like a women's bag," Shriver said.

"True. I picked it first until the zipper broke." Suspecting I might be the target scared me, but not as much as Sam's condition right now. "The police are on it. I'll let them worry about it."

"Good plan. I have to get back to the office. I have a court appearance this afternoon." Shriver gave me a hug. "Hang in there. I'm sure our officers will sort this out."

He left and I joined Caitlin and Greg in the cafeteria for coffee and told them what Shriver had to say.

Greg's eyes darkened. "Don't leave my sight. Sam would never forgive me if I let anything happen to you."

I kissed his cheek. "Thanks, but I don't plan on getting into trouble. Besides, they don't know if someone messed up or intentionally switched bags."

* * *

The next two days blurred but, by the third day, Sam sat up, ate on his own, and carried on an intelligent conversation. My biggest disappointment came when he tried to walk. He had stroke-like symptoms where he dragged one leg, then swung it around front in a straight-legged arc to take the next step.

"The proper exercises should relieve the walking problem," the on-staff therapist assured us.

"What should I be doing?" Sam asked.

"Right now? Rest and recover from the trauma. You can start therapy as soon as you return home." The doctor handed Sam a list of exercises. He suggested we investigate an in-home service.

Chapter Forty-One

It took a few days for Sam to recover enough to travel using a wheelchair. But by the weekend, we had arrived back in the States. Sam insisted he begin his therapy at the end of the week. We lucked out. A local physical therapist had an opening on Thursday afternoon.

* * *

Sam smiled as I joined him on the deck. "Glad you came outside. I'd hate for you to miss this glorious sunshine."

I lifted my face to the sky. "Mmm. It is wonderful."

"Have you been playing with dolls again?" Sam gestured toward the doll under my arm.

"You might say that." I laid Patsy on the table. "She needs a little more sunshine. I'm hoping to whiten up her frocks."

Sam scrunched up his face. "I don't think the sun will do it. You might want to try a solution of white vinegar and cool water on the clothing."

"How would you know that?" I cuffed him on the shoulder.

"I'm a fountain of useless knowledge. Besides, I watched my mother recondition old linens when my grandmother died. Sometimes, she'd soak them for days in the vinegar solution, but she managed to remove most of the stains."

"How did the fabric hold up?" I didn't want to destroy the antique cotton or linen.

"She never lost an item to the solution, but once, one of my sisters over-agitated a napkin until it disintegrated in the bowl."

"We'll see. I'll try my method for a while."

Sam's color had returned to a nice, healthy glow. His face tanned easily, so after the few days spent on the deck, he looked like Adonis. Well, maybe I was a little prejudiced, but he did look good.

"So, did you wrap up the case?" Sam asked.

"Not quite. I still have to submit my final report with proof documents, but the check is all but in the bank. And I've almost identified Jill's maternal lineage." Actually, I was positive but I needed documented proof.

Sam smiled. "I knew you wouldn't be able to walk away. You think she descended from Dorothy Arnold, and you'll be able to close another big hundred-year-old cold case."

I shrugged.

"What did Austin say? Did you ask him if he cared if you pursued the Arnold angle?"

"I did, and he said go ahead." I paused for a moment. "Harriet Parks Beauchamp is the unknown. And Camille's baby. I plan to research things from both directions, beginning with Harriet."

"This is where you just start beating the bushes and see what runs out, right?"

I nodded. "You got it."

"Be careful. Remember what happened with the last case."

"How can I forget? Somehow, I don't sense that this time my research will have the same effect. There aren't enough close living relatives who even know what's going on."

After thirty minutes, I stood, grabbed the doll, and headed for the door.

"I'll cook tonight," Sam said over his shoulder as he wheeled back into the house.

"Really?"

"Absolutely. Chinese or Italian?"

I turned to him, smiling. "How about Hawaiian?"

"You got it. One extra-large ham and pineapple pizza coming up." Sam held up his cellphone. "I'll call around five-thirty."

I saluted and retreated to my office.

Chapter Forty-Two

I t took less than a week to compile my notes from New Zealand. I'd found all I needed to close the case well within the six-month deadline. Conroy Parks was Roy A. Beauchamp. Lester's sisters would inherit Jill Hamilton's estate, no questions asked.

I had hoped somehow Lester would be eligible for a piece of the inheritance. I was still waiting for his DNA results, but I didn't have high hopes. As Ginny's official guardian, he could manage her money, but he wouldn't be permitted to use it for himself. Although rough around the edges, his honesty assured me Lester would never siphon off any into a personal account. He wasn't made that way from what I observed.

I needed to call Austin with my findings and update him on Sam's progress since he had inquired about it. With one call, I'd cover both topics.

"RaeJean. What can I do for you today?" Austin's voice set me at ease.

"I've pretty much solved the case. Conroy Parks and Roy A. Beauchamp are the same person. So, the Parks family in Idaho should inherit Jill Hamilton's estate. I'll have a report to you by the end of the week along with the required proof documents."

"Great. And two months before the deadline. Looks like you are in for a nice check. We're piling up the estate appraisal documents as each of our experts conclude their analysis. The townhome property appraisal came in yesterday, but there is still some kind of hold-up on the artwork."

"What's wrong with the artwork?" That familiar niggle reappeared. I spoke without thinking. "The Kuhn."

Austin didn't respond immediately. When he spoke, his tone had changed. "What do you know about the Kuhn?"

"Nothing really. But when I first saw it, I had this tiny voice niggle a warning. It has something unusual about it. I haven't had a chance to research it, but it is one of Kuhn's best clown paintings. Right?"

"It is. Jill paid top dollar for it." Austin didn't elaborate.

"And?"

"And that's all I can say about it right now."

"It's not a forgery, is it?"

"Like I said, I can't answer."

"Okay. No big deal. Since you are sorting out the estate value, and I have nothing lined up for work, I'll keep working on the case. I'm close to identifying Jill's maternal lineage. I realize it's not part of the assignment, but I'm interested to know who her parents were."

"Your time is your own. Go ahead. Let me know if there is anything I can do."

"I will. When I looked over Jill's research, she'd made a family tree with big question marks where her mother would be. She pressed so hard with the pen that she tore the paper. Now that I know Roy Beauchamp had a sister, I might be able to determine whether the sister was Jill's mother."

"Right." Austin's voice sounded neutral.

"If I can find her mother, maybe Jill will rest in peace."

Austin laughed. "Is she haunting you?"

"I meant that metaphorically." If only he knew. But I wasn't about to reveal to a logic-driven lawyer my connection to the doll. He'd never hire me again.

"I'd be interested in what you discover about Jill. You might consider calling on Joan Shannon again. She knows more than she's willing to share."

"I'll do that. She might be able to tie up a few loose ends."

I updated Austin about Sam's progress. "He should be able to walk on his own soon."

"Does the doctor have any ideas as to why he can't?" Austin asked.

"Swelling around the joints and some nerve damage that he's convinced will heal."

"A getaway might help. My lake property is vacant for the next three months. Maybe you can use it as a carrot for Sam?"

"Maybe. He's been depressed."

"We have kayaks, canoes, jet skis, and a boat for waterskiing. You can use all of them if Sam improves."

"Thanks. We might just take you up on that." Austin's idea sounded intriguing. At a minimum, it would give Sam a tangible goal besides walking without pain.

After I disconnected from the call, I heard Sam's voice echo from our back porch. I walked to the window to check on him and the dogs. He'd graduated from a wheelchair to crutches within days and now had shed one crutch. He'd made progress beyond all expectations because he pushed himself at therapy. According to his therapist, Sam's healing would be a step function. He would regain muscle control slowly. Each nerve had to completely rebuild itself before the muscle would respond, like climbing stairs instead of a ramp. But it didn't look like Sam planned on waiting. He had personal drive.

As I headed out of my office to join him and the dogs, I grabbed the doll. She needed another dose of sunlight. Her yellowed bib hadn't whitened, but the smell of dirty socks had disappeared. The remnants of gardenias set vibes in motion. '*I am safe,*' whispered in my ears.

My flickering thought about the message on the

postcard wasn't new information. Dorothy's parents received a postcard two months after she disappeared. Her father, Frances Arnold, blew it off. He insisted Dorothy had died and that the postcard was a sick hoax. He reiterated his attack-in-Central-Park theory, where thugs dumped her body into the lake.

As I descended the stairs, a quote from Shakespeare's *Hamlet* ran through my mind. "The lady doth protest too much, methinks." But in this case, the protestor was a man.

Maybe Arnold wanted people to believe his daughter died. But then, why did he spend such large sums of money looking for her? Unless he wanted to find her before someone else did to hide a family secret. Save himself from embarrassment.

When I walked out onto the porch, I noticed Sam's crutch leaning against the railing. He stood at the far corner overlooking our pool equipment. I grabbed the crutch and waved it. "Hey, did you forget something?"

He turned my way. His ashen face telegraphed a problem. "I guess I still need that."

I hustled to his side, handing him the crutch. "What were you doing?"

"Gave it a try and made the distance," he said as we headed back to the chairs. "But the old gams wouldn't respond to my commands to return."

Sam's recent nerve tests indicated common peroneal nerve dysfunction in his left leg caused by swelling and high fever. The nerve that branched from the sciatic nerve and supplied movement and sensation to the lower leg, foot, and toes retained damages such that Sam's left foot flopped and dragged when he tried to walk.

"Maybe you shouldn't try it unless someone is with you."

He retrieved his cellphone from his pocket and held it up. "Not to worry. I was a Boy Scout—be prepared."

"You still are one." I leaned over and kissed his cheek.

Sam's color returned. "What have you been up to while I've been getting into trouble?"

"Winding up loose ends with the case, mostly. I talked to Austin. He offered us the use of his lake house in upstate New York. Apparently, it's vacant for the next three months."

Sam looked confused. "That's odd. It's prime time over the summer."

"It is, but that's what he said." Austin's offer puzzled me once Sam noticed the timing.

"Sounds like fun if I can shed the prop," he said, pointing at the crutch.

"Soon. Remember, the doctor said nerve healing is a step function."

Sam stood, took a step on shaky legs, then returned to his chair. "Another week."

"Maybe two."

"Have Austin reserve August for us. That gives me two months." His eyes sparkled.

"I will." I could see his mind working out the

details. As much as I wanted to think about the lake house with him, my mind wandered to the unanswered question I'd been focused on.

Who had wanted me off the case, and why?

Chapter Forty-Three

The minute Sam's doctor entered, I knew the outcome of Sam's fertility tests. The doctors in New Zealand had warned us that his high temperatures might cause some type of permanent damage, including sterility. He'd suffered from a lasting erection for at least a day. An erection lasting over four hours caused a concern. I worried about the consequences, more for Sam than me. I had insisted on the tests.

We both sat in silence as the doctor delivered the news. "I'm sorry. Due to the long-lasting erection, called a priapism, the lab found no living sperm cells in your semen. Wait six months and be retested. Sometimes, the body recovers over time."

We thanked the doctor, then left. Neither of us spoke the entire ride home.

At home in our kitchen, Sam threw his jacket on

the counter. "Damn it, I'm sterile. So much for having our child."

Wrapping my arms around him, I leaned my chin on his head. "Maybe children are still in our future."

Sam stared up at me. "What do you mean?"

"We talked about adoption as an alternative." I peered into his eyes. "I'm game."

"Me, too, but not right away."

"I'm not ready, either. We've had too many crazy things happening in our lives this year." I'd expected a huge letdown and sadness, but my body wasn't crazy about pregnancy, the nausea, dizziness, and overall discomfort. I'd suffer through it for children, but it looked like I wouldn't have to. Besides, after reading the files of orphaned children in New Zealand, I wanted to help kids without a home.

I swallowed a lump in my throat. Time to move on.

* * *

We didn't discuss children or the possibility of adopting for another week. Finally, on Sunday morning at breakfast, Sam raised the topic. "Do you think adoption is better? I had a new thought. Maybe we could find a sperm donor?"

"A sperm donor? Where'd that come from?" I stared into his eyes.

"I'd love a baby regardless of its parentage." His lips pursed.

"Me, too. But it isn't just about loving them." I'd

wavered again as I thought about the cases I'd handled. Many adopted children had emotional issues regarding abandonment by their natural parent or parents. "Adopted kids can struggle when they learn they're adopted."

"I'm sure that's true." Sam looked away. "But don't all kids present their parents with unforeseen struggles?"

Where was this going? "I know I did. After a challenging moment with me, my mother would say, *Where did you come from?* and then she'd laugh."

Sam remained quiet.

"I'm not sure I'm capable of taking on an older child. With a baby, I can grow with it. I'd like to adopt an infant." I was ready to offer our child the moon. I wouldn't be like my mother and work all the time. She spent most of her time fretting about making ends meet. We had enough resources so I wouldn't have to work unless I wanted to.

"Before I'm willing to commit to anything, I need more information." Sam picked up his phone and searched for an adoption agency. "There's one in Wynnewood and two in Philadelphia. Want me to call and make an appointment at one of them?"

"Try the one in Wynnewood. What's it called?"

"Adoptions From The Heart. *We place thousands of children into loving homes.*" Sam read the listing.

"Is it international?" Several beautiful Māori children had been playing at Child Protective Services in Christchurch.

"It says it is. But not all countries allow international adoptions." Sam grabbed a notepad and scribbled down the contact information.

"Let's leave our options open," I said.

"So, no donor from a fertility clinic?"

"Not yet. I haven't rejected the idea, but truthfully, pregnancy is no picnic."

"Raising a child won't be a picnic, either, but I'd like to give it a try." Sam leaned over and kissed my forehead. "It's your body. You can decide once we gather the facts."

"It's a deal." The tension released from my neck. I needed more information, but my gut said adoption. I closed my eyes to hide the tears. What I wanted was Sam's baby, but I wasn't sure it was possible. Or was it? Caitlin had blathered on about gene splicing during one of our calls. I hadn't listened at the time. I promised myself I'd look further into it, as well as any other possibility that led to Sam and I having the family we so badly wanted.

Chapter Forty-Four

I hadn't been in my office for over a week. Sam and I had spent time together, taking the dogs to the local dog park where Sam also exercised by walking along the fence without using his crutch.

Before I did anything, I shot off an email to Austin asking him to reserve August at the lake house for Sam and me. He responded with a thumbs-up emoji. After traveling halfway around the world to New Zealand and nearly losing Sam, the thread of my solution to Dorothy's mystery had disappeared. Thankful for my index cards that captured her sightings and the theories, I'd use their information to retest my hypothesis. After that, I'd check into the less important connection between Roy A. Beauchamp and Lester Parks.

A dozen index cards listed all the theories about Dorothy's disappearance mentioned in my research. I eliminated the absurd media rantings used to sell papers, then used logic to eliminate a few others. It left me with six possibilities.

Theory 1: Dorothy Arnold was attacked and killed in Central Park.

I stared at the card. Nobody except Dorothy's father, Francis Arnold, bought this theory. He suggested the killer or killers threw her body into a reservoir in Central Park in December's freezing temperatures. By the time the authorities decided to check, the reservoir had iced over. In the spring, police dragged the waters and didn't find a body or any evidence of Dorothy Arnold. Nothing in this theory seemed viable.

Theory 2: Dorothy slipped on ice, struck her head, and was hospitalized with amnesia.

No patient with a head injury had been admitted to local hospitals in the area at the time of Dorothy's disappearance. Plus, not one witness came forward from the busy New York City streets claiming to have witnessed a falling accident on that day. It's possible nobody noticed her fall, but I doubted she then wandered around New York City not knowing who she was and disappeared. With no evidence at all to support this theory, it also felt like a dead end.

Theory 3: Dorothy was drugged and abducted.

Nobody believed this was a feasible theory, but the police entertained it because Francis Arnold owned a successful import business besides having benefited from a considerable inheritance when his parents died. He'd be a prime target for extortion. This theory implied Dorothy had been alive and was held for ransom. This opinion was more feasible than the others, except that no ransom demands ever materialized. If Dorothy had been abducted, the perpetrators would have contacted the Arnolds with a ransom proposition. I discarded the card.

Theory 4: Dorothy committed suicide by jumping off an ocean liner.

George C. Griscom Jr. believed Dorothy committed suicide, depressed over the rejections she received on her writing. When the lawyer, Keith, found scraps of burnt paper in her fireplace, he theorized that they were remnants of her rejected stories.

But when her friend, Gladys, met Dorothy in front of Brentano's bookstore, she reported that during their brief encounter Dorothy seemed in good spirits. Dorothy had purchased a book and a box of chocolates. Some theorists felt this purchase indicated she was preparing for a trip.

As wild as jumping off a ferry sounded, the proponent of the theory based it on autosuggestion. Andrew Griscom, George's cousin, had committed suicide by jumping off an ocean liner. Keith had found brochures in Dorothy's room, plus a dock worker reported she had queried him about ships leaving for the West Indies before her disappearance.

Several of New York's ferry services didn't require passengers to register. Dorothy may have boarded one, then jumped into the Hudson to her death. But her body never surfaced, nor did anyone of her description board a ferry that day in December. I kept this card as a feasible explanation even though the suicide may have been by some other method.

Theory 5: Dorothy was alive and in hiding *somewhere.*

On February 11, 1911, Francis Arnold received a postcard bearing a New York City postmark. *I am safe.* Signed with Dorothy's name. The handwriting matched Dorothy's.

This message supported my strong suspicion that she ran away. It's possible Dorothy had a friend send the letter to her parents after she'd had enough time to travel and get settled in her hideout. Or she arranged for a stranger to post the letter on a prearranged date.

Dorothy's face had been plastered all over the newspapers for months, even years, after her disappearance. I found it difficult to believe she hadn't been spotted if she remained in the States. She could have colored her hair or changed her looks some other way, but if she used New York City resources for any purpose, someone would have spilled the beans. She may have arranged her disappearance while living a double life until she escaped. She wanted freedom and the opportunity for self-expression.

Mostly, she wanted to become a published author. Living under her father and mother's rule didn't support her passion. Just the opposite. Being stifled by ridicule and laughed at when she faced rejections must have become unbearable, enough so that she had found an apartment in Greenwich Village where she wanted to live among successful authors. In a final blow, her father threatened to stop her allowance if she moved out. I kept this card.

Theory 6: *The Arnolds hid her in a convent or asylum because of her behavior.*

This theory made no sense to me at all. The Arnolds claimed to have spent thousands of dollars looking for their daughter. Perhaps they used the money they claimed to have spent to find her to institutionalize her. Nothing supported this theory. I didn't believe it happened that way. I dropped it on the discard pile.

She may have remained in New York, at least for a while. Either way, she could have orchestrated her disappearance. Dorothy had the spunk, motive, and means. She'd already shown her wild side when she spent time in Boston with Junior Griscom. That is, if Junior Griscom and Dorothy stayed together. I began to wonder if he conspired to help Dorothy run away with someone else.

Did she plant the European ocean liner brochures Keith found in her room as a decoy? Or maybe Keith also aided her in her ruse. He could have wasted the first month as a delaying tactic to give her a solid head start before recommending Pinkertons. That way, she was able to escape in any direction—from any port to anywhere in the world.

Once the police joined the hunt, they ran down tips, including an interesting sighting in Alabama. An experienced traveler, Dorothy had the ability to find her way to a city and port that would take her to the opposite side of the globe.

I reread a newspaper article from February 15, 1911, reporting a Dorothy lookalike dining with a man in an upscale hotel restaurant in Mobile, Alabama. According to the authorities, this lead went nowhere. Nobody knew either the man or the woman. I'd need the files kept by the Pinkerton Agency during their investigation of the incident. They'd followed through on most of the tips.

Knowing from past experience that those files had been retained at the Library of Congress, I visited their online index as a starting point. The agency had digitized their files, documents, and correspondence for the period from 1853 to 1999. Although incomplete, they included materials from Chicago, New York, and Philadelphia.

After scanning the New York file index and finding nothing about Dorothy Arnold, I began scanning all indices in alphabetical order. Bryn Mawr College was easy to find. 'William Henry Allison's diaries, 1868-1940' jumped out at me. He kept diaries of his life during the time he taught history at Bryn Mawr. Dorothy attended and graduated during the same period. He might have noted something in his journals. I applied for access to them. It'd be a long shot I'd pursue if nothing else emerged.

I checked the time. The dogs would need a break soon.

"The diaries are a stretch, for sure," I said aloud.

Sophie stood and shook herself. Eli had already walked to the office door as soon as he heard my voice.

"Okay, guys. I get the hint." I closed my laptop and headed for the backyard.

As I watched the dogs cavorting, I pondered my afternoon's work so far.

* * *

Once back at my desk, I changed directions. More often than not, pursuing a different lead would precipitate a breakthrough. I reached for Roy's folder. Lester and his sisters came to mind. I'd never asked for photographs of him or Ginny. Greg's facial recognition program might find a match to someone I'd already logged into the case database.

I called Lester and asked about pictures.

"Ginny's got a couple of books. She ain't gonna let those go. She's still cranked over the pictures you took."

"Why is she upset over those?"

"Who knows? You can't reason with her sometimes."

"I'd like a couple of pictures of her for my files."

"I doubt she'll agree, but I can trick her, so you get what you need." Lester laughed. "I'm an expert at trickin' her."

"How will we do that?"

"Bring your good-lookin' man. Ginny ain't stopped talkin' about him."

"I'd like to come up in a few days, but Sam's not

ready to travel long distances yet." I considered his offer. "You think, between the two of us, we can convince Ginny to relinquish a few photos?"

"I don't know 'bout that, but you can sneak phone shots when she ain't lookin'."

"That'll work. Thanks. I'll call back when I have firmed up my plans."

After scheduling a flight for next Wednesday, for fun, I reserved the Principal's Room at the same bed and breakfast I'd stayed at previously.

I looked forward to the scenic drive from Spokane, but I didn't relish confronting Lester about his biological father.

Chapter Forty-Five

"You knew all along Conroy wasn't your biological father, didn't you?" I faced Lester, but he avoided eye contact. "Les, why didn't you tell me? Knowing would have saved my client several thousand dollars."

"I ain't proud of myself, but Roy raised me good, and I didn't want to shame him."

"You wouldn't have shamed him. Besides, he isn't alive." I scowled.

"It's not just him. Ginny and Margie don't know we have different fathers." Lester sipped his coffee. The same waitress at the Chic-n-Chop approached us with our meals. Lester ordered the special, meatloaf, and I ordered a chef's salad. After his first bite, I congratulated myself on my choice. The meatloaf had carrots in it.

"I wouldn't have told them. I still won't. Do you know who your biological father was?"

"Yup. But I ain't about to spill." He glared at me.

"Is the man still living?" He didn't have to tell me. I'd already figured it out.

"Nope. He got his penance. The river swept him up." Lester spit out the words without thinking. His face showed regret. "Darn! I ain't saying nothin' else."

"You don't have to. Trust me, I'll never say a word." It had to be Conroy's drinking buddy who'd drowned years ago.

I changed the subject. Maybe he'd feel better with a collaborative effort. "Ginny's DNA indicates she's related to the woman found dead in Central Park. I'd like to test Margie."

"Don't waste your time. Margie's Daddy's baby. I'm sure of it."

"How can you be so sure? Your mother—"

Lester cut me off. "My mother was within days of fifteen when she had me. Daddy said the sun rose 'cause of her. He never looked at another woman. Besides, they had to take care of Ginny. She was always slow. When she was little, she'd have fits."

"Fits." A mental image of Sam's seizures surfaced—his contorted body, wide eyes, slack face, and the choking, muttering sounds like he'd swallowed his tongue.

"Ya. She'd fall and flop around." Lester's eyes rounded as he recalled the scary episodes he'd witnessed as a boy.

"Epilepsy?"

"Maybe. Never quite sure. Daddy said he held the blame for Ginny. Claimed he carried a bad gene."

Lester shook his head. "Hard for me to believe. He didn't have a mean bone in his body. Said he was a bad kid before he learned his lesson."

Lester's fond memories of his father dredged up dark feelings. I'd resented my mother when my father showed up unannounced and she wouldn't let him see us. I never knew why, then. Now, I realized he was likely drunk.

"Does your sister, Margie, have any issues like Ginny?" I wondered if she'd been spared.

"Not as bad. She gets prickly. Been divorced five times. She ain't a keeper. Lousy cook and quick temper." Lester grinned. "I'm the one kid in the family who's okay."

"I'd guess you had an interesting childhood." I smiled. Honesty flowed from him and warmed the room. I liked him for that. And yes, he was okay. Just a little rough around the edges.

"Yes, ma'am. I sure did."

"How did you discover Conroy wasn't your father?"

"Momma told me." His eyes filled. "Broke her heart to admit it, but I'd worried myself silly about having fits. One day, Momma got disgusted with my naggin' and dragged me to the shed. Confessed her sin to me, but she wouldn't reveal the guy's name."

"It must have been difficult for her. How old were you, then?" My hands began to shake in sympathy. Lester was hurting.

"Eight." He sniffed and wiped his nose on his sleeve.

"Wow." He almost had me crying.

"Momma said Daddy knew, but he didn't care." Lester smiled. "She never let on to him that she told me. And Daddy never slighted me."

Envy and fear prompted my next question. I wondered if I would be sorry to learn about my own father. "Sounds like he was a good man. Did you ever wish you didn't know?"

"Naw. I was too busy fishin' and huntin' with Daddy to worry about it."

"But you discovered who your biological father was at some point."

"Yup. Daddy got mail from a lawyer in New York. Momma's curiosity got to her, so she opened it before he got home. After she read it, she tore it up and threw it in the trash. When she turned her back, I grabbed it." Lester shook his head. "I had a heck of a time piecing it back together. Used a whole roll of tape. Said something about if he didn't adopt me, it'd matter someday."

"So, your father never saw the letter from the lawyer."

Lester shook his head.

"Why would your mother do that?"

"No idea." He squinted at me. "You ain't gonna trick me into tellin' who my real daddy was. I ain't stupid."

I smiled. "No, Les. You are not stupid. You're a good man." I'd pressed him as far as I needed. Copies of the letter his father received might be in the Murbeck or MacVale archives. I had another solid lead.

"One last question. Do you remember the lawyer's name who wrote the letter?"

"All I remember, he had a French-soundin' name."

"Rousseau?"

"Could be. I didn't give him much mind."

The Chic-n-Chop dining room buzzed. It had filled without me noticing. Lester had mopped his plate with the last roll and was sipping his fourth cup of coffee when the waitress approached.

"Dessert?" she asked.

"I'll have one of those ice cream potatoes," he said, then turned to me. "It's a local specialty."

"Ice cream potato?" The combination turned my stomach.

The waitress described the dessert. "It's a spud filled with ice cream and drenched with chocolate sauce."

"I'll try the fried ice cream as long as it isn't coated with potato."

She laughed. "No, ma'am. It's rolled in cookie crumbs and coconut, then deep-fried for thirty seconds. Then, dripped with chocolate sauce. It's fabulous."

Lester devoured his ice cream potato. I didn't watch. I thought about trying it at home sometime, but not in public. Fried ice cream, however, could quickly become my favorite dessert.

"Ready to head up to the farm?" I asked Lester.

"Almost. Give me a minute to call Ginny." He pulled out a flip phone and made the call. "We're on our way. Okay, okay. I'll bring you a couple of baseball cupcakes. Right. Not lemon."

* * *

Lester chattered the entire drive to Good Grief. He pointed out every productive hunting and fishing spot along the way. I'd fallen in love with the idea of Roy Parks by the time we pulled into Ginny's driveway. He represented the father I never had.

I loved my father. What I remember of him, anyway. He made me laugh when he was sober. But he never understood us girls. He'd bring us used toys, Barbie dolls with ratty hair. They looked like he dug them out of someone's trash or bought them at a yard sale. I'd throw mine in the back of the closet, and Caitlin would give hers to our dog Radar to chew. When Caitlin turned eleven, she screamed at him to quit. "We don't play with dolls. Most of all, not dirty ones!" He never came back.

When we approached the cluster of buildings the Parks family called a farm, I saw a gray Toyota Corolla parked next to the cabin. It matched our rental car.

"Well, I'll be. If it ain't Marjorie," Lester said. "I wonder what she's doin' here."

"Hey, Les. You got the cupcakes?" Ginny yelled from the cabin doorway. Standing beside her was a woman who had to be Jill Hamilton's niece or the first doppelganger I'd ever encountered.

Lester held up the white box holding six chocolate baseball cupcakes.

"What brought you home, sis?" Lester asked.

"Mama." She paused for a moment, tears forming in her eyes. "I talked with a tribal elder who said Mama wasn't doing so well. I wanted to see her before she died."

"Shoulda come sooner. She mighta known you," Ginny said. "Mama don't know nobody. Bet she won't know you, neither."

"It doesn't matter. I just want to see her." Marjorie disappeared into the house.

I glanced at Lester, and he shrugged.

Ginny broke the silence. "Hurry up. I made coffee. I want one of them cupcakes now."

Lester looked at me and mimed snapping a picture.

I followed the two siblings into the house. The smell of gun oil wafted up from the 20-gauge shotgun resting against the counter by the door.

Lester grinned and pointed at it. I wasn't sure what he was up to, but I smiled uneasily.

"You offered us coffee," Lester said to his sister.

"I'm gettin' it right now." She ignored me and pulled out one mug from the cupboard.

"Ginny..." Lester hardened his voice.

She turned to me. "How 'bout you, ma'am? Coffee?"

The cabin hadn't been touched since our last visit.

My first reaction was to refuse, but when I looked at Lester, he made a face suggesting I should accept the offer. "That would be wonderful. Thank you."

Ginny retrieved another former-white-but-now-brown coffee cup. I swallowed when I recognized the mugs from the Chic-n-Chop.

"I ain't sharin' the cupcakes, but I still have a few graham crackers left if you're hungry."

I smiled. "I'm stuffed. We had lunch at the Chic-n-Chop. Thanks, anyway."

"I'll have one." Lester took a cracker, inspected it thoroughly before taking a bite, then dragged a chair over to the cluster of living room furniture where Marjorie had taken a spot on the couch.

"We gonna look at pictures, Margie." Ginny sat in the middle of the couch and patted the empty side. "Sit here, ma'am. I'll show you Mama and Daddy's weddin'."

Ginny had pulled out several photo albums and placed them on the coffee table. She ran her hand across a single photo of a young Roy Parks and a beautiful Indigenous woman. Roy Parks smiled as he draped his arm around his new bride's shoulder. The woman stared up at him with adoring eyes.

"Mama and Daddy loved each other." Ginny smiled at me. "Daddy loved me."

"You're very lucky to have such good parents." My heart melted with her child-like smile.

Ginny's eyes filled as she looked at Lester. "Mama don't know me. Ain't that right, Les?"

Lester nodded.

"She don't know you or Margie, neither." Ginny sniffed, then wiped her nose with the back of her hand.

"It's okay, Ginny girl," Lester said. "Mama still loves us. She just can't tell us."

"Right. That's what the nurse lady said." Ginny stared at the floor.

Marjorie remained silent while she patted Ginny's back. A tear leaked from one eye.

When Lester finished his coffee, he placed his cup in the sink, and then inspected the shotgun. "Gun looks pretty good. Did you clean it today?"

Ginny handed me the album and joined Lester in the kitchen area. "I did. Looks pretty good, don't it?"

Lester gave me a quick nod as he rotated the gun and examined Ginny's work. "Look here, Ginny. How'd this happen?" Lester continued to distract Ginny with his thorough inspection of all parts of the gun.

"What are you doing?" Marjorie whispered as I snapped about two dozen pictures with my phone, more than enough for the facial recognition software to analyze.

I mouthed, "Lester will explain later."

She nodded, but she looked concerned.

"I done a good job, didn't I, Les?"

"You sure did. Daddy would be proud."

Ginny beamed, returning to the couch. "Wanna see a picture of Rover? He was my first dog."

I expected to see the Bluetick hound named Rover

we left sleeping on the stoop outside the front door. "Sure. I love dogs."

Ginny grabbed the other album and found the picture she mentioned. "Here he is."

"He's adorable." Rover was a black and white mutt with one blue eye and one brown eye. Ginny must have been five or six in the picture.

"I got another one." She flipped the pages ahead to a brown shepherd-lab mix. "His name's Rover, too."

I looked at Lester.

He laughed. "Ginny named all four of her dogs Rover. It's her favorite name."

"Rover's nice." At least she wouldn't call a new dog by the wrong name.

We spent another hour with Ginny and Marjorie. Ginny's developmental disability didn't extend to her ability to love. Her emotional glow lit up the cabin as she described the events captured in each photo. Lester sat back in the recliner and listened with obvious pleasure as she told me about the picnics, fishing expeditions, and hunting successes.

"And I caught the biggest fish that day, didn't I, Les?"

"Yup, a twenty-eight-inch salmon. Biggest we caught that year." Lester stood up. "That's about it. We didn't have money for lots of pictures, but Mama wanted a few."

Marjorie never joined in, but she listened and watched the entire time. After Ginny finished going through the albums, Marjorie put her finger to her lips, then signaled she'd allow me to take her picture.

Ginny stood and hugged the biggest album to her chest. "Can I take the pictures to show Mama? It might make her remember me."

"Sure. Next time we go on the reservation, you can take 'em." Lester winked at her.

Ginny smiled as she left the room. "Mama loves me. She just can't say it. That's what the nurse lady said."

I snapped a few photos of Marjorie as Ginny disappeared through a doorway.

This visit changed my opinion of Ginny. After observing her while she showed us the album, I saw a different girl. Her innocence reminded me of myself when my father left for good. I'd sit in my room and say, "I know you still love me, Daddy, even if you don't visit anymore." My opinion has never changed. But Caitlin never forgave him for leaving us.

Chapter Forty-Six

Back at home at my desk, I returned to my pursuit of Dorothy Arnold. I'd pretty much concluded that Dorothy ran away. After sorting the index cards for the millionth time, I'd narrowed the clues to those that supported my conclusion. That's when things started to gel.

Dorothy wasn't the person characterized by her parents or presented in the newspapers. I had to get a better image of her. A study of her friends and other influencers in her young adult life could help.

Some data existed for Theodora Bates, a friend and classmate from Bryn Mawr. I reviewed a summarized version of the strange Thanksgiving visit with Theodora where she claimed Dorothy had received a package by general post. But the post office didn't deliver on Thanksgiving Day. Someone else had to have delivered the package.

According to Theodora, Dorothy never opened it,

as if she already knew what it contained. I had doubts about the alleged delivery. Dorothy could have gone to Theodora's to collect something already there. She'd planned all along to leave the next morning, even though her parents had expected her to spend the weekend. The trip felt like the beginning of Dorothy's escape plan, and Theodora had aided and abetted her disappearance. She would need some type of documentation for her new identity. Maybe that's what Theodora had.

Besides her friendship with Theodora Bates, Dorothy had made other connections at Bryn Mawr where the protected little rich girl had evolved into an independent-thinking adult.

There were no shortages of influencers at college. First, there was the college president and well-known suffragette, Carey Thomas. Second, Dorothy's English instructor had married Alfred Hodder, a muckraker and former English instructor at the school, who published articles in *Harper's Magazine* and *McClure's*. Coincidentally, his best friend married Neith Boyce, a name Jill tagged in her copy of *Lorenzo in Taos*.

If Dorothy had been influenced by someone who promoted female independence, then Neith Boyce fit that profile. During Dorothy's early teens, Neith Boyce wrote a controversial column in *Vogue,* challenging the traditional roles of women. Boyce's spirited articles dominated New York City conversation at that time.

By 1903, the year Dorothy entered Bryn Mawr,

Boyce had published her first book, *The Forerunner*, depicting the struggles of an independent woman. Her book became an immediate success. She followed with three more novels. Her final book, *The Bond,* became a top seller in 1908. Boyce's nontraditional portrayal of marriage influenced Dorothy's generation. Plus, Boyce visited Greenwich Village during this time to promote her works. Dorothy could have met her or at least heard her talk. To give even more support to my theory, Dorothy's parents described their daughter as an avid reader.

I looked down at Sophie, who rested at my feet. "She must have read Boyce's novels."

Sophie opened one eye but offered no opinion.

"Right."

After graduating from Bryn Mawr, Dorothy frequented Greenwich Village and became so enamored with the place that she wanted to live there to mingle with the creative and artsy community. Her father flat-out denied her permission, threatened to cut off her allowance, and ranted in front of the entire household about how a good writer could write anywhere.

Dorothy's actions and behavior suggested she'd acted with a clear intent to conceal something. But somehow, rejection letters didn't seem like a big enough impetus. A different life-altering experience may have been the cause, like falling in love. Her disappearance had to have been planned over time with the help of others.

The Boston trip with George Griscom could have been a ploy with George as a participant, a smoke-screen to misdirect inquiries while she orchestrated her escape. By all accounts, he was a mama's boy and no Don Juan. Plus, she traveled under her own name, showing her independence, and leaving an easy trail for the police to follow during that Boston excursion.

When she disappeared, newspapers portrayed Dorothy as a demure, poised, and quiet young woman who didn't make waves. This described the woman her aged father wanted her to be. She wasn't willing to play the role. This became the *why* of her motivation to leave without a trail.

My suspicion was that she'd played the part so well that no one anticipated her departure.

Chapter Forty-Seven

My next big question revolved around Keith, the lawyer. He had to have been involved in the *how* of Dorothy's departure. Frances Arnold played right into Dorothy's scheme when he asked Keith to find his daughter, claiming he wanted to protect the family name. This gave Keith and Dorothy the opportunity to erase her trail and create false leads. I shook my head, recalling reports that Keith searched Dorothy's room for anything missing. He was the wrong person for that job unless he spent time in her bedroom, which I doubted.

I pulled out the index cards of reported sightings of Dorothy during the few years after her disappearance. The one that caught my eye was the report at the hotel restaurant in Mobile, Alabama, two months after her disappearance. Another guest spotted and reported a woman fitting Dorothy's description having dinner with a man about her age. As I tapped the desk, a faint glimmer appeared in its quartz tulip inlay.

I stood. "You're back!"

The light disappeared, but a tingling crept up the nape of my neck. When I looked at the doll, one of her eyes had opened to a slit.

For no apparent reason, Eli growled and jumped down from the chair, disturbing Patsy as he moved. The doll landed in a sitting position and both eyes popped wide open. I picked her up. The tingling on my neck raced up the back of my head.

"I'm on to something." I set her back in the chair, my confidence building.

"Dorothy was the woman." Identifying Dorothy's male companion at dinner would answer many questions. I suspected John Keith and scrambled for his index card.

Eli looked up at me, then jumped back into the chair with the doll.

"Keith had to have been assisting her, not hunting for her!" He had a connection to the West Indies with the sugar commodities market. He'd sailed out of Mobile numerous times to visit with the plantation owners.

Using a global search for John S. Keith, I connected him and his law partner, Lorenzo Armstrong, to multiple ship captains' logs where they sailed from Mobile to two locations, Havana and San Juan, on a regular basis. Plantation owners from those locations borrowed money using Keith and

Armstrong's loan operations, the Fajardo Sugar Company, and the West India Sugar Finance Company. Since land and predicted crop yield acted as the collateral for the advanced money, the men would have inspected the plantations before closing a deal.

On a hunch, I pulled ship manifests from January 1911 to the islands from the Port of Mobile in Alabama to Cuba and Puerto Rico. Keith's name was listed with a woman identified as his wife. He had traveled from Mobile to Havana during the six-week period he searched for Dorothy. Keith wasn't married at the time.

Maritime records showed two people disembarked in Cuba. Keith's name appeared a week later on a manifest for a return trip on the same ship. That same week, a man named H. Parks appeared on the manifest of a freighter leaving Havana, traveling alone on the *Wimmera* bound for Brisbane on the east coast of Australia. Dorothy could have disguised herself as a man. And the "H" in H. Parks on the freighter manifest could have been Harriet. My gut said yes. Harriet was the woman who'd married Roy Parks' father.

The Parks person disappeared from all documents after disembarking at the port in Brisbane. She could have caught a small craft to Wellington, New Zealand.

I pulled out the stack of index cards I'd prepared for the New Zealand Beauchamp family and checked the wedding date for George Beauchamp. "There it is! A tie to the Beauchamp family."

Two months after the freighter left Mobile, George Beauchamp had married a woman whose name had been vetoed on the official marriage documents. Within the year, the couple had a daughter, Camille. The birth wasn't a firm connection, but the timing was close to the disappearance of Dorothy Harriet Camille Arnold.

"What next?" Public records for their marriage didn't help. My recent trip to Bonners Ferry and the photos of Roy Parks' wedding gave me an idea. Beatrix had already said George's first wife refused to be photographed, but George and Harriet might have had a church wedding and there could be church records.

I jotted down the facts from the shipping records and placed the H. Parks card with the Beauchamp stack. It was still hardly irrefutable evidence.

"We don't believe in coincidences, do we, Sophie?" The dogs' favorite chairs sat empty. I checked my watch. When I turned to the door, they wagged their docked tails. "There you are. Time for dinner."

Both dogs barked.

I had another lead to follow after the dogs had a break. As I put away the cards, I reread the top card. "H. Parks." On my way to the door, I swung by the chair and picked up the doll. Her eyes stuck closed. "H. Parks was Dorothy, slipping away to start a new life, wasn't she?"

When I tilted the doll, her eyes lifted and locked with mine. The tingle I felt reinforced my confidence in my assumption.

Chapter Forty-Eight

O
n Tuesday, a package arrived from Austin's office. As requested, he had the original artwork removed from Jill's apartment and sent to Freedom Art Consultancy for verification of authenticity. The package contained photocopies of the certificates found in Jill's desk, all except for the Kuhn.

The consultant photographed the front and back of each piece and sent the digital copies to my email within a day. He had attached a brief note about the Kuhn, the one Jill had indicated in the museum catalog. The painting proved to be authentic but with a catch. The art expert suspected Jill's painting was part of a fraudulent transaction by a well-known art dealer in New York City.

Olivia's interest in the painting and her hovering near the Kuhn triggered a tangential thought about the missing box of documents Jill gave to Maggie. "I wonder why she had her take it home?"

"Who took what home?" Sam asked, walking into the kitchen with his empty coffee mug. He'd shed the last crutch a few days earlier.

"The art expert suspects the Kuhn was part of a fraudulent transaction."

"That means the estate isn't worth as much as we thought," Sam said. "Your fee will drop, depending on the appraised value of the artwork."

"Nothing I'd worry about," I said. "It's peanuts compared to the total."

"Then, you're right, I wouldn't worry about it." He kissed my cheek. "Coffee break?"

* * *

The art appraiser had valued the Kuhn piece between ten and fifteen thousand dollars. I didn't care about my compensation, but Olivia's interest bothered me, so I called Austin.

"So, you think Olivia showed an unusual interest in the Kuhn." Austin sighed.

"Yes. She indicated she didn't like the picture, yet she stopped and gazed at it every trip through the art gallery."

Austin remained silent for a minute, then spoke. "The chain of custody had a missing link, thus clouding its provenance. The Kuhn is the one questionable purchase Jill made. We never found a certificate of authenticity for that painting. I can't imagine she would have purchased it without certification."

"Me neither. My brief meeting left a similar impression. Maybe she had the document out and didn't put it back with the others. Maggie, the maid, took a box of documents home. Maybe Jill stuffed the certificate in there." Jill may have suspected she'd purchased the artwork unlawfully, but I couldn't picture her removing the evidence. It didn't make sense.

"It's a mystery," Austin said. "Is there anything else you need?"

The more I thought about the box, the more I realized I needed to speak to Maggie again. "I'd like to make one more visit to Jill's townhouse, if that's possible. You haven't cleaned it out yet, I assume."

"Gosh, no. Nothing will be removed until Roy Beauchamp or his relatives are identified. Let me know when you want to visit. I'll make sure one of the interns is available." He paused for a moment. "I'm not sure who'll still be around. We are getting close to the end of the semester, so we may have new interns."

"That's all right. I'm most interested in speaking with the housekeeper. I'd like to invite her to meet me there."

"No problem. She's called several times asking if we want her to clean the place."

I laughed. "Sounds like her. Routine and hard work help her grieving process."

"You're right. I hadn't thought of that. Next time she calls, I'll be more sensitive."

"I'll check our calendar. I'd love to bring Sam along to see the place."

"Just let me know when." Austin disconnected.

"Bring me where?" Even with a limp, Sam made a stealthy entrance into my office.

"I'm about to set a time to revisit Jill's Manhattan apartment. Would you be interested in accompanying me?"

"I just set up an appointment at Elegant Findings Antiques in Boston for Tuesday to show one of Paul Logan's clients the German pinwheel clock."

An idea popped into my head. "We could visit Caitlin over the weekend, then drive to Boston on Tuesday and New York on Wednesday."

"I better check with the Canine Fitness Camp first. This is short notice." Sam called while I waited. When he disconnected, he said, "All set. The doggie camp has plenty of room."

"Great. I'll check with Austin on the timing."

Once again, Austin insisted that someone be present. He agreed to inquire with the interns. Their internship had ended, but being students, I was willing to bet they'd accept extra work.

I just hoped, after what I'd confided to him, Austin wouldn't send Olivia.

Chapter Forty-Nine

A sparkling new silver Toyota Land Cruiser sat parked behind Caitlin's car when I pulled Sam's Jeep into her driveway. Sam had driven part of the interstate, but his left side tired easily. I'd taken over in Ludlow on the Massachusetts Turnpike.

Greg and Caitlin spilled out the back door, followed by Caitlin's Yorkie, Nellie. The dog sniffed my feet as I slid out of our vehicle.

"Hey, Cub. Good to see you." Caitlin wrapped her arms around me and whispered in my ear. "Greg told me about Sam."

I shrugged. "We can talk later."

"Right."

Greg slipped on a chef's apron he was carrying. "Anybody hungry? I'm ready to fire up the grill. We've got burgers and dogs ready and waiting."

Nellie pawed at Greg's pant leg at the mention of food.

Caitlin reached down and scooped her up. "Not you, Nellie. You're always hungry."

I laughed. "It's a dog thing."

"I'm with Nellie," Sam said. "I'm always ready for grub."

Caitlin had outdone herself by baking my favorite homemade chocolate chip cookies. Once we finished the meal, the guys headed inside to watch the sports channel. Caitlin and I cleaned up and settled on the back patio with a fresh glass of wine.

She broke the silence. Her expression warned me I'd be getting "the talk." She was never at a loss for advice. "Sam looks good."

It wasn't that I didn't appreciate her concern or respect her opinion. But she presented them like they were the gospel. Being older didn't always make someone wiser, but I must admit her self-education never stopped, so I planned to listen to what she had to say.

"Have you and Sam talked about a family since his diagnosis?"

"We have, and we still want one." I swallowed. "We aren't sure if we want to adopt or consider a sperm donor."

"Adoption is safe for you." She patted my arm. "After the last..."

She didn't finish the sentence, and it didn't matter. We'd been through it a million times. My depression.

My visions with the desk. "It is. I'm open to it, but Sam suggested that I'd bond better if I carried a baby, even if it wasn't his. He could be right."

Caitlin stood, holding out her empty glass. "Refill?"

I finished the last sip of mine. "Sure."

"Be right back."

Nellie stayed with me while Caitlin went into the house. I was grateful for the quiet company. As always, I knew Caitlin would be full of advice like she had been when I lost the baby. She'd read the Nessa Cary book and had become a believer. Actually, more like a crusader. She had convinced me Carey had valid conclusions. This supported my fears that I'd inherited a paternal stress-induced trait from our father, his susceptibility to depression.

Carey's a Brit who specialized in molecular biology and biotechnology. As fascinating as the theories in epigenetics were, Carey summed it up by saying, "Even though geneticists have made enormous progress, they still don't even know all the questions to ask."

Apparently, cells read genetic code in DNA more like a script to be interpreted than a pattern that replicated the same result each time. And it could be that my DNA booted a line when I lost my baby boy.

I'd been nibbling on chips while I contemplated our impending conversation, and I'd left a few in the bowl. Drool hung from the corner of Nellie's tiny mouth. "Sorry, Nellie. Chips aren't in your diet."

"That dog has no manners." Caitlin handed me my

wine. She had a book and magazine tucked under her arm.

I rolled my eyes.

Her eyes rounded, feigning innocence. "What?"

"More to read about science." I fought back a groan. "Let me guess. Genetics."

"One is and one isn't. Keeping abreast of science is not a bad hobby." She handed me the magazine entitled *The CRISPR Journal*. The cover displayed a bionic hand cutting a red strand of DNA. "There's a great article in here by Kevin Davies."

"The British journalist who follows and reports major advances in genetics." I'd read several of his published works trying to understand the genetics behind a serial killer. He didn't have the answers.

"Yes, that's the guy. Read his article. Maybe you and Sam could consider CRISPR."

"Caitlin. Really. All I can think of is the genetic material in the movie with Dwayne Johnson and the albino gorilla. An albino..."

"Exactly. The movie was a bust, but CRISPR is for real. There's a lot of speculation that it will revolutionize medicine. Read the magazine. The crux of the CRISPR discovery is that affordable technology exists for gene splicing." She stared at me for a few moments before continuing. "I'm just saying, you could use a donor and splice in some of Sam's DNA. It would be like having Sam's baby."

The whole idea sounded ludicrous, but so did a lot of Caitlin's scientific subjects. Surprisingly, many she followed had come to fruition, like cell therapy. "What's the catch?"

"Well, right now, it's not legal. Can you imagine something that powerful in the hands of the wrong people? Sadly, people in the world still suffer while criminals make a profit. Plus, there are those who say it's like playing God."

"Ridiculous. God gave us the tools. He'd want us to use them." I'd heard all the arguments before and I wasn't convinced it was sinful, but I understood the risks. "So, what are you suggesting?"

"Nothing really. The technology will be here in a few years. If the timing works for you and Sam, maybe it's an option." Caitlin took a long sip of her wine.

"When you say years, what are you talking about? I'm not getting any younger." Being in my early thirties, my biological clock for reproduction continued to tick down.

"Three to five years at most. Read the article in the magazine."

"Okay." I found it easier to comply with Caitlin than to debate. Besides, genetics advancement was a topic I'd always followed. Not for human reproduction as much as understanding human behavior.

"What's the book?"

She pushed a copy of *Infinite Awareness* by Marjorie Hines Woollacott across the table. I'd seen it during a search for answers about my experience with the desk, but never read it. I picked it up and read the back cover. "Interesting."

"Read it. It might help you understand why you reacted to the desk the way you did."

"Maybe."

The back door swung open just as I had started to tell Caitlin about Patsy. Greg peeked in. "We're in the living room. There's a game on—Boston and Atlanta. The Braves are ahead two to nothing, top of the second. Looks to be a tight game. Come join us."

Caitlin stood. "Let's go! The Sox need me."

Since they weren't playing Philly, I'd support Caitlin's team for this game. "Are the Phillies playing today?" I asked as I entered the living room.

"Tonight," Sam said, jumping to his feet. "Tie game! Bogaert scores!"

I stared at him as he hopped up and down. "Sam! Look at what you are doing!"

He stopped dead, gazed down at his left foot, then smiled. "Welcome back, buddy."

"What happened?" Caitlin rushed into the room.

"Boston tied up the game and Sam's left foot decided to work," Greg said.

"How can that be?" Caitlin asked.

"Hamburger therapy." Sam laughed. "No, really. I haven't felt this relaxed in months. Maybe that's what it took to get the nerve to respond—relaxation."

"The doctor said it would heal in time, but nerves don't work gradually. They are either connected or they're not."

"I'd say it's connected." Sam walked around the room.

"Take it easy, pal," Greg cautioned.

Sam took his seat, then turned to me. "How about another beer?"

"Sure thing. But if you think I'll be your servant forever, think again. You're walking and your strength will return!" I kissed his cheek, then got him the well-deserved drink.

* * *

Greg left on Monday afternoon. He had a client meeting in Philadelphia the next morning. "It's been great. Keep me in the loop." He put his arm over Sam's shoulder, then he winked at me. "Maybe we can go dancing during our next visit."

Sam laughed. "Please, no. You know I've always had two left feet."

Caitlin and I watched the two guys clown around. She smiled. "Greg and Sam love each other. It's a joy to watch them."

"It is. You and Greg seem comfortable with each other, too."

"Mmm. Greg's easy to be around."

I didn't press, but her eyes said it all. She was in love.

* * *

By Tuesday morning, Sam had mastered his balance, but he still walked with a slight limp.

While we loaded the car, Caitlin and I argued with him that it was better to be safe than sorry. She suggested he should take things a little slower, but he would have none of it.

"Exercise is the right therapy now. The more I use it, the better it feels."

Sam took the first leg of the drive while he felt rested and energized. I rode shotgun. Once we entered I-91 north toward the Massachusetts Turnpike, I slid *The CRISPR Journal* from my purse and opened it to the Table of Contents.

Sam glanced over. "What have you got there?"

"Another one of Caitlin's reading suggestions." I showed him the cover.

"Just like in the movies," he said and laughed.

"Yup. Just like in the movies." I tossed the journal into the backseat. I didn't want to think about it now. I'd read it later. Maybe after I'd solved the case.

Chapter Fifty

S am estimated a two-hour trip from Granby to
Elegant Findings Antiques on Charles Street
in Boston. He'd been to Paul's store dozens of
times and navigated the maze of streets near Beacon
Hill like a professional.

"The clock's a little bulky, but it isn't heavy." I'd
held the pendulum while he loaded our suitcases into
the trunk. Both clock pieces now sat on our backseat.
"I'll carry the smaller piece."

I caught glimpses of the Charles River to my left as
we sped along Storrow Drive. Once off Storrow, a
predominance of brick, four-story buildings mixed
with brownstones, the majority being Federalist style,
lined both sides of the street. It looked so much like
London that I expected Sherlock Holmes to appear in
a doorway at any moment.

"Almost there?" I asked. "This is worse than Philly
or New York. Where will we park?"

Sam laughed. "Legend has it, the streets in Boston were former cow paths. We'll park at the Charles Street Parking Garage. It's two-tenths of a mile north of Paul's place. It's possible there are spots on the street near him, but unless I need to unload something big, I always use the garage," Sam said. "It's safer and worth the cost."

Music played on the car radio as we entered the heart of the city. Sam switched it off. "Time to pay attention to my driving. Not sure if the spider venom dulled my driving reflexes."

He found his way without a problem. We parked, collected the clock from the backseat, and then headed south toward Elegant Findings. As we approached Paul's shop, I admired how Paul had made the street level of a three-and-a-half-story attached brick building stand out. Freshly painted steps led up to white-trimmed arches with side windows that dominated the rest of the black trim on the building. I almost missed a vacant shop that sat half below ground level.

Paul stood at the counter when we entered. "You made it, Sam. Any problems finding a place to park?"

"None. We're at the garage."

"Good idea." Paul looked at me. "This must be the little, umm...your wife, RaeJean." His neck reddened. My diminutive size obviously shocked him. Although Sam had worked with him for several years and I had spoken with him numerous times, we'd never met in person.

Sam grinned, patting my head. "This is her. A pint of high test."

"Don't feel bad. I get that all the time." I stood tall, shifting the clock piece to my other arm.

"Here. I'll take that." Paul reached out. "The pictures you sent looked great, but let's see what it looks like in person."

Sam and Paul laid out the clock pieces on the counter while I browsed the showroom. Cases and shelves of magnificent porcelain pieces lined the walls. I didn't see any clocks. That may be why Paul wanted to broker the piece as opposed to selling it in his store.

Paul oohed and aahed over Sam's find. "It's the most elaborate pinwheel I've ever seen."

"It *is* nice." Sam's eyes gleamed as he watched Paul examine the antique.

Paul checked his watch. "I sent the photos out to three of my clients who are serious clock dealers. They should be here by nine-thirty. Help yourself to coffee."

We'd taken a few sips when the first bidder arrived a little after nine. A middle-aged man dressed preppy in khakis and a navy blue sweater stuck out his hand toward Sam. "Sean Delaney of Delaney Antique Clocks."

"Help yourself to coffee." Paul pointed toward a Keurig behind the counter.

"Don't mind if I do. The traffic made me thirsty." He laughed.

Next, a woman dressed in black strolled in off the street. Her wild red hair accented the dark blouse and slacks. "Hey, Paul. Where's this clock you're teasing me with?"

Paul stepped forward to introduce her to Sam. "Laura Cousineau from Upstairs Downstairs Antiques a few blocks south on Charles."

Sam shook her hand. "Pleased to meet you. I've heard your name mentioned at more than one auction."

"All good, I hope." Laura laughed and brushed a stray lock of hair from her eyes, then turned to me. "Ah, another redhead, but yours looks natural. Mine comes from a bottle."

"Yours is a beautiful shade," I said. "It becomes you."

She shrugged. "It's fun, and I like change."

The door opened again. In walked a very tall, bald man. "Have I missed the party?"

Paul laughed. "Nope. It's about to begin. Once you get a coffee, that is."

"Ed, good to see you." Sam turned to me. "Rae, this is Ed Stuart from European Country Antiques in Cambridge. You've heard me speak of him."

"Nice to meet you." I craned my neck to smile up at him. He had to be over six feet tall.

Sam fussed with the clock, attaching the pinwheel pendulum to the timepiece. He pulled an emery cloth from his pocket and dusted a few spots along its edge. Once satisfied, he lifted the piece and held it at chest level. "This is the bad boy. I've never encountered such a clock."

Sean Delaney didn't hesitate. "Thirty thousand."

My knees wobbled. Sam had paid fifteen hundred for it. Obviously, the dealer at Bonners Ferry had no idea what he had.

"Thirty-five." Laura entered her bid.

Then, Ed stepped forward. "Forty thousand dollars."

Paul raised his hand. "Wait. Everyone submits a closed bid, and we'll go from there."

"I'm out," Laura said, admiring the clock once more. "It's worth more than my budget will stretch."

Delaney and Stuart looked at each other, grinning as if they'd done this before.

"Here you go, fellas." Paul handed them each a pen and paper. "Give us your best!"

Ed pulled out his cellphone. "I've got a buyer. Let me see what his budget looks like." He swiped his phone screen a few times, obviously consulting past correspondence with the potential buyer, then wrote down a number, folded the paper, and handed it to Paul.

Sean had already recorded his final bid. "Read it and weep." He grinned at Ed.

Paul compared both bids and whistled. "Close, but we have a winner."

Both men watched and waited for Paul to identify who got the prize.

"Ed's the winner at forty-five thousand dollars."

Sean shook his head. "I thought about going to fifty, but then my profit margin would be too narrow without a buyer in the wings."

Ed grinned. "Lucky me. My buyer is willing to pay a lot more than my bid."

"Give us a hint," Sean pressed.

Ed shook his head. "Not a chance. Let's just say I'll earn a sweet chunk of change."

Paul handled the transaction while Sam visited with the other two dealers. I wandered around, admiring the cut glass and thinking about the profit Sam made on the deal. Even with Paul's fee at twenty percent, he'd clear thirty-four thousand dollars. He'd be flying high the entire ride to New York.

Chapter Fifty-One

We got a later start than planned, but once we left Boston, we took the Mass Pike and headed west. As we buzzed along the Pike, my recent theories about Neith Boyce tumbled around in my head.

"It's getting close to lunchtime. Let's find a place to dine just off the highway," Sam said.

"Sure. Let me see what I can find." I searched for a restaurant nearby but didn't find anything special. "Nothing looks interesting. We may have to get further off the turnpike to find something decent."

As I scrolled the map along our route, I spotted Petersham, Massachusetts, to the north. The Hapgood family, Neith Boyce's in-laws, owned a summer home there. In fact, she and her husband were both buried there in the East Street Cemetery. I'd read her obituary in the newspaper archives.

"Are you up for a side trip?" I asked Sam.

"I guess. What are you thinking about?"

"I'd like to visit Petersham."

"Where?" Sam scowled.

"Petersham, a tiny town in Central Mass. There's a —" I paused. "Guess."

"Oh, this is a tough one, Rae." Sam feigned deep thought, tapping his chin. "It has to be a cemetery."

"Good guess," I explained its significance.

"Sounds like fun." Sam reprogrammed the directions in our navigator to take us to Petersham. "Says it will take about forty-five minutes to get there using the Palmer Exit through Ware and Gilbertville. Looks rural. Can you wait an hour to eat?"

"I can wait provided they have a restaurant. I'll check." I found two eating places in the town. "The Country Store sounds fun and it's on the corner of Main and East Street. The cemetery is located about a mile out of town from there."

The road from Palmer wove through several small towns, including Ware, Gilbertville, and Hardwick. According to the map, we drove parallel to a huge body of water labeled Quabbin Reservoir. I Googled it on my phone. It was the major water supply for Boston. We also passed several small cemeteries along the way. I would have loved to stop to see if any notable people had been buried in them.

Sam looked over and smiled as we passed a cemetery on a hillside north of Hardwick. "I can see your longing, but not today or we'll never make it to New York."

"Right. But small towns—such treasures." I admired the monuments atop the hill as we passed.

Our approach to the center of Petersham on Route 32 brought us up a moderate incline. Colonial homes lined both sides of the street. At the summit, two buildings appeared, first a red brick one with what had to be the town hall on its left. East Street ran between the town hall and The Country Store.

"This is so New England," Sam remarked. "It has a common area surrounded by beautiful old homes." He pointed to his left. "That one over there looks like a church. And look, a bandstand."

"This is it." We parked parallel to the sidewalk just past our destination. I admired the two-and-a-half-story home fronted with white pillars next door. The two building fronts matched. A small group of folks I guessed to be locals stared at us when we entered.

"Welcome." A middle-aged man greeted us from behind a display of fresh vegetables and fruit. "I'm Ari. May I help you?"

"We're hoping to get lunch," Sam replied.

Ari pointed to the rear of the store. "We have a soup and sandwich bar in the back. We also have vegan selections. All our food is grown locally. We also offer a sandwich made to order. Oh, and the soup is fresh every day."

"Perfect," I said.

We found our way back to the sandwich bar. I ordered the mango curry chicken salad and Sam ordered a Cuban panini.

We sat discussing the Hapgood house while we waited for our sandwiches.

Without warning, a lady I guessed to be in her sixties chirped from another table, "I know where the Hapgood house is located. My Aunt Louise worked as their maid when I was a kid."

Her friends rolled their eyes as she stood and approached our table. One lady with short, wavy hair smiled and said, "She's always been this forward. Loves to talk to anyone who'll listen."

I smiled back, wondering what to expect.

She stuck out her well-endowed chest and announced, "Hi. My name's Janna. I grew up in this town. Is there anything in particular you're trying to find? Maybe I can help."

Her silver and gray haircut framed a delicate-boned face tanned from the weather. Her clothing consisted of knee-high leather boots, fitted jeans, a turtleneck, and a leather jacket—all black. A wide belt with a large silver buckle cinched her ample waist.

I stared for a moment before I could speak. "We're hoping to find the Hapgood house and the East Street Cemetery."

She dragged over her chair and sat cowboy style, the chair back facing the table.

Sam covered his mouth with a napkin. His eyes twinkled.

"No problem. I'm familiar with both of them. Ask me something difficult." She grinned at Sam, cocked her head, then added, "I ride a motorcycle."

"I wondered if you did," Sam said, making a good recovery.

"Have you heard of Neith Boyce Hapgood?" I asked, figuring this would stump her.

Janna thought for a moment. "I'm familiar with the Hapgood name. Anyone raised here knows of them. My mother and her two sisters worked for most of the rich families who summered here from New York back in the late 20s and early 30s. They did the cooking, cleaning, and watched their bratty kids." She paused, holding up her right hand, closing her eyes, and drumming the fingers of her left hand on the table. After a few seconds of what I could only assume was the act of rummaging through her memories, she opened her eyes. "Got it! She was a writer, right?"

I nodded.

She drummed again, then beamed. "She was a playwright and actress with the Provincetown Players."

"Right again." Meeting people like Janna made visiting local spots worthwhile. They knew a lot about their town's history. Usually more than they even realized. All I needed was the right question to unlock a clue. But what was the right question?

"Anything else?" She pursed her lips as boredom set in.

"Did you ever hear any stories from the Hapgood household about Neith?"

She shook her head.

"What about visitors? Did the rich people who

summered here ever bring notable people to visit while your aunts worked at their homes?"

"All the time." She smiled. "Aunt Louise met famous writers at the Hapgood home on North Main." She paused. "I don't remember any of them, but when Neith and Hutchins Hapgood visited, they'd bring along an entourage of writers."

"Makes sense." Without names, she wasn't much help except to confirm the tight clique of writers from New York. "If you think of anything else about Neith Boyce Hapgood, please call or text me." I handed her one of my cards.

She smiled when she read the card. "Bloodline Forensics. A snappy name."

"So I've been told."

When our sandwiches arrived, Janna returned to her group at the adjacent table.

We ate in silence. Even though I was starving, the high quality of the food didn't escape me. "This is the best chicken salad sandwich I've ever had."

Sam nodded, unwilling to pause from devouring his Cuban panini.

I grabbed the menu and began to read. "All-natural roasted chicken, cashews, dried fruit, celery, mango chutney, lettuce, tomato, red onion, and mayo on a wheat wrap."

"Geez. It's loaded." Sam took another bite, gave me a thumbs-up, then mumbled through a mouthful. "Mine's excellent, too."

Once we finished our lunch, we drove north to

where Sunset Lane connected from the west. The trip took about two minutes and was about sixteen hundred feet up the street.

Sam laughed. "We could have walked here."

"Better to drive. Two days ago, your foot perked up. That's fantastic, but not a victory yet." Sam still had a strange gait as his left foot remained weak.

"True. But I'll be like new with more therapy."

The Hapgood house lived up to its hype. The two-and-a-half story colonial faced North Main. A granite stone porch supported two-story high pillars. Someone kept the grounds immaculate. An addition to the back, a summer kitchen or a woodshed, had been remodeled into a living space commensurate with the rest of the house.

"Nice. Seen enough?" Sam asked.

I nodded. "Let's check out the cemetery."

Sam navigated a U-turn back to The Country Store, then a left onto East Street down a steep slope past the building. After a mile, the East Street Cemetery appeared on our left. Sam turned into the second drive and followed the one-way arrow. We crawled along a perimeter road, reading the headstones and searching for the Hapgood plot. About halfway up the second side, near a small pond, I spotted the Hapgood name. "There it is."

We got out of the car and walked the few yards to the markers. Weather had taken its toll. A greenish-white lichen had grown along its edges. Neith and Hutchins shared a headstone.

I kneeled beside it. "A modest tribute for two people who lived flamboyant lives."

Sam shrugged. "Maybe so, but they lived with fame. They don't need it in death."

A sadness spread through me. Not because the burial site wasn't what I expected. Because Neith Boyce Hapgood, a pioneer who craved independence, declared independence, didn't even get her own monument. In life and in death, she remained subservient to her husband.

I stood. "I've seen enough. Let's go."

Chapter Fifty-Two

Our drive to New York City proved uneventful. We got lucky and found a place to park on the street near our favorite spot in Manhattan, the House of the Redeemer.

As soon as I walked into the lobby, the docent appeared. "Oh, good. Here you are. I was just getting ready to leave." She handed us our key. "You have the same room as always on the fourth floor."

I'd already taken care of pre-payment with a credit card. "Great. We know our way."

"Stairs or elevator?" Sam asked. He was feeling chipper since his breakthrough.

I raised my eyebrows. "You're sure you can make the stairs?"

"We're traveling light, and we know the way." He laughed. "Besides, the elevator's a relic of questionable reliability."

"True." Still, I worried he'd wear out before we reached our floor.

We settled in, then ordered takeout from Three Guys on Madison Avenue.

I reminded Sam that Maggie planned to meet me at Jill's apartment at ten in the morning.

"You sure you want me to go with you?" Sam asked. "I can check in with my contacts here. There's plenty I can do."

"Come with me. I want you to see the apartment. If it takes me longer than planned, you can hook up with one of your antiquing friends once the house-keeper arrives."

"Good idea."

We both fell asleep immediately, exhausted from the drive.

* * *

The Murbeck limo pulled up at nine o'clock. An early arrival at the apartment allowed time for Sam's tour before Maggie arrived. They both deserved my undivided attention.

When the driver opened the door for us, Olivia sat facing the front in her favorite spot.

"Good morning. This is my husband, Sam," I said. We settled in, facing the back. "Sam, this is Olivia."

Olivia nodded.

Sam squeezed my hand.

At the townhouse, I gave him the grand tour. We

ended in the art gallery, where we found Olivia sitting near the Kuhn.

"All done?" she asked.

"Just about. I want Sam to see the pieces Ms. Hamilton collected."

Olivia raised her eyebrows. "Is he an art critic?"

"No, but he appreciates fine art, and this is an exquisite collection."

Olivia lowered her voice. "Did you hear the news?"

I played along. "What news?"

"The Kuhn. It's authentic, but Ms. Hamilton never owned it. Some kind of Kuhn clown fraud." Olivia laughed at her wit.

No response seemed to be my best answer. I approached the Kuhn for a final look. "What do you think, Sam? Do you like it?"

"I haven't seen a Kuhn I didn't like." He glanced at Olivia as he responded.

Sam and I had just finished viewing the Caravaggio when the elevator bell rang. When the door opened, Maggie stepped out, juggling far too large a box for such a small lady.

Olivia stepped forward to relieve her of the load. "Here. Let me take that."

Maggie clutched it like it held the family jewels. "Ner' you mind. I've got it!"

"No! Give it to me. Where do you want it?" Olivia raised her voice as her lips formed a thin smile.

Eyes wide, Maggie handed her the box. "Put it on the kitchen table, please."

While Olivia carried the box to the kitchen, I introduced Sam. "He came with me. I wanted him to see the apartment, but he's not staying."

Sam saluted her, then stepped into the elevator.

As the doors closed, Maggie turned toward the gallery where Olivia had settled after putting the box in the kitchen. "What's she doing here?"

"She's here on behalf of the law firm. No visitors are allowed without a chaperone until the estate is settled."

She glared at Olivia.

"What's the problem, Maggie?"

"Oh, nothing really. But that woman upset Jill the last time she visited. Some blarney about valuing the art collection. She and Jill didn't hit it off."

Olivia had visited the townhouse before Jill died. I wondered why she hadn't mentioned it to me or Austin. Or, if Austin knew, why he hadn't told me. "She's a bit abrasive."

Maggie scrunched up her face. "I'd say. Well, let's get to it."

Olivia remained in the gallery. Maggie and I retreated to the kitchen.

"Shall we?" She pointed to the box on the table.

"Absolutely." My heart fluttered as I slid onto the bench seat. Jill had removed these documents and letters from her townhouse for a reason.

Maggie had barely opened the lid when the elevator bell rang again.

"Now who's here?" Maggie called as she hustled into the foyer.

I recognized Tim's voice.

"What are you doing here?" Olivia had joined him in the foyer.

"Austin sent me over. Said he needed to see you at the office."

"He's there? He said he wasn't working today. Any idea what's up?" Olivia asked.

"I'll be right back," I said to Maggie, then joined them in the foyer. "This is a surprise. Now, I need two chaperones."

Tim fidgeted. "No. I'm here to replace Olivia. Austin wants to see her."

My antennae lifted at Tim's unusual demeanor. Austin may have confirmed Olivia's interest in the Kuhn.

"Okay, then. I'm off." Olivia collected her stuff. She looked confused as she stepped into the elevator.

"Maggie, the housekeeper, and I are working in the kitchen."

"I'll be in the living room if you need me." He dropped into a chair while I returned to the kitchen.

"How do you want to do this?" Maggie asked once I seated myself. She lifted a few documents from the box.

"Let's remove everything and sort it by relevance as best we can."

"Relevance to what?" Maggie asked.

I laughed. "No idea. Let's see what we find. Stack similar documents in the same pile."

"Gotcha." Maggie took out a handful of letters. "These all have return addresses. Is that relevant? Australia, United States, Italy..." Maggie paused. "How about I sort by country, and you sort each stack by city and province?"

"It's a plan."

We worked for about twenty minutes. When finished, we had a large pile for New York, small piles for Australia and New Zealand, and one tiny pile for the rest of the world.

I paused. "Everything keeps leading back to New York."

"And why not? Jill lived here." Maggie spoke as if it was obvious.

I rolled my eyes. "Exactly."

Maggie hopped to her feet. "How about a nice cup of coffee and some biscuits?"

"Sounds great." I needed caffeine or sugar to get my mind in gear.

The coffee had just finished brewing when Tim wandered into the kitchen. "I smell coffee. Is there a chance I can have a cup?"

Maggie pulled a third mug and a small plate from the cabinet. "Help yourself."

Tim glanced our way several times as he dumped four packets of raw sugar into his coffee. "Finding anything important?"

"Not yet." I wondered what he considered important.

"Thanks." Tim saluted with his mug, then sauntered back to the living room.

"He's an odd one," Maggie said. "Kept snooping while he fixed his drink."

"You noticed."

"Not much gets by these old eyes," she said, fluttering her lashes over deep blue irises.

The New Zealand correspondence consisted of letters Jill had sent to Saint Saviour's, inquiring about her birth certificate. She received stale, canned responses with instructions to petition the courts for further information. Correspondence with postage from other countries revolved around the history of her art pieces.

"All that's left is New York correspondence." Maggie patted the large pile.

"More sorting," I said. A quick fanning suggested we sort by returnee. The bulk of the pile belonged to Murbeck. Local art galleries comprised the remainder.

"Miss Jill was always on the lookout for collectible art," Maggie said. "She didn't have many vices—corgis and art. That's about it."

"Not bad vices."

"Art dealers first," I said, picking up the top envelope.

I dealt out the letters with the skill of a croupier. "Reputable, reputable, reputable," I said each time I recognized the gallery. "Here's one I don't recognize." I set it aside.

"That's all of them. I can't understand why Jill insisted I take home the box." She scratched under one of her braids. "It's nothing."

I picked up the envelope with the unknown returnee and slipped out its contents. As I unfolded the letter, my arm hairs lifted. "My God, the...Tim Donahue," I whispered, then I caught myself.

"What is it?" Maggie leaned over to read the document. Her eyes grew wide.

The letterhead listed Tim Donahue, the student intern in the living room, as a business partner. Then, I remembered the FBI had indicted the same gallery for selling art pieces without a proper title. The original owners had petitioned the court for their artwork to be returned, and the buyers wanted their money back.

I put my finger to my lips, but it was a bit too late.

"What have you found, Ms. Hunter?" Tim's soft voice had turned hard.

Both our heads turned toward the sound.

Maggie gasped. "He's got a gun."

He approached the table, waving a gun at me. Looking down, he spotted the document with his name on it. "You can give me that."

"Don't you do it, RaeJean. He's a thief." Feisty little Maggie elbowed her way between Tim and me.

"You shut up." He repeated his demand. "Give me the document."

The elevator bell announced its arrival. At the sound of the door opening, Tim's face turned pale. His hands began to shake. "Are you expecting anyone?"

"No," Maggie replied. She looked at me and raised her eyebrows.

"Me, neither." I prayed Sam hadn't returned. He'd be walking into an ambush.

"Who's there?" Tim called over his shoulder.

No answer.

He shouted again. "Who is it?"

Still no answer.

"This way." He waved us along as he backed out of the kitchen, through the library to the living room door. "Wait here and don't try anything stupid."

"Cover me," I mouthed to Maggie.

She stepped ahead to block Tim's view while I slid back into the library and hid the document in a random book on the middle shelf, making sure nothing looked disturbed. I took note of the title and the maroon and gold leather binding.

Tim scuttled along the wall to the door opening, then slinked into the foyer.

I reached over and patted Maggie, then winked.

She nodded.

"Today's your lucky day. Nobody's in the car, so I won't have to shoot you." His nervous giggling betrayed his lack of composure.

"Nerves," I whispered to Maggie. She nodded.

"Get over here where I can see you. There's something on the elevator car floor."

We inched into the doorway, watching as he reached down and picked up an envelope. Someone had used a wide-tipped black marker to write his name on it.

"It's for me." He ripped it open.

Chapter Fifty-Three

Tim stared at the message longer than necessary. Once again, his neck reddened as he balled it up and threw it on the floor.

"Well, Mr. Smarty Pants, what does it say?" Maggie's diplomacy lacked finesse, but she got to the point.

Tim seethed and groaned as he paced back and forth in the foyer, banging on the doorway to the gallery each time he passed by. "Crap! Crap! Crap!"

When he turned toward the gallery, I snatched the note and smoothed it open.

Gotcha! There's no way out, so let the ladies go. Anne Finley, FBI

Grace Walker was my FBI contact. I'd never heard of this woman. "Who's Anne Finley, Tim? Has she been chasing you since you stole the Kuhn?"

"Shut up! I didn't steal anything." Tim wiped his runny nose on his sleeve like he'd been crying.

"Put the gun down. You're already in enough trouble. Please..." I coaxed him as best as I could. He stared through me, making no attempt to shoot or relinquish the gun.

"Now, laddie! No need to ruin your whole life," Maggie added.

Tim's twisted look raised hairs on my arm, but his frozen silence suggested he had doubts about violence.

"Tim, put down the gun." I pleaded once more.

He groaned, turned, and hurled the gun into the art gallery, missing the Kuhn by fractions of an inch. Inconsolable, he collapsed against the wall and began to wail.

I ran past him into the gallery and collected the gun just in case his crying was an act. There was no way to get help until he was totally disarmed. On my way back to the library, I dialed Sam.

He answered immediately. "Rae, are you okay? I'm in the lobby. What's going on? It's full of cops and FBI agents down here."

"I'm fine. I'm sending the elevator down. Send up the FBI and an officer." I disconnected and pressed the elevator down button. Even though I held the weapon, I couldn't help but wince. The woosh of the car's descent reminded me I'd sent our escape route to the first floor. I crossed my fingers, then looked at Tim. Now, he'd buried his head between his knees. It didn't look like he was moving anytime soon.

Maggie stared at me with wide eyes, her arms akimbo. "What just happened?"

The elevator bell rang. When the door opened, people had filled the car to capacity. Olivia stepped out, flashing an FBI badge. She strutted over to Tim. Two more plain-clothes FBI agents, and five uniforms spilled out.

Olivia, Agent Finley as per her badge, crouched in front of Tim. "What's going on?"

He shook his head, refusing to answer.

One of the officers read him his rights.

"Tim, tell the officers what's going on," Agent Finley urged.

He didn't respond.

"We'll take him to the precinct. He'll talk there." Two cops sandwiched him, each slipping an arm under his, then jerked him to his feet. Tim snuffed and wailed, "I didn't do anything. I wasn't going to hurt them."

As the elevator closed, a cop said, "Zip it, buddy. Save your story for later."

"Tim's gun is in the gallery." I pointed to the handgun I'd set on one of the viewing seats.

Agent Finley led two FBI agents into the room and pointed toward the painting. "This is the Kuhn."

The agents began photographing each painting, spending longer on the one in question.

Agent Finley joined us in the lobby. "What happened up here after I left?"

"The lad panicked when we found an invoice with his name on it," Maggie blurted.

"It was for the Kuhn." I thought for a moment. "He

must have been watching or listening from the library. He heard me read his name. That's when he barged in, brandishing his gun."

"RaeJean held her ground. She wouldn't give him the paper." Maggie patted my arm.

I shrugged. "Stupid, I know, but he didn't strike me as a killer."

"And you know what a killer looks like." Agent Finley's disgusted look suggested I wasn't just stupid. I was an idiot.

I felt the blood drain from my face when I realized the gravity of my actions and the naivety of my statement. "Maggie. Oh, God. This could have ended in tragedy."

Agent Finley nodded. "It could have, and both of you could have been victims."

"But we're not." Maggie wrapped her arm around me. "I'm pretty shaken, but today we must have had divine intervention on our side."

"Or luck," I mumbled. "I'm so sorry to have put you through this."

She gave me a squeeze and wiped a tear from her cheek with her free hand.

My phone vibrated. Sam's name appeared on the display. "It's Sam. Can he come up?"

She shook her head. "No. I want a forensic crew in here. You can leave as soon as you give me the invoice."

My unease about Olivia, also known as Agent Finley, returned, but I was still trying to decide if I was dead wrong about her. Her badge looked authentic, and she wasn't alone. "How about a copy? I'll give the box of papers to Austin, and he can give you a copy."

"That'll work for now. We can subpoena the documents when we're ready for them."

She sounded legit.

Agent Finley looked around. "Right. So, where's the document?"

"I hid it."

The three of us went to the library. I hesitated as I glanced toward the book.

"Aren't you going to show her?" Maggie winked at me. "She's going to love it."

"Love what?" Agent Finley asked.

I reached up to the middle shelf, retrieving the book. I handed it to her.

She threw back her head, laughing as she read the title aloud. "*Praise of Folly*, Erasmus."

Maybe I could trust her. She had my sense of humor. "Can we go now?"

Agent Finley smiled. "Sure."

During the elevator ride, we remained quiet. On the ground floor, I held the close button on the panel. "Will you explain how you knew Tim was a threat?"

She nodded. "Sure, but not today. Not until we nail the rest of the ring."

"Fair enough." The door groaned open.

Sam stood outside the elevator. With one motion, he scooped me into a tight hug. "Quit doing this to me. I won't live to see forty."

Maggie stepped off the elevator and patted Sam's

arm. "Don't you worry about her, young man. She's tough as Irish wool and nowhere near as scratchy."

Sam laughed. "She is feisty."

On our ride back to The Retreat, my mind churned. I'd never suspected Tim. And I'd misread Olivia—that is, Agent Finley. Maybe.

I also still had a puzzle to solve. What did art fraud have to do with Dorothy Arnold?

Chapter Fifty-Four

We'd been back home for a week when my phone rang at midnight. Shriver's name appeared on the display. "Hello. Hang on while I go to another room."

Sam rolled over with one eye peeled open. "Who's calling at this hour?"

"It's Shriver. I'll get it in my office." I grabbed my sweatshirt and shuffled down the hall, both dogs tripping me with every step. "Okay. I'm ready."

"Sorry to bother you this late, but the Queenstown police had a breakthrough." He paused. "They interviewed the shuttle driver. He didn't remember seeing anyone suspicious or unknown hanging around when he loaded the gear."

"That doesn't sound like much of a breakthrough." I checked my watch. Twelve fifteen.

"That's not it." He cleared his throat. "I hate to

admit it, but the suspect had to be someone from my office working with a partner at Murbeck. But I can't imagine who."

Olivia came to mind again. She was FBI—with connections. I didn't say anything to Shriver. Instead, I listened.

"I wasn't going straight to the office the next morning. I figured you and Sam would leave early. So, I brought the bags to the office and left them there overnight. The driver picked them up on his way to get you and Sam."

"The bags stayed at the law office overnight," I repeated. "Did you lock your office?"

"Yes, but the interns, my receptionist, and the cleaning crew all have keys."

"Giving someone an opportunity. But what's the motive?"

"That's a good question. Why would someone think you are a threat?"

I wracked my brain, but I couldn't think of a reason why anyone at his office would care.

"There's more. The police forensic investigator found an online source for the spider found in the sleeping bag." Shriver cleared his throat.

"Online. They sell spiders online." I grimaced.

"Yes. A company called Bugs Online sells arachnids to a variety of customers all over the world through Amazon and guarantees three-day delivery regardless of the destination."

"A package labeled arachnids arrived in Wellington the day before you and your husband departed for Christchurch. We're tracking down the exact drop by NZ Post. They've upgraded their system, but it's not user-friendly yet."

"How did the perpetrator know we were going on a hike?"

"It had to be someone at our firm. There is no other explanation. I lent you the gear and someone on my staff had to have dropped the spider into the bag."

"But who?" I suppressed the thought that it might be Shriver. Austin had assured me he was clear of accusations in the firm's scandal. But maybe he had a different agenda.

"I've called Austin. He's going to pull phone records and email trails from his end, and I agreed to do the same here." Shriver hesitated. "Both our companies are international, so it's possible whoever's behind this is routing requests through other offices."

"How long will the investigation take?" I didn't like the possibility of a spider showing up at my house in Wyncote in an Amazon box. Sam and I ordered online all the time. Currently, I had a dozen items on their way—books and a couple of supposedly indestructible toys for the dogs.

"It's hard to say. We've hired a consulting firm that specializes in data capture and retrieval. They didn't want to commit. They could find a trail right away, or if the person is an expert at covering their tracks, it could take weeks or even months."

"Did you pack the bags yourself?"

"No. I had one of the other interns handle it for me. I had a meeting. But I doubt he did it. His father is a partner. He's a good lad. He's worked for us since high school. The police scheduled an interview with everyone who was at our office the two days the bags stayed here." Shriver paused, clearing his throat. "We may want you to return and testify."

"I'm not a fan of court proceedings. In my profession, expert testimony can be a part of the job, but I avoid it like the plague." That uneasy, sick feeling crept through my body. For inexplicable reasons, opposing attorneys liked to grill me. Sam believed it was my size. They saw me as a rookie, easy to discredit.

"Maybe Austin can record a deposition, but it would be more powerful for you and Sam to make an appearance."

"Let's hope it isn't necessary." I thanked Shriver for the update, disconnected, and went back to bed.

"What did he want?" Sam asked, scooching into a sitting position against the headboard, giving his left leg extra help. The muscle memory remained weak for certain movements.

"They found the origin of the spider in your sleeping bag."

"They did? Where did it come from?"

"Amazon."

"The Amazon rainforest in Brazil?" Sam's eyes widened.

"No, Amazon, the online company."

"You're kidding. I have a new appreciation for the power of the Internet markets."

"It gives me pause. I've got items in transit. Now, I'm worried. Every shipment could be a spider." I hugged my chest.

"Most of what you order is books. Spiders would get smooshed in a typical book envelope. Plus, the shipping label would indicate the shipper along with a sticker indicating a live arachnid."

"Just the same." I shivered. I filled Sam in on the progress and next steps. "If they find this guy, we may have to go back to Wellington to testify."

"I'd better get in shape for another vacation getaway." Sam grinned.

"It could mean that. If it does, we're providing our own gear this time."

"No kidding." Sam nestled back under the covers. "I'm game. I'd love to spend more time there when it's summer."

"Me, too. Although, I don't think it gets that cold. Just windy during the winter."

Sam glanced at the clock. "Man! It's almost two. I have a meeting at the airport with Paul in the morning. He picked up a clock at an estate sale over the weekend in Chester that he wants me to appraise. He's flying back to Boston at noon."

I yawned. Exhaustion couldn't wipe away the images of spiders crawling from Amazon boxes. I tossed and turned, dozing off around four-thirty. The alarm rang at six.

"Up and at 'em, Sherlock," Sam said as he rolled out of bed. "I've got to be on the road by eight."

Groaning, I slung my feet over the side of the bed and sat upright.

Hopefully, Austin would have answers soon. I wanted this case closed.

Chapter Fifty-Five

On Friday morning, I called Austin. He was unavailable, but I spoke with Agent Finley, who had been asked to help with office interviews. "We've questioned Mr. Bradley's entire staff. No one from this office committed an international crime."

"What about rerouting emails or messages through international partners?" I asked.

She didn't answer immediately. "It's possible. We've got a technical team on that."

"Thanks, Olivia...Agent Finley. Will you have Austin call me when he's available?"

"Sure."

When I disconnected, I sent Austin an email in case she forgot. I also sent an email to Grace Walker, my contact in the FBI, asking her to verify that Anne Finley worked for them. It didn't hurt to be careful.

* * *

So much had happened over the last six weeks that I'd forgotten about the Abbott photo of Jill with an unidentified woman. I'd planned to visit the Museum of the City of New York to review the Mayer correspondence, but I never did. I found my copy buried under a stack of papers. The woman in the photo might provide a link between Jill Hamilton and Dorothy Arnold.

My throat tightened as I studied the scene. Jill held out a bouquet of flowers in her left hand and Patsy tucked under her right arm. The face looked familiar, but I couldn't identify the woman or recall where I'd seen her before.

I called the museum again and spoke with the same archivist.

"Since our last conversation, most of the Abbott records have been categorized and dated. If Abbott took the photo in the early 1930s, we'll have a copy, a negative, or a reference to the scheduled shoot. If you send me a digital copy of the front and back, I will see if I can find it in the files."

She'd never asked for a copy during our initial contact. I guessed that she expected me to follow through with the Mayer correspondence. "Great. I'll send you a copy right away."

The archivist gave me her work email. "I'll check today at the end of my shift."

As soon as we disconnected, I sent off a digital copy of the picture and a short note.

* * *

The next day, the archivist responded, saying the woman in the photo was Marjorie Dubey, Dorothy Arnold's younger sister. Abbott had taken the photo in the Dubey's backyard on Old Chester Road in Essex Fells, New Jersey.

If their grandmothers maintained a lifetime friendship, it wasn't unreasonable to think the granddaughters, Isabelle Hamilton and Marjorie Dubey, would become friends. Isabelle would have wanted to introduce her daughter to her social circle.

I studied the picture. Marjorie's expression hinted at deep sadness as she stared into Jill's eyes.

Chapter Fifty-Six

When Dorothy disappeared, George Griscom Jr. also left for a family vacation near Florence, Italy, with his parents. Something felt amiss with Junior's trip.

Plus, Dorothy's brother John's movements during the time of her disappearance didn't add up, either. He was out of the country when Dorothy vanished. When he returned home, he acted surprised that she'd gone missing even though the news made the headlines in both national and international newspapers. After being home a short time, John believed Griscom knew of Dorothy's whereabouts, so he and their mother traveled to Europe in February 1911 and confronted Junior. Even after an alleged thumping by John Arnold, Junior claimed to know nothing.

One reporter suggested it was Dorothy and not his mother who traveled with John, and that John had whisked Dorothy off to Europe in a move to free her from her father's grip.

According to reports, Mrs. Arnold returned home first, followed by John Arnold several months later.

I looked down at Sophie, who slept at my feet. "That is, if she left in the first place."

Sophie opened one eye.

Both mother and brother swore they never found Dorothy. When Junior Griscom returned from Europe, he searched for Dorothy, too. He spent time and money, without success.

Next, I revisited my research about the Greenwich Village bohemians and their writing community, but I didn't find anything new. So, I redirected my attention to the writer from New Zealand, Katherine Mansfield. I spent the next few hours examining Internet photographs of Katherine Mansfield and following her whereabouts prior to Dorothy's disappearance. My gut told me she and Dorothy may have connected in Europe, somehow. I found nothing.

Finally, I ran a wide-open Internet search without a date restriction and found a 1920 photo that showed Katherine sitting with a group of people. The caption read, "George Gurdjieff, the mystic, expounding on his theory of *waking sleep*." Upon closer examination, I spotted a woman in the rear of the group who resembled Dorothy Arnold. Could Dorothy have been at Gurdjieff's institute in France where Mansfield studied?

I captured the photo, cropped it to isolate the

woman, and then emailed it to Greg along with several published photos of Arnold I'd found online. His facial recognition program would catch identifiable facial features the naked eye might miss.

Until this photograph, I had no indication Dorothy knew or associated with Katherine Mansfield. Nor did I have any indication, other than speculation, that she might still have been alive in 1920.

Seeing a potential photo of Dorothy in France, I searched for her name in 1920 to 1921 on ship passenger manifests leaving from America's east coast seaports to ports in Europe. Still nothing.

In previous cases where my trail had gone cold, I would brainstorm possibilities using the notion of six degrees of separation. First, I'd look at family trees for a link, then I'd look at the tree without the names. I'd compare town, city, county, state, or country of origin. I already knew Roy Beauchamp and Katherine Mansfield hailed from New Zealand. Using the commonality of the country, I searched for a lead in the South Pacific.

I found a woman named H. Beauchamp, a first-class passenger on a ship manifest leaving from New Zealand. The ship sailed into the port of Rotterdam in 1920, the same year as the group photograph. From Rotterdam, the Internet trail went cold.

H. Beauchamp could have been the same person as H. Parks, who appeared on a ship manifest in 1911.

Chapter Fifty-Seven

On Wednesday, I received the autosomal DNA results for Ginny and Lester. I found a match at the family level, so I'd order a complete analysis, Y-DNA for the father, and mtDNA for the mother.

There was a twenty-five percent confidence level for Ginny's match to Jill, enough to indicate she was related. They also shared an identical mutation in the marker table for the Beauchamp family.

In fact, the chromosome showed abnormalities associated with Down syndrome. In a recent study, scientists learned that people who suffered from depression, addiction issues, or bipolar behavior shared the same genetic mutation in combination with another gene typical in a Down's syndrome child. Jill and Ginny carried those markers. I ordered a complete analysis for both women.

Without cell samples from Conroy Parks, I had no way to determine his genetic map.

I stood and walked around the office, stopping at the window, and then patting both dogs. I even picked up Patsy for a moment. That's when it struck me.

"What's wrong with me?" I'd never pursued Roy's Kootenai wife. If I identified her genetic map, it was possible I could isolate the unique genes passed on by Conroy.

I called Lester Parks since it was now a reasonable hour in Bonners Ferry. "Hey, Lester, it's RaeJean Hunter. Got a minute to talk?"

"Sure. I ain't busy yet." He laughed. "Hell, I ain't busy at all. Going fishin' later with Frank Perkins, the guy spreading the rumors."

"You're friends with the guy spreading rumors about your dead father?"

"Sure. Why not?" Lester laughed. "You should hear what I tell people about him."

"Umm, I don't want to hear it," I replied a little louder than I intended.

"You sure? I got a great imagination."

"Positive." I'd heard enough. "Do you know your mother's heritage?"

"You mean who her mama and daddy were."

"Yes."

"Mama's mostly Kootenai. Her mama was full-blooded, and her daddy was a half-breed Kootenai. Kootenai's part of the Shoshoni nation. Me and my sisters get benefits from our Native blood."

"Are any of your mother's relatives still living?"

"Yup. Why?"

"I'd like to run a DNA test on your closest relative." I hoped he'd offer his mother.

"That'd be Mama—back on the reservation with her sister. What's it gonna do for us?"

"It'll help me isolate the genes passed on from your father."

"Hm. What good's that?"

"I can't explain anything else yet, but maybe soon. Your mother's DNA will help."

"Okay. I'll ask Aunt Lily. She might help. But it'll take a while. She ain't got a phone."

"No phone."

"Heck, no. I call the tribal elders, and they go talk to her. Then, they call back when they get good and ready. It's a big pain in the you-know-what, but it is what it is."

"Okay. I'll wait to hear from you."

We disconnected and I logged online to see if the Indigenous Americans Genealogy database had Kootenai samples. If all else failed, it could be enough. I lucked out. I'd be able to request a grid of markers if I was unable to get a swab from Lester's mother.

Chapter Fifty-Eight

Lester already confessed that Roy Parks wasn't his father. However, without proof that Roy adopted him, Lester would be excluded from an inheritance. And Lester had taped the letter back together, read it, then destroyed it. He said Morris Hadley, a New York lawyer, sent it.

I needed to talk with Joan Shannon again on the off chance that she might have known of the letter's existence. She'd wanted her father's files to write his memoirs. There could have been something in his papers providing a second confirmation of Conroy Parks' identity, or the identity of Roy Beauchamp's mother.

I called the Brookfield Senior Living Facility. The receptionist connected me to Joan.

"RaeJean, it's so nice to hear from you. Have you solved your case yet?"

I laughed. "Just about. But I'm still trying to identify Conroy Parks' mother."

"So, you've called an old lady for help." Joan sounded chipper.

"I've found oral evidence of correspondence between Conroy Parks in Bonners Ferry, Idaho, and your father."

"What do you mean by oral evidence?"

"Did your father ever mention a client in Idaho? A man named Lester Parks described a letter he had read as a child that came from your father's law firm. Your father had tried to inform Roy Parks that he'd need to adopt Lester if he wanted the boy to inherit anything from his and his wife's estate. Law firms keep copies of all their correspondence. I'm hoping the letter to Conroy Parks is in your father's files."

"Good luck with that. Murbeck refuses to let me have his correspondence."

"I might have an in." I had my fingers crossed that Austin could gain me access to the files.

"If you do, maybe you could sneak me copies of a few of his juicy cases."

"I can't promise anything. I haven't been allowed alone with any of their materials. Austin claims it's to protect the firm from litigation by Jill's family."

"He's right. No doubt, you'll read about a Hamilton cousin who sued for Aunt Adelaide's estate after she died."

"I saw it on the Internet." Sadly, I'd worked with enough families to know litigation wasn't unusual.

"Everyone's skeletons air at the speed of light online," Joan said.

"True. But it's a good source for researchers like me. The key is to check its veracity. The Internet is loaded with false or partially true stories."

"My father used to say, 'It must be true. It was printed in the newspaper.' Then, he'd laugh. He handled high-profile clients. You know, old money. He knew things that never made the papers."

"I saw he had some important clients. Did he ever mention the names Beauchamp or Parks?"

"Both. He dealt with a New Zealand lawyer who represented the Beauchamp family." Joan paused. "Didn't you say Conroy Parks changed his name before entering the States?"

"Yes. Why?"

"It is possible Father sponsored him by securing a temporary working visa. In 1944, to get into the country, people needed a sponsor and a job waiting for them. Father handled lots of those types of cases. To gain permanent residency, Father could have arranged his marriage for a price."

"Was that a common practice back then?"

"I believe so. People all over the world struggled after the war. Father wanted to help."

"That would explain how he knew about Lester's real father and Roy's need to adopt the boy," I said. "But why would Lester's mother tear up the letter?"

Joan remained quiet for a moment. "Where did this young man settle?"

"In Idaho, near Bonners Ferry. Why?"

"Is there any chance Lester's mother came from the reservation nearby?"

"As a matter of fact, she's Kootenai."

Joan cleared her throat. "Haven't you studied Indigenous American culture?"

"Not much, I'm embarrassed to say." It was on my bucket list of topics to research, but somehow, I'd never gotten to it.

"She feared being lost to her tribe and ancestors. From an early age, Indigenous people of the Americas are taught to value their culture and protect the well-being of their tribe. Adoption outside the tribe would mean the child is lost. If the mother is a party to the adoption, she could be lost, too."

"To protect Lester's heritage, his mother kept the letter from Roy. Wow." I thought about inheriting a variant gene and the spiritual connection of generations. "So, the Indigenous Americans believed their heritage passed on through generations, not through conquest like early settlers believed."

"You're getting the gist of it," Joan said. "I'm sure you'll find researching their culture interesting and informative."

"It sounds like I will. I appreciate your help," I thought for a moment. I had no idea if I could help Joan. "I make no promises regarding access to your father's cases, but I'll ask."

"Thank you." Joan sniffed. "I won't hold my breath."

I laughed. "Right. Not a good idea. I'll get back to you."

We disconnected and I searched online until I found an article, "American Indian Belief System and Traditional Practices," by Betty E. S. Duran, MSW, MPH at the University of Oklahoma.

I contemplated how to educate myself fast when my phone vibrated. I had a text message from Greg. *The woman with the mystic, Gurdjieff, shows a 94.85% confidence level when compared to Dorothy Arnold's photographs.*

The law enforcement industry threshold was ninety-five percent for a positive match.

This was a nail-biter. I had the ship manifest records leading to New Zealand, the DNA from Jill and Ginny showing shared ancestors, the note from Dorothy saying, "I'm safe," her mother's belief that she lived, Marjorie, Dorothy's sister, with Jill Hamilton, and now I had a near positive match to a woman in France with Gurdjieff, the mystic.

I stood and paced my office. After several minutes, I picked up Patsy. Her eyes stuck closed for a moment, then rolled open. A slight glint flashed, my head tingled, and I recognized the scent of gardenias. "It's Dorothy."

Chapter Fifty-Nine

M y phone vibrated on the table. Austin's name appeared on the display.

Tension swept through me. Would it be good news? I hadn't heard a word from him about the investigation into the spider. "Hello. What's up?"

"I just got off the phone with Carl Shriver from Rousseau & MacVale. They caught the person who smuggled the spider into the sleeping bag. I thought you'd want to know."

"Who was it?" I still somehow expected it to be Olivia even though I knew she was an FBI agent.

"A lowlife who accepts jobs through the Darknet."

"How'd they catch him?" My body relaxed with the news that it wasn't her.

"A local innkeeper saw a stranger hanging around in Queenstown and picked the guy out of a mug book. He has an extensive record and has spent time in prison."

"Do they know who hired him?" Tension returned as fast as it had dissipated.

Austin cleared his throat. "I'm embarrassed to say, it turned out to be one of our firm's interns who wasn't even involved with the case. The guy posed as part of the cleaning crew and got into Shriver's office."

"And switched out one bag."

"Yes. He removed the other bag from its frame. Since he thought Shriver purposely left them loose, the assistant transported them that way."

"But why? What did I ever do to your intern?" It didn't make sense.

"The intern needed money for college and heard about the terms of the Hamilton trust being discussed in the break room. He'd have qualified for a full scholarship to Columbia based on his financial need. He confessed to the crime once identified. He planned to delay your investigation until the six months expired. Plus, he used his real name and address to order the spiders."

"That was foolish. And he wants to go into law?"

"Maybe later. For now, he'll be studying from a jail cell." Austin paused. "It's hard to understand what makes people do bad things, but if all else fails, check out the money trail."

"Right. Follow the money." I felt better that I wasn't the target, but it still hurt to think how Sam had suffered. "Will we have to return to New Zealand for a trial?"

"He didn't say, but if I were to speculate, I'd guess

no. I'll see if you can testify virtually or provide an affidavit."

"Good." We had other things to concentrate on. Like a family.

"Don't worry about it. It should be an open and shut case." Austin paused.

I sighed. "Then again, when has it ever been an open and shut case?"

"You're right. There's no such thing. I'll keep you in the loop. I've got to go. I have another call." He disconnected.

Austin was right. Worrying about it now was pointless. I resumed my quest to find Jill's birth parents.

Beauchamp spoiled his son by bailing him out of every scrape he'd managed to get into. The clerk at the records office in Wellington was right. Roy lived a privileged life until he depleted his father's reserve of patience.

George, along with lawyers at Rousseau & MacVale, helped Roy change his identity and enlist in New Zealand's military as World War II erupted in the Pacific. Roy's war experience changed him. He no longer wanted to live in New Zealand where people knew him as the worthless son of a rich father. So, his father's lawyer at Rousseau & MacVale and Morris Hadley arranged a marriage, giving him the opportunity to immigrate to the United States.

Beatrix Rousseau had said that Harriet's mood swings appeared after delivering her son, Roy. She would retreat to her second-floor salon for days while the nanny cared for the baby. During this time, she claimed to be writing. With further research, I uncovered more of the story. As an infant, Camille exhibited abnormal behavior and suffered seizures. George Beauchamp struggled with his wife's mood swings on top of his child's afflictions. When the situation became unmanageable, George Beauchamp committed both his wife Harriet and his daughter Camille to Seacliff citing mental instabilities, a solution that wouldn't be allowed today.

"All the money in the world couldn't solve George's problems, Eli." I reached down and rubbed behind his ears. Eli rolled on his back. He moaned with delight as I scratched his belly.

Police reports, gossip shared by the records clerk, and my interview with Beatrix confirmed Roy Beauchamp was Conroy Parks. However, I still hadn't found concrete evidence that H. Parks and H. Beauchamp were the same person. My literary community research was my last hope.

Knowing that Katherine Mansfield, a Beauchamp by birth, and D. H. Lawrence had a close relationship for years, I retrieved my index cards for Lawrence. He left London in 1922 on a worldwide trip. He traveled to New York City and Taos, New Mexico, where he bought a one-hundred-sixty-acre ranch in exchange for one of his manuscripts. Then, after his purchase, he made one last stop in New Zealand before returning to London. According to a digitized record, Lawrence signed the guest register at Seacliff Lunatic Asylum and visited Camille Beauchamp.

I needed to learn everything I could about Seacliff Lunatic Asylum where Jill was born and the orphanage nearby where she spent the first four years of her life.

Between 1874 and 1884, builders worked on the hospital. For the first three years, the New Zealand architect, Robert Lawson, designed and oversaw the project that was to be the largest structure in New Zealand at the time. The Gothic Revival building, with its gabled roof and turrets projecting from every corner, sat on a hillside at Brinn's Point, north of Port Chalmers.

Three years into its construction, a major landslide destroyed a temporary building. Lawson had failed to account for the unstable soils for such a colossus. Authorities charged him with negligence and incompetence. They found him guilty of the charges and fired him.

Losing one of the buildings wasn't enough of a warning for the builders. Another building shifted in 1942, causing an electrical fire that ignited a women's ward. Per standard procedure, the staff had locked thirty-eight women in their rooms. All of them died in the fire. The main building survived another seventeen years, but it continued to shift until finally, the authorities required it to be demolished.

The next article I browsed sickened me. It described the fire where Camille died.

"In 1942, a fire broke out at Seacliff in Ward 5. The ward, a two-story wooden structure, held 40 women. All patients had been locked in their rooms, according to standard operating procedures since the war, and the shortage of nursing staff. Firefighters succeeded in rescuing two women. The rest died of smoke inhalation."

I cringed at the thought. "Those poor women."

Sophie woofed and tap danced by my feet. She needed a break.

"Pretty soon," I assured her, careful not to say *out* or the barking would begin. Eli stood, and both dogs sauntered to the office door.

After reading about Seacliff, my curiosity about Saint Saviour's Orphanage peaked. Before getting far into the research, I found a photograph taken at the orphanage during the timeframe that Jill stayed there. Greg could compare them to the photos of Jill when she first arrived in New York. He'd acquired a new tool, Resolution Photomatching, a product used to confirm the identity of sports memorabilia. It might pick Jill out of the crowd. I sent it to him.

Sophie woofed again. This time, Eli joined in the pleading.

"Okay. Time for a break. Let's go outside." Both dogs rushed to the door. I closed my laptop. Reading about the depressing conditions at the orphanage at that time would not solve my case.

Chapter Sixty

"So, you think Dorothy Arnold escaped to New Zealand via the Virgin Islands sugar plantations, married Katherine Mansfield's cousin, George Beauchamp, and they had two children." Sam set his wine glass on the table.

"I believe so. Their daughter, Camille, had mental and emotional issues. George had her institutionalized, which turned out to be another nightmare. Camille fraternized with male patients and became pregnant with Jill."

"As it turned out then, Camille Beauchamp was Dorothy Arnold's daughter. So, Jill's grandmother was Dorothy Arnold."

I nodded.

"How did Jill end up at Saint Saviour's?"

"At that time, all babies born at Seacliff went to Saint Saviour's, where nuns cared for them, or the church placed them with families. Apparently, Jill had issues, so she remained there until she turned four." I swallowed a lump in my throat. "She might have stayed there longer, but there's a likelihood she was molested by an older boy. That's when the Hamiltons adopted her."

"That's horrible!" Sam's eyes filled.

"Remember, I told you Maggie shared a story of an incident that caused Hamilton to cry after a phone call? That incident alerted the Hamiltons to Jill's danger and suffering."

Sam shook his head. "The poor woman."

"Hamilton had been monitoring Jill's progress. He also helped Adelaide send money. He brought Jill to the States because even after the incident, the New Zealand Beauchamp family refused to take her in. Jill had shown signs of inheriting the same mental issues, and George and his second wife had three children of their own to raise."

"Bless the Hamilton family for their compassion." Sam sipped his wine.

"And bless Jill's corgi companions who adored her." I reached down and patted Eli's head. After a few moments, I said, "Lester won't be getting a direct inheritance."

"That's a shame. His two sisters split the forty million dollars, and he gets to be a caretaker of Ginny." Sam thought for a moment. "Why didn't Roy's wife, Rozine, inherit the money?"

"I asked Austin that. He said it was because of her dementia. A clause in the trust provided for the cost of care, but not a full inheritance. When Lester's mother developed dementia, Lester applied for, and was granted, Ginny's guardianship. His mother returned to the reservation to receive care and support from her tribe."

"And Lester looked after Ginny."

"Right. As Ginny's guardian, he provided for her personal care and well-being. Under the Idaho Code, a guardianship is ordered by the court to the extent required by the ward's actual limitations, with those powers and duties specified in the court order."

"And?" Sam asked.

"And with Austin's help, Lester petitioned the Idaho court to grant him a reasonable income from Ginny's inheritance that would allow him to care for her without worrying about his own financial security. The court gave Lester a substantial annual income with increases tied to inflation. The bulk of Ginny's inheritance will be managed through a trust set up by Murbeck partners. She'll have whatever she needs."

"That's good. I can't imagine Lester handling that large chunk of money." Sam paused. "He'd eat every meal at the Chic 'N Chop."

I laughed. "Maybe, but he's no dummy. He talked with Austin about the original trust stipulations where the estate would go to Columbia University if I hadn't found the family."

"And?"

"And he convinced Ginny that after both their deaths, any residual amount should go to the university. She agreed as long as she got a weekly allotment of chocolate baseball cupcakes."

Sam laughed. "A reasonable exchange for Ginny."

* * *

I collected the mail and sifted through the various items as Sam watched. He expected his payment for the pinwheel clock.

"Is that it?" Sam asked as he reached for a business envelope with a window. He grinned as he ripped it open. "This is it!"

I continued sorting. A statement from our investment firm, a genealogy magazine, and three pieces of junk mail. The next item was a large, brown envelope with a return address for the FBI. I waved it at Sam. "This is what I've been expecting."

"The dossier on Agent Finley?"

"Exactly." I ripped it open. "I can't believe this."

Sam leaned over my shoulder. "Hmm. It's been redacted."

I scanned the document until I found something. "In her background check, it says Finley's mother was a Hamilton."

"She wanted the money to go to Columbia University. I'm calling Austin." I grabbed my phone and placed the call.

"Hey, RaeJean. You got the dossier on Finley." He chuckled.

"What's so funny?"

"Just that I knew you'd call." He paused for a moment. "And I'm glad you did."

I felt my heart return to normal. "Why is that?"

"Olivia confessed that her discomfort with the case wasn't with you, other than she knew you were good at your job. Her discomfort lay in her inability to make tuition payments at Columbia. She wouldn't be eligible for tuition aid from the FBI until she completed her probationary period."

"So, if I found the beneficiaries, she was out of school."

"Exactly. She'd have to drop out. But—"

"But the Parks sisters made a nice donation to Columbia."

"Right. And as a Hamilton descendant, she would benefit from the endowment per stipulations in the scholarship fund. She gets to finish her degree tuition-free."

"Good for her." I'd suspected her of something more sinister than being broke. I felt guilty for doubting her motivations. For once, I was glad to be wrong.

Chapter Sixty-One

Sam and I spent the month of August at Austin's lake house. We relaxed, worked on Sam's rehab, and researched spider venom side effects, hoping to find an answer to his sterility. Typically, a redback wasn't lethal. We didn't find anything that explained our situation.

On our last day, we decided to spend it without our phones.

"We can do this," Sam laughed.

The day turned out to be one of the most relaxing ones of the month.

"We should have tried this sooner."

When we plugged back into technology, Sam found a message on his phone from his doctor. *The forensic genealogist has pinpointed something about your DNA that explains a lot. Call me if you can't wait for our next appointment.*

"Do I wait, or should I call? I don't want to spoil the day."

"Call." I knew Sam would worry about it until he found out what the doctor had to say.

Once he connected with the doctor, he put his phone on speaker.

"It turns out Sam carries a recessive gene that makes him more susceptible to the venom than most people. He is one in a million with this issue. It's quite possibly the same gene that caused the stillbirth, but it's so rare that I'd never heard of it until now. Apparently, it doesn't always affect a fetus. We can go into more detail at your visit."

"If I understand this correctly, then my fertility issue is a random occurrence." Sam glanced up at me with unabashed concern in his eyes.

"Yes. In your case, the DNA fragmentation caused one of the twenty-three chromosomes to be missing or doubled in the fetus, but it isn't likely to happen with every potential pregnancy."

"We will wait to talk more at the next visit." Sam disconnected.

The news unsettled us both.

"I think waiting applies to us, too. Let's not discuss this until we understand exactly what it means." Sam wrapped his arms around me and kissed the top of my head.

* * *

Sam sat waiting on the deck with a bottle of wine and glasses when I brought Patsy down for her sunbath. Her clothes would never look like new, but the sun and white vinegar had worked wonders. This would be her last outing.

Her glass eyes rolled open as I righted her to smooth her frocks. All I felt was contentment. No tingle. No great insight.

"I like her best when her eyes are closed," Sam said.

"She grows on you. This doll provided Jill with years of comfort." I tipped her back and laid her on the table next to me. I didn't confess to Sam that I agreed with him. Somehow, I wanted to love her like Jill did. Maybe in time.

I never discovered who gave Jill the doll, but the way Lester talked about his father, I wouldn't have been surprised if Roy Beauchamp, also known as Conroy Parks, did. After all, he was her uncle.

Eli pattered over to me, put his front paws on the table, then pushed his nose against Patsy and sniffed. Satisfied, he lowered himself to the deck and stretched out on the cool floor beneath us.

"See? Eli loves her."

Sam nodded. "He does."

We sipped our wine in silence for a few minutes.

I glanced back at Patsy as I posed my next question to Sam. "Are you ready to talk about having a family?"

Sam's wine glass froze in midair. He set it down. "I am."

"And?" Butterflies erupted in my stomach, but I couldn't put off the dreaded conversation any longer.

Sam locked eyes with me. "After mulling it over, I think we should pursue both adoption and a donor. See what happens. With my diagnosis, I'm not willing to put you through what would feel like Russian roulette. What do you think?"

Unsure how to answer, I didn't agree right away. "Why both?"

"Hedging our bets." Sam gulped down the rest of his wine. "You'll be a heck of a mother either way, but if you carry a baby..."

"I know. I might bond sooner. That is, if I can carry it to term." I gazed toward the birdfeeders where Sophie lay in wait for a cardinal who taunted her from the top of an oak tree.

"The doctor said you're fine. And we know I'm broken. I'm the bad seed in our marriage."

"You're not a bad seed. You've inherited something that you have no control over." I squeezed his arm. "You're perfect to me."

He didn't answer, but his eyes teared up.

I had hoped gene splicing might be an option, but with Sam's recessive gene, would it even be viable? I'd need to follow up with Dr. Eisenstein and maybe read more about the science behind it.

I still wanted Sam's baby.

Chapter Sixty-Two

I t had been several months since I'd wrapped up the Dorothy Arnold mystery and the inheritance from Jill Hamilton. I'd earned enough money to take a few years off if I wanted. But I wasn't sure that was a good move. I preferred to keep busy. This morning, I decided to run another DNA match, looking for my father.

I'd just finished submitting the comparison program when I received a reply from Kevin O'Leary. Months ago, I'd asked him about his father. I'd given up on hearing from him.

I read his email.

I spoke with Aileen. She didn't see any reason to withhold information about our father. He's alive and in a nursing home nearby. It's Peace Care Saint Joseph's on Pavonia Avenue, Jersey City. He's mentally alert, but not ambulatory. Aileen said she'd meet you there. His name is Sean O'Leary. We have no idea if he knew your father.

I responded and asked her to set a time for a visit. I still hadn't involved Caitlin in my latest quest, but with this new information, I decided to call her. She answered right away.

I could hear Greg in the background. "Are you going to tell her?"

"Tell me what?"

"Greg popped the question, and I said yes." Caitlin let out a hoot. "I'm not going to be an old maid after all."

"Hallelujah! That's fantastic. When's the big day?" My entire body began to tingle at the thought. I wanted Caitlin to have a relationship like Sam and I had. I wanted to hoot, too, but I waited for her answer.

"Right away. We don't want a big wedding. Just you and Sam as witnesses, and a few close friends. We were in the middle of planning when you called."

"Of course. I can't wait to tell Sam."

Caitlin remained silent for a moment. "He already knows."

Greg chirped up in the background. "He helped me make the decision. But I made him promise not to tell you. I didn't want to steal Caitlin's thunder."

"You guys and your secrets." I grinned from ear to ear. She and Greg, like Sam and I, were soulmates. "I am so happy for both of you."

"It's like a dream." Her voice had gone all moony.

"I'll let you go back to planning," I said. There was

no way I would spoil her moment with potential information about our father.

When I disconnected, I saw I'd already received a response from Aileen. *Any day within the next two weeks.* She included her phone number.

I texted immediately. *How about next Monday?*

She sent back a thumbs-up. *Let's meet for lunch at Kevin's pub and go from there.*

I replied with a thumbs-up of my own. My stomach fluttered. Was this the lead that would take me to my father?

Chapter Sixty-Three

Visiting nursing homes and elderly family members was a big part of a genealogist's job. My visit to Sean O'Leary was one of many forays into urban senior living centers. The train from Philadelphia brought me to the Pennsylvania Station at eleven o'clock. An Uber would get to O'Leary's Pub by noon. I texted Aileen my ETA.

She met me at the front door. I'd seen her picture on Facebook, but I wouldn't have needed it to recognize her. Red curly hair. Pale skin and freckles. Thin. We could have been twins, except she was taller by three or four inches.

"RaeJean Hunter, I presume." She laughed, holding out her hand.

"That's me." When our hands touched, my head tingled as it had with the desk and the doll, suggesting another spiritual connection.

"Follow me. Kevin's whipping up a special treat.

Irish nachos." She smiled. "If you're related to me, you're gonna love them."

"I'll take your word for it." My eyes adjusted to the dimness as we entered the bar. I spotted Kevin with his back turned, working a very crowded bar. It looked like the locals had invaded for lunch hour.

"Hey, Kev. My twin is here," Aileen shouted.

He turned, waving a beer glass at us. "Hey, RaeJean! Nice to see you again. Two 902s?"

Aileen looked at me.

I nodded. Sam and I loved the Hoboken 902 craft beer we had on our first visit.

"Sure, and the Irish nachos to start." She led me toward the last table in the corner.

"Is it always this busy on a weekday?"

She hesitated. "I might have told a few people you'd be here. They all wanted to see my doppelganger."

"We are not doppelgangers. We're biological relatives. DNA doesn't lie."

She laughed. "Right. You're the expert. I hope you won't be disappointed if my dad doesn't know or remember anything about your father."

I shook my head. "I won't. But I'll follow every lead until there are no more."

"I understand."

I wondered if she did. She'd had her father for her entire life.

Kevin arrived with the Irish nachos. "Two 902s and nachos for the ladies."

"French fries!" I laughed. "What's on them?"

"Ranch dressing, cheddar cheese, and bacon." He smacked his lips. "Can't beat the flavor. Boy, you two gals do look alike."

"We could be sisters," Aileen said.

My stomach rolled. "Or cousins."

"Right! Cousins," Kevin said. He'd caught my uncomfortable look.

The Irish nachos were to die for. Kevin followed up with Mrs. O'Leary's melt, a well-done burger with lettuce, tomato, cheese, and a special dressing. He'd remembered I liked my burgers well done.

"What's the deal with the cow on the menu?" I asked.

Aileen straightened. "Don't you know about Mrs. O'Leary's cow and the Chicago fire of 1871?"

I'd heard the story. I nodded. "And what does a cow on your menu in New Jersey have to do with it?"

"The fire started near Catherine O'Leary's home. It destroyed about a third of Chicago, but miraculously, it spared her property. She was blamed because the fire started in her barn. People accused her of being drunk. She and her husband owned a saloon where they promoted gambling. The papers made her and her family's life so miserable that it's rumored they changed their name to Walsh and moved to the southern edge of the city."

"I didn't know that story, but I do know the Irish got blamed for a lot of things." Their low positions in society at the time made them easy targets.

"Us being O'Learys, Kevin decided to honor the poor cow who got blamed for kicking over a lantern."

I made a note of the name *Walsh*. It just seemed important.

Once we finished our lunch, I called an Uber to take us to Saint Joseph's to visit Sean O'Leary. The two-mile trip took close to fifteen minutes with traffic.

"Here it is," Aileen said.

I stared at the four-story brick building with a fifth level below ground. There was no grand entrance like Joan Shannon's senior living facility. No grass. No sense of outdoors. Just brick and mortar, windows with black frames, and A/C window units in some rooms.

We walked through the front door into the common area filled with a dozen patients in beds and wheelchairs. A few heads turned in our direction, like a nest of baby birds when the mother arrived, heads pointed up with beaks open in anticipation. A few smiled, but most just stared or turned their eyes back to the door.

"There's Dad, over there." Aileen rushed to where a frail man lay staring out the window. She leaned in and kissed his cheek.

"So, this is the lass you told me about." He eyed me up and down, smiling. "Yup. You're an O'Leary."

"Let's go to your room where we can talk with one extra pair of ears instead of a room full," Aileen said.

"No worries. My roommate passed last night. I have a private room for three days."

"I'm sorry to hear that," I said.

"I'm not. He was a wailer. Cried and moaned all night long. Didn't know his name most of the time." Sean closed his eyes. "He's at peace now. Poor fellow."

We settled into the room, drawing up two chairs next to Sean's bed.

He spoke first. "Go ahead. Ask your questions, but I don't know much."

I got straight to the point. "Did you know Patrick O'Leary? He was my father. We lived in Baltimore."

"Aye. I knew several men by the name Patrick O'Leary, but only one who'd abandon his family." A deep sigh escaped him. "That'd be my youngest brother. He was a drinker. Started in high school. Last time I saw him, he was on the run."

"When was that?" I held my breath.

He rubbed his untrimmed beard as he tried to remember. "It was after Aileen was born—twenty-five, maybe thirty years ago."

"What was the occasion?"

"Same as always. He needed money." Sean looked out the window. "Said he had to disappear."

"Why?" Maybe I'd find out why Caitlin resisted finding him.

"He wouldn't say. Just said he planned to dry out. Wanted to go somewhere nobody knew him and start a new life."

"Did he say where he was going?" I figured this would be hopeless, but I asked, anyway.

"No." Sean reached out and took my hand. "I shouldn't be telling you this, but I gave him a little cash and wrote a check for five hundred dollars. You know, him being my baby brother."

I nodded.

"He cashed the check in a small bank in upstate New York near the Canadian border. If I remember correctly, it was Ogdensburg. I looked it up when I got the canceled check. It's right on the St. Lawrence River." He lay his head back and closed his eyes.

"Ogdensburg." I had another lead. "Did he stay there?"

"No idea. Never heard from him again."

"Never, Dad?" Aileen asked.

Sean shook his head. "That boy was battling demons. No idea what happened to him."

"Did you search for him?" I asked.

Sean glared. "Of course, but I found no trace. I've always suspected he changed his name."

"Officially?" I might be able to find a filing in court records.

"No idea. He wanted to disappear, and he did."

We chatted a little about family. I talked about Caitlin and how our mother died in a car crash. He was sympathetic, but I sensed that he didn't have the energy to care deeply.

Aileen looked at me. "Anything else? Or are you ready to go?"

We'd visited for close to an hour. I'd exhausted Sean O'Leary with all my questions.

"Mr. O'Leary, thank you for your time." I drew in a

deep breath, then asked, "Do you want me to notify you if I find him, or find out what happened to him?"

"Yes. If I'm still kicking and you want to. But if you come back, please call me Uncle Sean." He gave my hand a squeeze. "You're the spitting image of your grandmother. Just like Aileen."

Aileen said her goodbyes and we left the facility. "I'd like to know what happened to your father," she said. "Let's keep in touch. After all, we are family."

"And I didn't think I had any on my father's side." My eyes filled. "I've got plenty of time to catch the train back to Philly if I hustle to Journal Square."

"Let's go." She draped her arm over my shoulder. "I'll get off at the second stop. It's close to home. You've got a long ride ahead...cousin."

I caught the train and rode back to Philadelphia. During the ride, I thought about Catherine O'Leary and her cow. I wasn't sure why, but I had a fleeting thought that it somehow related to my father's disappearance.

Epilogue

S am and I sat enjoying our late afternoon glass of wine on the deck when my phone vibrated on the table. Austin's name appeared on the display. "It's Austin."

Sam arched an eyebrow as he took a sip of his wine and watched me put the phone on speaker.

I'd pretty much concluded that I wanted to go back to my old job working with the FBI.

"Austin, how are you? Sam's here, too." I winked at my husband.

"Hello, Sam." Austin greeted him, then he cleared his throat and looked at me. "I have another cold case I thought you might be interested in pursuing for me."

I didn't reply.

"The Border Patrol at El Paso, Texas, has confiscated female remains found among items from a Mexican antiquities dealer. They found them while

413

searching for drugs. The dealer claims they belong to Yda Hillis Addis, a woman who disappeared in 1902."

I took a deep breath. "Austin, that's a hundred and twenty years ago."

"I know, but your track record says you are the genealogist for the job."

I made a face. "Enough! I won't succumb to your flattery anymore."

Sam grinned.

Austin laughed. "It doesn't hurt to try. Just the same, the fee is reasonable. Not like your last case, but the client is willing to pay all expenses as well as double your hourly rate."

"Are there any secrets or conditions you're withholding?"

"Not that I'm aware of. How about I send you what I have, and you can decide?"

"That sounds good to me."

Sam nodded his approval. Not that I needed it, but it was a plus when we agreed.

"I'd like your answer in a week. If you don't take the case, I'm not sure who I can get."

We disconnected and I looked at Sam. "What do you think? One last historical case before I go back to work for the FBI?"

"It's your call, Sherlock."

Sam was right. It was my call. Or was it my calling? Maybe I'd never work for the FBI again.

I looked at the doll. Her left eye rolled open.

Author's Note

My fascination with genealogy began at least 40 years ago when my mother received an original copy of her family tree dating back to the American Revolution. It wasn't until the last decade that my interest turned to action. I studied the genealogist's methods, their conclusions, and their supporting data from diaries, letters, photographs, public records, and more.

Solving cold cases using genealogical methods and DNA has revolutionized criminal investigations. So far, the oldest case solved dates back to 1956 when teen lovers in Great Falls, Montana were found murdered. A breakthrough in technology using a single sperm cell, genetic genealogy, and the cooperation of the murderer's children provided the evidence needed.

The announcement got me thinking that if a case 65 years old can be solved, how far back is it feasible using the current technology? This led to my first book, *The Desk from Hoboken.* During my research, I found

another famous New York City case, the disappearance of Dorothy Arnold, which led to this novel.

The research techniques RaeJean Hunter used to
solve the mystery are based on knowledge I acquired
by reading *Forensic Genealogy*, co-authored by Colleen
Fitzpatrick, PhD, and Andrew Yeiser, and *The Family
Tree Problem Solver* by Marsha Hoffman Rising, and
augmented by reading articles online and subscribing
to genealogical magazines.

After reading dozens of articles about Dorothy
Arnold's disappearance, I believe one or both of her
parents knew what happened to her.

Most of the historic characters in the book existed
(Armstrong, Beauchamp, Boyce, Hamilton, Mansfield,
Von Arnim, Parks a.k.a. Parker, and Samuels). I created
fictional historical characters and relationships where
necessary to make the plot work. I found no evidence
that the soldier, Louis McLane Hamilton, married or
had children, but he died at age twenty-four in 1868
while leading a charge under the leadership of General
George Armstrong Custer at the Battle of Washita
River. Jill's father, William Hamilton, is a character
from my imagination.

Dorothy Arnold wanted her independence to
pursue a writing career. Hampered by the limitations
forced on her by her father, I believe she ran away with
the help of friends. She sought independence, a dream
held by many women.

Most of the documents used to "solve" the case are
imaginary but are of the type a forensic genealogist

would use. After 110+ years, any intimate relations are speculative.

In truth, I haven't solved this historic cold case. But within this book, I've attempted to reimagine and piece out what might have happened. I've used RaeJean Hunter to investigate the mystery.

Have I gotten any closer to solving the case? In reality, the one new piece of information I uncovered is that a person, H. Parks, sailed from Mobile, Alabama, to Australia in the same timeframe a woman resembling Dorothy Arnold was spotted in a restaurant in that same city.

Most indications are that Dorothy ran away. My story is one of many possibilities.

Acknowledgments

Thanks to my publisher, Harbor Lane Books, LLC, and their team who have helped me get my book ready to market.

Thanks to my Beta Readers (Courtney Hitson, William "Bud" Humble, Tom Nowak, Janet Richards, Rebecca Young) for once again doing an outstanding job finding the plot holes and providing insightful input.

Thanks to the many unmentioned folks who helped bring The Doll from Dunedin through the many steps in a writer's journey to reach publishing, then marketing.

About the Author

ML Condike has published short stories in anthologies that include *Strange & Sweet*, (2019), *Tall Tales and Timeless Stories*, (2022), *Malice in Dallas, Metroplex Mysteries, Volume 1* (2022), Reckless in Texas, Metroplex Mysteries, Volume 2 (2023), Notorious in North Texas, Metroplex Mysteries Volume 3 (2024), and won first place in the fifteenth annual Writer's Digest Popular Fiction Awards, Mystery/Crime category (2019), and 2nd Place in the Tennessee Williams Short Story Contest, Key West Art & Historical Society (2022).

She's an associate member of Mystery Writers of America Florida Chapter, Sisters in Crime National, Sisters in Crime North Dallas (Treasurer), Granbury Writers' Bloc, and Key West Writers Guild.

Her debut novel, and the first book in a genealogy mystery series, *The Desk from Hoboken*, received the 2024 Readers' Favorite Gold Medal Award for Fiction – Mystery – General, and recognition as a finalist in Best New Fiction in the 2024 American Fiction Awards.

Website: https://mlcondike.com
Facebook: https://www.facebook.com/marylou.condike
Facebook Author: https://www.facebook.com/mlcondike
Instagram: https://www.instagram.com/mlcondike/
LinkedIn: https://www.linkedin.com/in/mary-lou-condike-b16117187/

About the Publisher

Harbor Lane Books, LLC is a US-based independent digital publisher of commercial fiction, non-fiction, and poetry.

Connect with Harbor Lane Books on their website www.harborlanebooks.com, TikTok, Instagram, Facebook, X, and Pinterest @harborlanebooks.

harbor
lane
books

Milton Keynes UK
Ingram Content Group UK Ltd.
UKHW030705021124
450460UK00005B/9